Running WILD

Cathryn Fox
Delilah Devlin

What the critics are saying...

ജ

LION IN THE SHADOWS
Delilah Devlin

"Lion in the Shadows is a very intense story that grabs the reader from page one and never lets go. Any lover of the paranormal and ghosts should read LION IN THE SHADOWS as it is in a class all by itself" ~ *Love Romances Review*

"Lion in the Shadow is a wonderful novel about a persons willingness to grow through love, as well as the struggle she goes through to get to that point. Not only is it an emotional story, but a highly sensuous one as well. ~ *A Romance Review*

"...an intriguing novel about love, acceptance and sacrifice. Beautifully written, Lion in the Shadows has all the elements of a great book. Action, adventure, mystery and of course hot sex! ~ *The Romance Studio*

"Lion in the Shadows is a supernatural thriller with plenty of the steam that readers have come to expect from Ms. Devlin. Did I mention the heat? Whew...it's always a sure bet that Ms. Devlin's books will be packed with superb, sexy and inventive love scenes, and this book is no exception." ~ *Road to Romance Reviews*

UNLEASHED

Cathryn Fox

"Unleashed by Cathryn Fox is molten lava wrapped in spun-sugar, with explosive potential. Ms. Fox has created one whopper of an awesome story. It is stories like this one that keep husbands busy in the bedroom, boyfriends thinking wow and women believing that love can find a way, along with a very healthy dose of mind shattering sex. ~ *ECataromance*

"Deliciously decadent...Cathryn Fox has created a scintillating blend of intrigue, sex, and danger into an explosively climatic story..." ~ *A Romance Review*

"For an engaging read that includes sweltering sex scenes, may I suggest a reader look no further than Unleashed. It is definitely a keeper ~ *Coffee Time Romance*

"Cathryn Fox provides readers with an erotic story, portraying two unique characters with secrets and doubts about their ability to emotionally love someone. Unleashed offers readers an erotic paranormal with a touching love story. ~ *Fallen Angel Review*

An Ellora's Cave Romantica Publication

www.ellorascave.com

Running Wild

ISBN 9781419955082

Edited by Briana St. James and Heather Osborn
Cover art by Artist

Trade paperback Publication May 2007

Content Advisory:

S - ENSUOUS
E - ROTIC
X - TREME

Ellora's Cave Publishing offers three levels of Romantica® reading entertainment: S (S-ensuous), E (E-rotic), and X (X-treme).

The following material contains graphic sexual content meant for mature readers. This story has been rated E–rotic.

S-*ensuous* love scenes are explicit and leave nothing to the imagination.

E-*rotic* love scenes are explicit, leave nothing to the imagination, and are high in volume per the overall word count. E-rated titles might contain material that some readers find objectionable—in other words, almost anything goes, sexually. E-rated titles are the most graphic titles we carry in terms of both sexual language and descriptiveness in these works of literature.

X-*treme* titles differ from E-rated titles only in plot premise and storyline execution. Stories designated with the letter X tend to contain difficult or controversial subject matter not for the faint of heart.

RUNNING WILD

ജ

UNLEASHED

Cathryn Fox

Chapter One

ꟗ

This had to be some sort of joke.

Paranormal task force agent Jace Garret avoided psychics like the plague, and the last thing he wanted was to join forces with one. He'd rather solicit the help of an Ebola-ridden monkey than team up with the infamous Skylar Bray. It wasn't that he questioned her tracking abilities or feared she'd botch his surveillance.

Oh no, those weren't his reasons at all.

If she discovered the secret he'd been hiding for the last thirty-one years, he'd go down faster than a two-dollar whore.

Like a caged panther, he paced around his captain's office, his rubber soles squeaking on the polished tile floor. The throbbing in his head began beating a steady rhythm with each heavy footstep.

"Forget it, Captain, I won't do it." Jace gave a quick disgruntled shake of his head. "And I don't give a shit how good you say she is. I don't need her help." He clenched his jaw and scrubbed a hand over the day-old growth speckling his face. "I can track this werewolf on my own, and you damn well know it." Jace slammed a manila file onto Captain Mike Sanders' desk and continued to glare at him.

Defying gravity, Sanders was leaning back in his seat. The chair legs teetering under his heavy weight. Drumming his meaty fingers on the wooden armrest, he planted his rather large feet on his desk, and met his gaze straight on. "Listen, Jace..."

Sanders' subtle body language indicated that the issue had already been resolved. Changing the Cap's mind was like changing a blown-out tire mid-chase. It was impossible, and Jace knew it. Feeling ticked off, Jace grunted and starched his spine.

How in the hell was he going to get out of this one?

He made one more desperate attempt. "Come on, Captain—"

With a wave of his hand Sanders cut him off. "You know as well as I do that we've been having trouble tracking the newest breed of werewolves encroaching upon the city. Since they're able to evade us at every turn, we can use all the help we can get."

Jace raked his fingers through his hair and grunted something incomprehensible. He couldn't argue that point. Lucas, a powerful alpha wolf, was the main suspect in a recent rash of murders throughout the city. But without any solid proof, they had to catch him in the act in order to make an arrest. They needed to do it fast, before widespread pandemonium broke out. If the public ever found out there were werewolves—not simply a wild pack of dogs—terrorizing the city, the department would have one hell of a situation on their hands.

Sanders jerked his thumb toward the window. Jace's gaze followed the movement. Silvery stars began to dot the evening sky as the descending summer sun kissed the horizon. Jace snarled, the darkening sky a fitting match for his mood.

"The full moon is only a couple of days away and we have to remain tight on his tail until he transforms. That's why we need Skylar's help," Sanders added. He hooked his fingers through his belt loop and leaned back another inch.

Great. What a way to top off his perfectly shitty day. As if being partnered with a psychic wasn't bad enough. Now fate had thrown a full moon into the equation to really complicate matters for him.

Jace resisted the urge to kick his Captain's chair out from underneath him. The juvenile side of him enjoyed the mental image of the robust man thudding to the floor. Instead of acting on his anger, he fisted his hands and continued to stalk back and forth.

He'd be smart not to piss off the Captain again. Walking the beat was right up there with babysitting a woman with supersensory powers.

A fresh wave of anger pitched though him. "I don't need a psychic to help me track him. All I need is a few more days, a big-ass Uzi and a clip of silver bullets," he snapped.

Blood pounded through Jace's veins as he fought to keep his rage in check. Just how competent was Skylar? He knew the department had used her to track before, but was she skilled enough to discover his secret?

Jace lowered his voice and switched tactics. "Come on, Cap, call her off."

"Too late." Sanders' gaze zeroed in on a spot just beyond Jace's shoulder. "She's already here."

A stream of profanity spewed from Jace's mouth as he twisted around. All hope seeped out of him like smoke from a chimney. There she was, leaning against the doorjamb, her expression serene, unreadable.

He did a slow perusal of the woman before him. He'd seen her around the office before, had quite often admired her sweet body from afar, but he'd always been careful to avoid contact. This was his first encounter with her up close and personal and there was no denying it, she was exquisite. Her honey-tanned face was a combination of sculpted angles and soft curves. She had a perfect nose with a sexy little slope tipping the end.

She lifted her gaze and met his. The minute their eyes met Jace felt a familiar stirring deep inside his groin. Her eyes were a fascinating color of green, rimmed by a halo of warm golden flecks. Cat eyes—eyes that could see into the very depths of darkness. Jace shivered.

Skylar took a tiny step forward and offered her hand.

His heightened senses were immediately assaulted with her arousing feminine scent, leaving him feeling slightly lightheaded. It took a moment to register that the sharp intake of breath he heard was his own.

She smelled like the beach on a warm, summer day. A dangerous mixture to a guy who spent his time hunting wild beasts. A wave of lust gravitated to his cock as he inhaled her delectable aroma. At that moment all he could think about was whether she'd taste as sweet as she smelled.

He widened his stance and closed his hand over hers. Heat curled through his body when skin contacted skin. He gazed at the petite woman smiling up at him and shifted his glance downward. She wore a summery, knee-length skirt that hugged her curvy hips and a yellow, flowery, sleeveless blouse that exposed just a hint of cleavage and revealed she spent many hours in the sun. He rolled his tongue around a suddenly dry mouth as his attention drifted back to her face.

Sexy, mysterious eyes peeked out from underneath long, silky lashes. Buttery curls framed her flawless skin and billowed over her slender shoulders.

His gaze settled on her mouth. And what an exquisite mouth it was. She had the most amazing, luscious lips. For a moment he wondered if that glossy lipstick of hers would smear if she slid her gorgeous mouth down the length of his body. His cock tightened and he smothered a moan that gathered in his throat.

Damn. She was hotter than his leather car seats during a heat wave. He sidled closer and towered over her. Once again, he was swamped by her evocative scent.

She graced him with a becoming smile. This woman emitted an aura of quiet confidence and strength of character that he found rather fascinating. When she opened her mouth and touched her tongue to her pretty pink lips, a heady rush of adrenaline fired his blood.

"I'm Skylar Bray. It's nice to meet you, Agent Garrett."

Her sultry voice was as bewitching as the woman herself, and he felt himself being pulled under by her spell. He shuddered involuntarily and blinked his mind back into focus.

"Call me Jace," he mumbled and tried not the think about the way his entire body tightened at the sound of her voice.

He took a moment to note his physical reaction to her then fought to clear his arousal-fogged brain and gain control over the situation.

He wanted to step back, to break away from her delectable aroma as it perfumed the air, but something compelled him to remain close. His legs wouldn't carry him away from this intoxicating woman.

How was he supposed to concentrate on anything when his senses were overcome with her hypnotizing scent? He somehow had to find a way, because he needed his wits about him in order to gauge the strength of her powers.

Would she be able to sense the wolf stirring within him?

He watched the play of emotions cross her face and wondered what she was thinking. Was she trying to reach into the depths of his mind, to glimpse the area that he'd kept suppressed for so many years?

"I guess we're going to be partners for the next couple of days," she said. There was something about the lilt in her voice that drew him in. It got under his skin and warmed his body like the buzz of a fine wine.

"Guess so," he mumbled. Did she have any idea what she was getting herself into? Tracking a werewolf was a far cry from a day at the beach. She could get hurt or, even worse, killed.

"Don't worry, Jace. I know what I'm doing." She folded her arms across her chest and met his gaze unflinchingly.

Great. Now fate had tossed in a little mind reading to really fuck things up. He frowned and shook his head.

She flung her wavy curls off her shoulders and quirked a small smile. "No, I can't read your mind. Captain Sanders warned me you'd be leery."

He cocked one brow in the Cap's direction. Leery? That wasn't the word he'd choose. More like downright opposed.

His Captain stood and moved to the front of his desk. Arms folded across his barrel chest, his gaze darted between Jace and Skylar. "You two play nice." With that, he made his way out into the hall. "And keep safe," he tossed over his shoulder as he disappeared from their line of vision.

Jace turned his attention back to Skylar. He studied the petite woman before him. The first woman in a long time to rouse such a primal reaction in him.

The one woman he had to keep his distance from.

God dammit!

* * * * *

Skylar tried not to focus on the tingling sensations that poured through her as she looked at the handsome, rugged detective towering over her. The attraction between them had been instant.

He was tall, much taller than her, forcing her to crane her neck to look him in the eyes. His long, midnight hair was a tousled mess, and she resisted the desire to comb her fingers though it. She took a tiny step back to release the pressure on her spine and to free herself from his earthy male scent. That was when she noticed his attire. He looked as though he hadn't seen a shower or a fresh change of clothes in days. She noted the weariness around his eyes and suspected he hadn't had a decent night's sleep in a while.

"I was on a stakeout." His voice was low, rough and softly seductive.

She tilted her head and smiled. When she looked into his eyes she was taken aback by the unwavering strength and determination she found there. "And you accused *me* of being a mind reader," she challenged.

She couldn't help but admire the cocky grin pulling at the corners of his sexy mouth. "I guess you'll need some sleep before we begin our plan of attack." She tried hard to see into the depths of his mind, but there was a part of him that she couldn't reach.

Was there more to this paranormal task force agent than met the eye?

Was there something about him that he didn't want her to know?

Perhaps that was the reason why he was so strongly opposed to working with her. She'd come across opposition before, of course. So much so that she'd gotten used to it. Usually it was an ego problem. The big, bad-assed agents hated to admit they needed help from a girl. Oddly enough, she sensed Jace had different reasons, reasons that had nothing to do with his self-importance.

She made another attempt to read him but his shields were too strong to penetrate. How interesting. She was both confused and intrigued at her inability to touch his mind. But certainly not deterred.

Jace shook his head and leaned in close. Close enough that her whole body tightened in response to his nearness. She found his total disregard for her personal space seductive and began to quiver in the most interesting places. Ripples of sensual pleasure danced over her flesh.

"I'll sleep when I'm dead." The heat of his breath assailed her neck. Warmth pooled between her thighs, filling her with a restless ache. Moistening her lips, she took another small step backwards, widening the distance between them.

She stole another quick look at him. Well-worn, tight jeans hugged his hard, sculpted thighs. His navy T-shirt strained over broad shoulders that tapered to a tight waist. Her gaze tracked back to his face where she spent an extra moment looking at his eyes. They were rich and dark, like Belgian chocolate. The kind that sent her taste buds on a wild excursion and fired her senses into overload.

Why she was noticing such a thing was beyond her. She'd sworn off men long ago, and wasn't looking for any kind of relationship, physical or emotional.

Past experiences had taught her that men feared her power. Whenever a lover discovered her psychic abilities, they'd close themselves off, and eventually the relationship would fizzle. Skylar knew men wanted her for one thing and one thing only—sex. When it came to sharing their heart with a woman like her, they disappeared quicker than the last donut at the precinct.

Those were complications she didn't want or need. Now she was a no-nonsense, career-oriented woman who dedicated all her spare time helping the Paranormal Task Force track vicious werewolves, like the ones that had killed her parents years ago. Living a double life, she spent her days running and operating her own flower boutique while her nights were spent helping the department track wolves.

She'd do whatever it took to bring the animals to justice, even if she had to go undercover with a man as dangerously handsome as Jace Garrett—a man who aroused desires in her she'd been able to suppress for years.

"Perhaps you'd like to take a shower before we begin?" she asked.

The provocative thinning of his lips drew her attention. With one easy step, he closed the already too small gap between them. "Well now, Skylar, if I didn't know better, I'd think that was some kind of invitation." A rakish grin curved his mouth while the heat in his smoldering gaze stroked her in other places.

She knew he was playing with her, trying to get a better handle on who she was and what she was all about. She was anything but an easy read, and wasn't about to let him bait her.

She pursed her lips. "Then I guess during the rest of the investigation, we'd better leave the thinking to me." With a quick twist, she flung her hair over her shoulders and sauntered out the office door. His mumbled curses reached her ears and brought a smile to her face.

"Hurry up, Garrett. If we're going to work together you can't always be two steps behind me."

Chapter Two

ꕥ

A short while later Jace stood in the small bathroom of his condo and adjusted the water on his shower nozzle. He stepped under the hot, needlelike spray and let the warmth soothe his tired body.

Two steps behind her. Her words rang in his ears and fired his blood. He huffed and shook his head. No one had ever accused him of being two steps behind before. There was no doubt about it. Skylar Bray had been put on this earth just to annoy him.

But did she have to be so damn sexy while she was doing it?

He knew where Lucas had gone. His own surveillance team had tracked him to an upscale fantasy resort forty miles outside of town. Jace knew the kinds of activities that played out in that particular resort. Married couples looking to liberate their secret desires and experiment outside their relationships frequented the place. He assumed that was another reason the Captain wanted Skylar on the team. They'd have to go undercover and pose as husband and wife in order to infiltrate the erotic playground.

Jace grabbed the soap and began lathering his body. As he slid the bar over his cock, his thoughts returned to the fiery woman who waited for him in his living room. He'd damn well like to show her who was two steps behind. As his mind conjured up the numerous ways he could accomplish such a delightful task, he felt his cock grow in his palms.

He threw his head back, stroked his shaft and imagined the hands sliding over his thickness were those of another. As he recalled Skylar's delectable summery scent, he pictured her tight little body lying naked on a bed of sand, her legs spread wide, exposing her sex as she beckoned him to come to her. Her damp pussy glistening in the sunlight as she toyed with her pale nipples. Jace licked his lips and could almost feel her rich female texture and taste her delicate feminine juices. He increased the rhythm and tempo of his strokes as a delicious warmth spread over his skin.

He knew it was against the rules to get intimately involved with a partner and that it would cost more than his badge if she discovered his secret. Even though his mind warned him to keep his distance, the primitive beast inside Jace played by different rules. The problem was, he'd been hunting Lucas for weeks now and hadn't had the time to sink into a soft, fragrant woman. Since the tempting Skylar had been crossing his path for far too long, he suspected that if the opportunity to touch her or kiss her presented itself, he'd become too lost in his carnal hunger to consider such matters.

Jace knew that the animal in him had control of his primal urges and once the blood drained from his head, he couldn't be held accountable for his actions, regardless of the consequences.

He had a good idea what would happen to him if Skylar discovered his biological father was a werewolf—a vicious animal who had sexually assaulted an innocent woman in a dark alleyway. Jace had been born as a result. No one would care that Jace had been raised by a sweet, gentle woman who had showed him how to control the animal inside him.

Memories while in his wolf form were scattered, violent and downright primal. In order to avoid hurting, or—even worse—killing another, he always handcuffed himself in his soundproof room just before the change. Even though he took measures to protect the public, no one would care. All anyone would see was a wolf masked in a man's body—and sooner or later, the hunter would become the hunted.

A sound outside his door drew his attention. Cursing, he quickly pulled his hand away from his swollen cock and stepped further under the spray. With Skylar waiting for him, he didn't have time for such an indulgence.

* * * * *

Skylar listened to the rush of water behind the closed bathroom door as she padded softly through Jace's condo.

Talk about a minimalist, she mused. Containing only the basic bachelor necessities, like a recliner, corner table and big-screen TV, his condo was clean and orderly but lacked any kind of warmth or comfort. Without any photos or pictures on his walls, she had a hard time grasping who he really was and what made him tick.

She moved down the narrow hall to his bedroom. When she pushed open his door, a smile touched her mouth. This room presented her with a clearer insight into the psyche of PTF Agent Jace Garrett.

Dark curtains were pulled back, providing her with a view of the skyline and the lively city sprawled below. Jace must have had the room soundproofed for sleep, because she couldn't even hear the dull roar of traffic. Overhead, the stars twinkling in the velvet black sky created a calming, soothing effect. It was easy to tell this room was his private sanctuary—a place he'd retreat to in the evenings in search of peace and tranquility after a long day on the hunt.

She found herself wondering if he brought many women here.

His four-poster bed looked soft, inviting. A thick, cozy blue duvet had been haphazardly thrown over the king-sized mattress. Walking quietly across the polished oak floors, she made her way to his bed and began rubbing the cushy material through her fingers. Without realizing what she was doing, she pulled it to her nose and inhaled. Jace. She drew another deep breath as her body registered the effect of his earthy, male essence.

Suddenly, her mind began playing out the kinds of activities that assuredly took place on his luxurious bed.

Hot, naked, primed bodies pressed against one another. The glistening light from the crescent moon slicing through the window, bathing them in a sensual, dreamy glow. Hushed tones of lovers murmuring to one another, their soft, secret laughter sending intimate messages. Discarded clothes hastily torn away, mingling on the wooden floor. Erotic music playing in the background while condensation pooled on a forgotten, half-empty bottle of wine, as the couple became lost in each other's nakedness.

Her eyes drifted shut as she suspended reality for a moment and envisioned herself sprawled across his huge bed. Jace hovering over her, licking a path of moisture down her neck until his burning mouth closed over her breasts, claiming her, branding her with his heat. His finger opening her dewy folds so he could dip in and out of her slick, tight crevice. His thumb flicking and tickling her clit until she became feverish with longing.

She sagged against the bedpost as her heart picked up tempo. A moment later, her lids fluttered open and she spotted his handcuffs lying on the nightstand. Her glance darted to his headboard. Scuff marks in the rail gained her full attention. She wondered if he used the cuffs for sexual bondage.

Did he chain his women and have his way with them? She touched her fingers to her throat and swallowed hard while her mind wandered. Would he anchor her legs to the bedposts as he drove his cock in and out of her soaked cunt? Unconsciously, Skylar's legs widened.

Would he be fast and furious or soft and gentle?

Perhaps it was he who liked to be bound. She could climb over him and press her damp pussy onto his waiting face, where she could ride his tongue until she tumbled into orgasm.

Pleasure shifted inside her and her whole body began to moisten and vibrate with indecent thoughts. She sucked in a tight breath and fought down the torrid warmth seeping into her skin. She was surprised by the foolish way her mind and body responded, considering she was only standing inside Jace's bedroom. But there was something raw, primitive and carnal about him that sent her hormones into overdrive.

Gaining control over her desires, she turned her attention to a small pine bureau nestled in the corner. Moving closer, she noticed a small silver-framed picture. She picked it up, but it slipped from her fingers and clunked onto the bureau. She glanced over her shoulder to make sure Jace hadn't heard the noise.

Satisfied that the shower was still running, she picked the frame up and held it between her palms. The woman in the photo was exquisite. With dark skin and midnight hair, her features were strikingly similar to Jace's—she had to be his mother. She did a quick scan of his room, but found no pictures of his father. Interesting.

Lost in her thoughts, she hadn't heard the shower turn off or the footsteps approaching.

When she looked up and came face to face with Jace, the picture once again fell from her hands and landed on an oval area rug. Air rushed from her lungs in a loud whoosh. He stood before her naked, looking wild, dark and dangerous. A muscle in his jaw twitched.

She was taken aback by his lack of modesty, but soon found herself admiring his masculinity. He was so handsome. The dim overhead light shimmered on his wet, slick body. The wispy shadows covering his face did little to diminish his good looks. In fact, they gave him a sexy edge. She did a slow perusal of his sculpted muscles but her gaze kept straying back to his thick cock. Skylar shivered. He looked so masculine, feral. Like an untamed animal stalking its prey.

"That's my mother." The profound emotion in his voice surprised her. The intimate smile he gave her made it a struggle for her to remain standing. For a brief moment she suspected she'd gotten a glimpse of the inner man—a gentle, sensitive man well hidden beneath a tough exterior.

Skylar bent down, picked up the delicate, framed picture, and placed it on his bureau. When she turned back around, Jace had taken a small step closer to her.

She touched his mind and tried to read him. He seemed to be waging some kind of internal war with himself. She sensed his carnal hunger for her, felt it with every fiber of her being. Even though he wanted her, *needed* her on a sexual level, a part of him was fighting it, struggling to smother his desires.

Heat flamed through her as her gaze once again settled on his beautiful cock. It was thick, swollen and ready. A shiver swept down her spine as her fingers anticipated a touch, to see if his engorged shaft felt as thick and hard as it looked. She moistened her lips as her mouth watered for a taste.

Hunger moved through her, swamping her with desire. She had no idea what was happening to her. She'd never felt like this before. Never felt such intense primitive longing. She wanted to taste him, to touch him, to kiss him.

When he looked into her eyes she knew he felt her passion. His jaw clenched. He stiffened and made a move to widen the distance between them. She understood his hesitation. It could cost him his badge to get involved with her but she couldn't help herself. She needed him on an intimate level. Fueled by her desire, she reached out to him.

"Jace," she whispered his name and moistened her lips, letting him know with just one word that she wanted him. That what happened between them, stayed between them. His eyes glazed with lust and she felt his resolve melt around the edges.

"Skylar." His voice was whispery soft, gentle and filled with such need her blood raced through her veins. He stalked closer. His every movement was sensual, seductive.

When she looked into his eyes, her breath stopped. "Yes?"

His burning gaze left her face and slowly tracked down her body. "How bad do you want to capture Lucas?" The warm timbre of his speech seeped into her skin, filling her with heat.

"Bad." Her words came out as a soft, sexy moan.

He leaned in and breathed into her mouth. "I assume you do know where we're going?" His fingers surfed along her skin. His touch was hot. Tempting.

When his scent reached her nostrils, a soft moan of surrender rumbled in her throat. Unable to find her voice, she nodded and bit down on her bottom lip. Jace carefully watched the movement.

His eyes locked with hers as he delved beneath her skirt and slid his hand between her thighs. She dragged in a shuddery breath.

"Then you know we have to pretend to be lovers, right?" His hand trailed higher and lingered only inches below the warm apex centered between her legs.

"What...what are you suggesting?" Desire burned in her veins and undoubtedly colored her cheeks a hot pink. She resisted the urge to arch into him.

He looked at her with pure lust. "I think perhaps our best chance of pulling this off is to spend a little time getting to know each other. Intimately." The hoarseness in his voice felt like a rough caress.

He held her gaze as he smoothed her hair from her forehead. Warmth settled low in her stomach. Jace Garrett was a powerful, ruthless hunter, yet he was so gentle with her.

Skylar believed that somewhere deep underneath that gruff façade existed a sensitive, compassionate man.

The logical part of her warned her to be careful. Not to get too close. No matter how handsome he was, or how deeply she fell under his spell, Jace was a man who could undoubtedly break her heart.

"I think you should kiss me, Jace." They both knew it was an excuse to touch each other. The raw, animalistic pull between them was too powerful for even the strongest of minds to fight.

When he captured her mouth in a kiss full of sensual promises, all coherent thought vanished. She became too lost in the sensations to think rationally.

She felt her body splinter into tiny pieces when his tongue swept through her mouth like a windstorm. A low growl rumbled in his throat. His passionate, demanding kiss quickly overshadowed sensibility.

His primitive nature aroused sensations in her unlike anything she'd ever felt before. She should stop, she really should. She should run away and put an end to his sweet kisses, but his primal essence completely overwhelmed her. She knew she couldn't end this even if she wanted to.

His fingers skimmed her panties and she let out a little gasp. Like a pebble tossed into a placid lake, ripples of pleasure moved onward and upward through her body.

"Mmm…" He moaned his approval as a reckless grin tugged at his mouth. "Why so wet?" His deep voice was hot, rich and flowed down her spine like warm honey.

The need to lose herself in him became so intense it was almost painful. She began breathing heavily, trembling from head to toe.

"You have to ask?" Need made her voice husky.

Her fingers skated over his shaft and it pulsed in response. She stroked him and watched him grow another inch. She'd never seen a cock as big or as thick before. How would they ever fit together? She shuddered just thinking about him pushing his engorged erection deep inside her pussy. An intoxicating mix of heat and fire poured through her.

His male juices dripped from the tip of his cock. She ran her fingers over it and watched in fascination as the bulbous head darkened and swelled in her hand. White-hot desire claimed her. She swallowed the saliva pooling in her mouth as she envisioned herself brushing her tongue over the warm tip of his arousal.

She squeezed him. "So nice..." A moan escaped from her throat as his liquid heat lubricated her hands.

"Tell me you want me." There was a soft growl beneath his gentle voice. He pulled her in close and she collapsed against a wall of thick, hard muscles.

When she tipped her chin, she became captive by the turbulent gaze in his dark eyes. "I want you," she said breathlessly.

With that, Jace threw his head back, moaned, and pressed into her hand. In a motion so fast it took her off-guard, he delved further under her skirt, and in one fluid motion ripped off her panties.

Chapter Three

ꟹ

Jace wanted her like he'd never wanted another woman before. He craved her with an intensity that was as scary as it was arousing. When she first reached out to him, he fought down his carnal craving and started to pull away. He almost succeeded until her heady feminine scent reached his over-sensitized nostrils, curled through his bloodstream and awakened the beast within him.

"Jace," she whispered breathlessly. The sound of her seductive voice made him forget all rational thought, allowing need and desire to rule his actions.

Her heat scorched him, while her exotic aroma sent fire pitching through his veins. The beast inside him howled and the need to feed his hunger curdled his blood.

As his fingers continued their gentle assault beneath her skirt, he looked deep into her eyes and surfed his other hand along the delicate curve of her jaw. The long column of her neck was warm satin beneath his stroking fingers. His thumb brushed her swollen lips. Her mouth was so soft and smooth, like the whisper of silk over his skin. A fast, erratic pulse drummed against his touch. He leaned in to caress the deep hollow of her throat with his tongue. Her whimper of pleasure resonated through his body.

"You taste exquisite," he whispered, his voice a rusty growl.

When she moaned her approval, he rewarded her by dipping a finger into her cunt.

She gasped and let her head roll to the side. Like a musician plucking strings, he strummed her clit until it sprang out from beneath its hooded flesh.

He continued to caress her delicate pearl until her juices moistened her slick pussy. Her feminine scent beckoned, enticing him.

"I need to taste you, Skylar."

"Yes, please. Taste me…" Her voice was richly seductive. She thrust her pelvis forward, urging him on.

"Let me undress you first."

She nodded her consent.

His nimble fingers worked the buttons on her blouse before he peeled it open and slipped it off her shoulders. Her nipples tightened under his appreciative gaze. When he licked his lips in anticipation, her breathing became labored. Skylar cupped one breast, rubbed a finger over her hard nipple, and offered it to him.

As he leaned in to suckle her, the wet tip of his cock pressed between her silken thighs. His nostrils flared and he called on every ounce of strength not to bend her over and fuck her right then. But it was too soon for him to lose control. He wanted to take it slow, to savor every delicious minute, and stretch the night on forever.

Before his composure vanished, he moved in for a more thorough taste of her tight nipples. She moved restlessly against him and he felt her body quiver beneath his pillaging tongue. He pulled one puckered pebble into his mouth and gently ran it between his teeth. Skylar's body melted all over him as he wrapped an arm around her waist and anchored her to his hips. Her uninhibited responses to his touch sent a riot of emotions through him.

He stroked her breasts and tongued her nipple until animal lust took over. The urge to sink into her heat overwhelmed him, but before he gave into such indulgence, he needed to ravage her sweet, dripping pussy.

With agonizing slowness, he worked the button free on her skirt. As he dragged it down her long legs, he purposely nudged her swollen clit. He grinned when she moaned, thrust her hips forward, and arched like a bow. She gave a needy, not-quite-satisfied sigh.

He inhaled her. Deeply. Her enticing scent nearly drove him over the edge. The sweet torture made his cock throb. "Get on that bed and spread your legs for me."

Obediently, she kicked off her shoes and took a few steps back, pushing his duvet aside and sinking onto his mattress, her sensuous body warming and scenting his cotton sheets.

The sight of her long hair pooling across his pillow while the silvery moon bathed her body left him weak.

Licking her lips, she widened her legs and caught his gaze. She slid her small hands over her breasts and lower, until she touched the glistening dark patch at her center. Her curls were damp with passion. Jace growled and began panting heavily. She parted her dewy folds, probed her drenched cunt and then brought her hand to her mouth. She slipped her finger between her pretty pink lips and moaned. "Mmmm." Once again she dipped into her pussy and held her finger out to him. "Want some?"

A tremor racked his body. Jace growled and dropped to his knees. "Jesus, what are you doing to me?" He gripped her ankles, spread her legs wide apart and climbed in between. Moving his mouth to her creamy white thighs, he breathed in her intoxicating aroma. His lips climbed higher and higher until he reached her wet pussy. Shivers of warm need moved through him.

As he parted her silky strands with his tongue, heat flowed over him with a slow molten burn. He felt her skin tighten beneath his invading mouth. Her clit was hard, inflamed. She wrapped her fingers though his hair, pinning his mouth to her cunt.

God, she tasted like heaven.

He lapped at her and licked her sweet juices until she writhed and moaned like a wild, wanton woman.

"Jace, please. I need more. I need you inside me. Now."

"I'm not nearly done tasting you, sweetheart," he said, and probed her opening with his tongue. "I want you to come in my mouth. I want to taste your juices." He toyed with her clit and felt her muscles quake. "That's it, baby, just relax and let it happen." Changing the tempo and rhythm of his tongue and fingers, he worked her into a sexual frenzy.

She fisted his hair and drove his face deeper into her pussy. Her muscles began to pulse and clench with her mounting orgasm. She took deep gulping breaths as he pushed a finger inside and slowly curled it around her G-spot. Skylar threw her head to the side and pitched her hips forward. "Yes," she cried out. She palmed and squeezed his sinewy shoulder muscles as he worked another finger tight inside her. She began trembling and panting. A low moan sounded deep in her throat as his burning mouth pressed hungrily against her cunt and massaged her puckered clit. She watched him feast on her pussy. Her erotic whimpers filled the room. She threw her head back. "Yes, Jace," she whispered, as the rippling waves of an orgasm took hold. In no time at all her milky-sweet release poured into his mouth.

After he lapped up every last drop, he slowly slid up her body. His lips hovered only inches from her. "I've never tasted anything sweeter."

"Show me." Her gaze was drowsy, sexy.

He moaned and pushed his cock against her thigh. "Dear God, Skylar. You're making me crazy." He smoothed her hair from her face and closed his lips over hers for a mind-numbing kiss. She drew his tongue deeper into her mouth and wrapped her legs around his back.

"Very sweet," she murmured into his mouth.

A moment later she broke the kiss and looked deep into his eyes. "When do I get to taste you?"

He knew the second her warm, sensuous lips closed over his cock, he'd explode in her mouth. "That will have to be next time. Right now I need to fuck you."

Her eyes glazed over. "Yes, Jace, fuck me."

He loved the way she spoke his name. So soft, so intimate. He eased into her. Offering her only a few inches.

"More," she demanded and bucked against him. She hugged her legs tighter around his ass and drove him inside her.

"Yes!" she screamed, when his thickness pushed open the tight walls of her pussy.

"Yes, Skylar, that's my girl. Take what you need." He buried himself into her tight, hot sheath and luxuriated in her silky heat.

The bed began to rock as he thrust into her. She kissed him with a passion so intense he lost all track of time and place. As she clung to him, he felt her come apart in his arms. Her muscles tightened around his cock and he knew her next climax was only a few strokes away.

He grabbed her wrists and pinned them above her head as he pushed impossibly deeper. He wasn't just seeking her heat, her warmth. He was in search of something else, though he wasn't exactly sure what. He needed her to be one with him.

He pushed that thought to the far corners of his mind to consider later.

She moved under him. Meeting and welcoming each delicious thrust. He felt that first tight clench of her muscles that told him fulfillment was only a heartbeat away. He slammed into her, deep and fast, giving her what she needed to take her over the edge. She screamed and writhed as another orgasm racked her body.

He glanced up into her eyes, the desire reflected there his undoing. His body began to pulse and throb. A low, animal growl rumbled deep in his throat as her sultry tang saturated the room. His skin grew tight and his balls constricted as pressure built deep in his groin. He took deep gasping breaths in an effort to fill his lungs.

"Skylar..." Flames surged through him. His body tensed. His senses exploded when he bucked forward, driving his cock impossibly deeper. Perspiration beaded his skin as her juices seared his dick. Jace threw his head back and groaned.

When her muscles tightened around his cock he pumped harder and then stilled as his seed erupted deep inside her.

As he lay on top of her, he worked at regulating his breathing. "You're incredible, sweetheart," he whispered into her ear as their juices mingled deep inside her pussy.

Her smile was warm and tender. She pushed his damp hair off his forehead and feathered her fingers over his jaw. Her touch was so gentle, so loving. A cocoon of warmth encompassed him as he leaned into her hand.

He shifted his body weight and curled up beside her. She snuggled into him while he stroked her hair and looked deep into her eyes. Now that he'd pleased the beast within him, rational thought returned. He watched her, gauging her reaction, checking to see if she'd been able to sense the animal pacing below the surface. Fortunately, he'd spent thirty-one years mastering the ability to hide *what* he really was. Relief washed through him when she smiled at him, still oblivious to his true nature.

"That was amazing," she whispered breathlessly.

He rained kisses over her cheeks and grinned. "I do aim to please," he teased.

Skylar grinned in return. "Lucky for me."

God, he couldn't believe how emotional he was feeling. He'd had great sex before, but those experiences paled in comparison to what he was feeling now. He wanted to know everything about her. She got under his skin and touched something deep inside. Something he hadn't even known existed. And that scared him more than a silver bullet aimed at his head. Because if he gave in to those emotions she'd surely sense the wolf.

"Tell me something about yourself that no one else knows."

She gave a quick shake of her head. "Forget it," she said and pinched her lips tight.

He swiped his tongue over her lips and she automatically opened for him. "Come on," he coaxed. "Tell me something that you wouldn't even tell your closest girlfriend."

She frowned, sadness apparent in her eyes. "I don't really have any close girlfriends."

He lifted a brow. "No? Why not?"

"Because most women think I'm a freak. Sometimes it's hard for me to hide my abilities and women feel threatened by me." She forced a small smile and turned the tables on him. "Tell me something about yourself that no one else knows."

Jace's heart went out to her. He understood loneliness all too well. "I'm a freak, too." He shrugged. "What do you know? We have something in common."

"No friends?" she asked, cuddling in tighter as they shared a common connection creating a bond between them.

Yeah, that…and I'm a werewolf. "I'm kind of a loner."

She smiled at him. "So what happens after two loners have sex?"

As he held her in his arms, a wave of anger welled up inside Jace. Fuck! He hated that he was cursed with werewolf blood. Hated that he could never have anything more than a physical relationship with her. There was no way he could let her in, show her his true emotions or get too close. As much as he loved the idea of marriage and children, he couldn't possibly have such a thing. Not when deep inside him a werewolf stirred in his blood.

Once a month he chained himself to his bed for fear of unleashing the animal within. He had no idea if he could tame the beast in the dark corners of his mind and wasn't about to give himself an opportunity to find out. Wasn't about to put a woman in jeopardy. Especially this woman.

He exhaled a weary sigh and tried to separate himself from his emotions. He could never be anything more to a woman than just a wild time.

The rich scent of their lovemaking reached his nostrils and he growled. Cushioning her in his arms, he looked deep into her eyes, and knew he wanted her again. She might not be his forever, but she was his tonight.

"I believe after two loners have sex, it's customary for them to do it again."

"Again?" she asked, grinning. Her voice was a sleepy whisper.

"Again," he said and captured her lips in a searing kiss.

* * * * *

Hours later, silence fell over them as Jace drove his car along the highway. Skylar studied the picture of two young kids hanging from his rearview mirror.

Skylar nodded to the picture. "Are those your kids?" She really had no idea if he had a family somewhere.

He shook his head and smiled. "No, those are the Cap's twins. They're great. Michael likes to go fishing with me and Michelle likes to put curlers in my hair. She says if I'm going to wear it long like a girl then it should be styled like a girl's." A low chuckle rumbled in his throat.

Skylar's heart melted in her chest. There was so much more to this tough agent than she knew. If he liked kids so much, why didn't he have a family of his own? Before she had time to ask him, he pulled his car into a parking space in front of Paradise Resort.

He twisted sideways to look at her. "Any questions before we go in there?"

Apprehension began moving through her. Lucas was here. She felt it with every fiber of her being. The small hairs on the back of her neck began tingling, alerting her to the imminent danger that lay ahead.

Jace moved closer. He leaned in and slanted his head. His mouth was so close to her ear she could feel his warm breath. "Don't worry. I won't let anything happen to you," he murmured. His fingers closed over hers, warm and strong. He gave a gentle squeeze. "Just remember, no matter what the circumstances, we have to play along."

Skylar drew a deep shuddery breath. It amazed her how in tune he was with her emotions.

Without realizing what she was doing, she entwined her fingers through his. The compulsion to lean into him, to find solace in his embrace suddenly overcame her.

As she stared at him for an endless moment, her heart did a little pitter-patter in her chest. She might consider herself a self-reliant, independent woman but there was something in the way he treated her that made her feel absurdly safe.

She couldn't believe how close she felt to him. There was no awkwardness between them after what they'd shared. Instead, there was warmth and familiarity. And she found that very disconcerting, given the fact that there was still some small part of him she couldn't read.

She suddenly became aware of the way her body was reacting as Jace idly stroked his thumb over her hand. "Do you think we'll be able to pull it off and fool people into believing we're lovers?" She eased her hand away, folded her arms across her chest and hugged herself. She immediately missed the heat from his touch.

Despite having changed into a pair of jeans and a sweater, the night air had dropped a few degrees, leaving her feeling somewhat chilled.

He hooked a finger under her chin and lifted her face to his. When he smiled at her, she lost her breath. Her body warmed all over, in spite of the cooling temperatures outside.

She watched the cords in his throat work. "I do now," he said, his voice an intimate whisper. She watched, transfixed as his burning eyes left her face and slowly scrolled the length of her. Sexual tension hung heavy in the air as the corners of his mouth lifted suggestively.

Skylar smiled and ran her tongue around suddenly dry lips. The heat firing between them began steaming up the windows. She forced herself to get her emotions under control. Her whole reason for being there was to capture Lucas, not fall into Jace's arms again.

"Okay, let's do it." She hated that her voice sounded so tight.

She opened her door, climbed from the passenger seat and circled the car to meet Jace. She waited for him while he grabbed their luggage from the trunk. He slung her bag over his shoulder and tucked his case under his arm. His large hand swallowed hers as he led her to the main building. The warmth of his fingers over her skin left her body tingling.

Secluded amongst a cluster of old pine trees, towering oaks and shrubs, the main building of the resort remained draped in utter darkness. Long fingers of silvery moonlight broke through the canopy of willow branches that hovered over the cobblestone walkway. The fragrant smell of lilac and honeysuckle perfumed the air. Skylar listened to the crickets chirping and frogs croaking a melodic love song nearby. Somewhere further in the distance the sound of rushing water mingled with the soft murmur of voices.

Jace pushed open the front door and Skylar had to quicken her steps to keep pace as his long strides carried him to the front counter.

She felt as if she'd just walked off the city street and into an African safari. The walls were dressed in a striped, zebra motif. Beautiful, lush palm trees draped with tiny fairy lights were strategically positioned throughout the lobby and provided a warm blend of soft light and romance. Ivy garlands hugged the ceiling, while potted ferns climbed the textured walls. Tiger-skin throws were haphazardly tossed over a leopard print sofa and matching loveseat. The neutral-colored ceramic tile beneath their feet reflected the earthy jungle feel.

The overall decor proved to be seductively alluring.

Jace stepped up to the counter. "I have a reservation under the name of Garrett." He dropped their luggage onto a nearby cart.

The clerk behind the counter pursed his lips and scrutinized his reservation book. "Yes, we've been waiting for you."

Jace cocked one brow suspiciously. "You have?"

"Uh-huh." He nodded and winked. "The festivities are already in full swing."

"Ah, yes, of course," Jace said.

Skylar watched Jace play along. He remained cool and collected under pressure. She knew he had no idea what festivities the clerk was referring to. She admired his confidence and self-assurance.

"My wife and I have been looking forward to these *festivities*—" he said, returning the clerk's wink, "—for weeks." He wrapped his arm around Skylar and pulled her closer.

She snuggled into him and, like the adoring wife she was supposed to be, pasted on what she hoped was a seductive, bedroom smile.

A wide grin spread across the clerk's face. He handed Jace a sheet of paper to sign. "Once you've completed your initiation ritual, I'll show you to your suite." He folded his hands on the countertop. "You're booked into the Wet and Wild suite."

"Initiation ritual?" Skylar piped in, trying not to look too alarmed.

He frowned and raised an eyebrow. "Surely you've read the pamphlets?" The clerk gestured for the concierge.

"Well..." She shrugged apologetically.

"It's customary for first-timers to be initiated."

Skylar's eyes widened in surprise. Her heart did a somersault. The concierge came up beside her and she turned her attention to him. "What's involved—?"

In a movement so fast it took her off guard, Jace's mouth closed over hers as he silenced her protests with a long, sensuous kiss. He pressed his lips to hers. Hard. Possessively. He traded wet, heated kisses with her for so long it left her shaken. She was out of breath when he finally released her. By the time she gathered her wits, she noticed the delighted expression on concierge's face.

Jace spoke up. "I know all about the initiation rituals," he assured the clerk. "I was saving the intimate details as a surprise for my wife." He lowered his voice and looked deep into her eyes.

Skylar's knees turned to warm liquid when she caught his smoldering gaze and reckless grin. It was the way he always looked *at* her, not through her, that knocked her off balance. It was as if she were the most important woman in the world.

He framed her face with his hands. "She just loves surprises. Don't you, sweetheart?" The pleasure in his voice sent a shudder rippling through her.

Skylar worked past the knot in her throat and tried to keep her voice low and sultry. "Of course I do, honey." Pressing her lips together, she stood there basking in the glow of Jace's touch, thankful that he was so patient with her foolish mistakes.

Jace rubbed his hands together in anticipation, and suddenly Skylar wondered if he'd known exactly what these "festivities" were all along.

The concierge nodded and motioned with a wave. "If you'll follow me then," he said.

With Jace's arm carelessly draped over her shoulder, they followed the concierge down a long hallway. It seemed the most natural thing in the world for Jace to touch her in such a familiar way. She supposed he was doing it on purpose, to make them blend in and look like every other married couple in the resort.

The thought that he was just doing it for the sake of the job inexplicably disappointed her, even though she knew it was what was expected of him.

They stopped just outside a set of thick oak doors. Skylar heard soft music mingling with the murmur of husky, seductive voices. Blocking out everything around her, she concentrated hard to see if Lucas was behind those doors. Both relief and disappointment flowed through her when she realized he wasn't. She was surprised to discover just how apprehensive she was about this operation. In the past, the PTFA had never allowed her to accompany an officer on a hunt. They must have suspected she was in capable hands with Jace Garrett.

If only they knew exactly how capable those hands were.

The concierge pushed open the wide double doors and gestured to a tall, casually dressed man on the other side of the lavish room. The man nodded his acknowledgement while a waiter stepped forward and handed her a tall glass of champagne.

Skylar graciously accepted the drink, took a generous sip to help relax her frayed nerves, pressed the delicate crystal glass into Jace's hand and then followed him further into the room. The jungle theme from the main lobby carried through into the large lounge area. Once inside, Skylar stopped dead in her tracks. The scene playing out before her left her shocked, speechless. Her stomach took a nosedive.

Jace must have felt her withdrawal. When he nudged her, she schooled her face and remembered they were to remain undercover at all times. No matter how difficult the circumstances were, no matter what situation they found themselves in, they had to play along if they wanted to catch Lucas.

She leaned into Jace and he tightened his hold. Enclosed in the safety of Jace's arms she scanned the room. It was filled with couples, some semi-clad, others completely naked. A few shared glasses of champagne and talked quietly amongst themselves while others were oblivious to anyone around them as they engaged in heated sexual activities. In one corner, underneath the pale glow of a lighted palm tree, a man pushed his cock deep inside a woman while he traded passionate kisses and kneaded the breasts of another. Similar acts took place in every dimly lit corner of the spacious room.

The host stepped up onto an elevated stage and raised his hand. A hush fell over the crowd. All eyes turned to the front, even the men and women in the corners fell quiet.

Skylar pressed against Jace. "What's going on?"

He shrugged and led her to a table where they quickly seated themselves. Jace swallowed a mouthful of champagne and handed it back to her. Skylar took another large gulp from the glass. She wasn't much of a drinker, and suddenly felt a little dizzy. She blinked her eyes into focus and tried to concentrate on what the man was saying.

"Our last guests of the evening have arrived," the host announced and waved his hand in Skylar's direction.

Skylar swallowed as all eyes turned on them.

"Now, if I could have all the men in the center of the room, we can begin." He drew a circle in the air and indicated an empty space in front of the stage.

Jace made a move to rise but Skylar grabbed him. "Don't go."

He leaned in and brushed his lips over her cheek until his mouth was close to her ear. "Everything will be fine," he assured her, but the way the other men stared at her with hunger in their eyes left her feeling a little uncertain.

She watched as Jace's long, muscular legs carried him to the center of the floor where he stood beside the rest of the men. Skylar estimated that twenty or so other guys stood with him. She glanced around the room. The women watched the festivities with bright-eyed enthusiasm. Skylar had no idea what was about to happen, but by the excited look in everyone's eyes, she suspected it was something big.

As she finished off the cool, sweet liquid in her glass, warmth spread over her body and she felt herself begin to relax. She drew a long breath and let the champagne work its magic.

"Now, let's all give a warm welcome to Skylar as she begins her initiation ritual," the host said, clapping his hands enthusiastically.

At the mention of her name, Skylar felt all her blood drain to her feet. The sound of clapping was like thunder in the room. She shot Jace a sidelong glance and he gave her a quick, short nod.

Skylar swallowed her apprehension and scanned the room. If she blew her cover and didn't go along with the festivities, the PTFA would never allow her on a hunt again. And that was something she couldn't let happen, because she'd made a vow years ago that she'd do whatever it took to bring down every last werewolf until they were obliterated from Earth.

"Skylar, if you would," the host said, motioning for her to rise.

A young woman, who looked to be about the same age as Skylar, grabbed her arm and lifted her from her chair. Another older woman jumped up and pushed Skylar forward while she shouted words of encouragement. Many other women joined in, chanting their reassurance. Skylar drew a deep breath, fueling her courage.

The room seemed to sway as she walked slowly over to the assembled group of men. She had no idea how her rubbery legs managed to carry her. The men stepped aside to let her in. When she broke through the circle, all chanting stopped and she became acutely aware of the silence settling over her. She felt like she'd just entered the lion's den.

Her mind began racing, trying to understand what was expected of her, but she couldn't seem to keep a coherent thought. Unsuccessfully, she tried to shake the buzz from her head.

She turned toward the host and worked at quieting her heartbeat as she awaited further instructions.

"Now you will undress." His voice was deep, gravelly.

Skylar's breath came in a ragged burst and she felt her whole body go slack. Then she quickly realized he was talking to the group of men encircling her. Hastily, many of them had begun to tear their clothes off in anticipation. She touched her tongue to her lips and grinned when she caught Jace's gaze. Perhaps this initiation ritual would be more pleasant than she'd originally anticipated.

She gave him a playful look.

The crowd of women seemed to grow restless as they watched the men discard their clothes. Once again, they began clapping and chanting for the men to "take it off". Their low, murmuring chants grew louder as they became more and more excited. It all seemed so tribal, so primal.

Skylar glanced at the men surrounding her, but there was only one man in the circle that held her attention. She watched, mesmerized, as he peeled off his T-shirt and exposed his broad chest and tight abdominal muscles. He had a six-pack that would intoxicate any woman. Without realizing what she was doing, she licked her suddenly dry lips.

A moan caught in her throat when he worked the zipper on his jeans. She immediately recalled how he'd pleasured her only hours earlier. A wave of passion washed over her as saliva pooled in her mouth. He slid his jeans and boxers down his thighs and kicked them aside. His every movement was sensual, suggestive. He was staring straight at her, clearly aroused. His huge, thick cock sprang to life right before her eyes. His breathing was ragged.

She lifted her gaze to his and noticed the sparkle in his eyes. Her whole body quivered in delight as she ached to lose herself in him once again.

Her mind and body relaxed and began swimming with indecent thoughts. Thoughts about how she'd like to take his throbbing erection into her slick mouth and suck until his juices erupted deep in her throat. Her legs widened involuntarily. Skylar felt her nipples tighten painfully and resisted the urge to cup them with her hands. She had to lock her knees to steady herself.

All around her, men impatiently tossed their clothes aside. She felt her internal temperature rise as cocks of all shapes and sizes began to grow beneath her appreciative eyes. It didn't take her very long to figure out what was expected of her.

The sound of the host's voice drew her attention. She reluctantly tore her gaze away from all the naked flesh and turned toward him. She ran her tongue around her desert-dry mouth. Her whole body felt light, like she was floating. She felt a little disoriented.

What was in that champagne?

"Skylar, you may pick one man and bring him onto this stage where you will perform whatever sexual act you desire."

She groaned with unexpected pleasure.

She looked deep into Jace's eyes. They were dark, scalding hot, and filled with raw hunger. A jolt of desire singed her blood.

The chanting began again. The smell of sex fired her blood. In no time at all she became caught up in the frenzy from the crowd and felt herself being pulled into the excitement.

She felt her body flush as her sex juices begin to flow. Lust settled deep in her loins. She savored the sensations that rushed through her.

When the men began to masturbate, the women in the crowd who were still dressed began removing their own clothes. Their chanting changed in beat and loudness. Many produced vibrators and began probing their hot cunts or using them on the women beside them. Skylar felt her breathing become heavy, labored, as she walked slowly around the circle. She stopped to give consideration to every single man.

She knew the situation was escalating beyond her power to stop it. It felt too good, too right. Her whole body was on fire, yet there was only one man in the room who could extinguish that blaze.

She paused in front a dark-skinned, muscular man and let her gaze drop to his cock. "Very nice," she said to him as she stroked his engorged phallus. He moaned his appreciation and reached out to touch her breasts. Totally caught up in the moment, she groaned and threw her head back while he played with her tight nipples through her sweater.

Feeling like a kid in a candy store, she moved around the circle and studied the different men, but the whole time she knew exactly who she wanted. Exactly who she'd choose. There wasn't a guy in the place that stood a chance against Jace Garrett.

He was such a beautiful man.

Apparently she wasn't the only one in the room who thought so. Many women eyed him while they licked their lips and pushed their sex toys further inside their drenched pussies.

She was shocked by the wave of possessiveness that washed over her.

Skylar turned her attention to Jace. With long, easy movements she crossed the room to stand before him. He reached out and brushed a wayward strand of hair from her face. She craved the feel of his skin against hers. She leaned into him, letting him know she welcomed his touch. The wet tip of his arousal brushed between her inner thighs and her pussy became slick with excitement. Her skin grew tight and needy.

Gone was the tenderness she'd seen earlier in his eyes. In its place existed raw, primitive lust. When his deep eyes were looking directly at her, it was possible to forget every sane thought.

A jolt of uneasiness filtered through her when she realized exactly how much she wanted him again. Deep down she knew that having sex with him had nothing to do with protecting her cover. She wanted him on all levels.

When he put an arm around her and pulled her up against him, she quickly reminded herself that what she felt for him was lust. Pure and simple. There were no emotions between them, nor did she want there to be.

Skylar knew that when it came to relationships with her, nothing lasted forever. Undoubtedly, that small unreadable part of Jace's mind was his way of closing his feelings off to her. Jace was no different from all the men from her past. He'd never give himself emotionally to a psychic.

He caressed her neck and quickly made her forget all coherent thought. Desire twisted inside her and fired her blood. "This is the man I choose," she said boldly, leaning in to graze his lips with her own. Jace deepened the kiss. Champagne mingled on their tongues. She savored the sweetness of his mouth.

He grabbed her hair and held her against him. "Why me, when you can have your pick of any man in the room?" His voice was a gruff whisper.

She pulled back and looked into his eyes. A sly smile slanted her lips. "Because I never did get to taste your cock."

Chapter Four

ꙮ

Silence descended upon the crowd as Skylar slipped her hand into Jace's and led him to the stage. Her fingers felt so small inside his powerful grasp. Her body came alive just thinking about how the thickness of his fingers had probed deep inside her pussy and given her an earth-shattering orgasm a short while ago.

Jace willingly followed her onto the elevated platform. His eyes were dark and full of lust. By now her nipples were excruciatingly hard and her pussy was dripping wet. She ached for him to tongue-fuck her, to bury his long fingers deep inside her cunt once again. But that would have to wait, because right now her mouth craved the tangy taste of his cock.

After they situated themselves on the stage, Jace pulled her close and trailed the backs of his fingers down her cheeks. His smile was filled with tenderness and concern.

"You don't have to do anything you're uncomfortable with," he assured her. The longing coloring his voice told her how much he wanted this.

It was sweet that he was concerned about her, but she wanted this as much as he did. "I know," she whispered. Even though she knew what she was doing wasn't rational or smart, she was too caught up in the moment to consider putting an end to this sweet torment. The only thing important to her right now was this moment and this man. She knew there was no turning back now.

Skylar positioned herself between his legs and wrapped her delicate fingers around his thick shaft, her gaze taking in the sight of his huge cock. His size and thickness thrilled her all over again. Her pink tongue snaked out and caressed the tip of his sex. She inhaled his musky scent.

"I can smell your arousal," she whispered.

When her warm breath fanned his cock, it pulsed in response. She listened as his breath came out in a low rush. She looked up at him. He looked so damn sexy, so hot. He cupped her cheeks in his palms and guided her head forward.

"This is what you do to me." He threw his head back and groaned when she flicked her tongue out for a more thorough taste.

The crowd erupted into cheers when she began her initiation ritual. A moment later they broke off into smaller groups and delved into their own sexual escapades.

Skylar was the only one in the room that remained fully dressed. She smiled up at Jace. His face had taken on a ruddy hue, his eyes deep and glossy.

She leaned forward and scraped her teeth lightly over his erection. Jace growled, fisted her hair and pushed his pelvis forward.

She slowly drew the bulbous head into her mouth and moaned in delight when his warm, velvety cock easily slid to the back of her throat. She stroked her tongue down the length of him and kissed him lightly. She felt his whole body tense in response to her slow seduction.

The heat of his cock seared her mouth. Flames surged through her when she tasted that first salty drip. He groaned and threaded his fingers through her hair, pushing his cock deeper between her lips.

With a catlike stretch, her exploring fingers grazed his inner thighs. Her fingers climbed higher and sifted through the tangle of dark hair at his groin. She grasped his heavy sac, gently massaging and cupping his tight balls in her hand. She lowered her mouth to stroke and taste them with her tongue.

Jace reached down and thumbed her nipples through her sweater, evoking a low groan from her that grew louder and louder, until her moans of pleasure mingled with his.

His head lolled to the side. "Skylar, sweetheart, you're damn near killing me." He pinched her nipples and made her gasp.

She eased back and looked deep into his glazed eyes. "Then perhaps I should stop." She chuckled easily when he gave a quick shake of his head.

"You should never stop," he growled viciously, and drove his cock back into her mouth.

The fact that she was pleasing him gave her great satisfaction. She wasn't sure why his pleasure was so important to her.

Encouraged by the moans of approval from the frenzied crowd, she once again drew his entire cock into her mouth. "Mmmm…" With little finesse and much greed she laved the swollen head and drank the salty, dripping semen emerging from the tip.

His breathing grew labored. She teased and caressed his erection, taking time to savor every delectable inch. Soon her panting matched his.

"Do you like doing this, baby?" His voice was silky soft. "In front of all these people?"

When she moaned her reply, he gave a satisfied sigh.

"Does it make you wet?" He pressed his foot between her thighs and she pushed against him. Like a cat on a scratching post, she purred and rubbed against him.

"If I slipped my fingers inside your panties would I find you wet for me?" The masculine tenor of his voice sent fire reverberating through her blood. She spread her legs further in silent invitation.

"You make me so hot, my pussy is dripping wet," she murmured seductively around a mouthful of cock. Warm and wicked sensations washed over her.

"When you're done, sweetheart, promise me you'll let me taste your sweet juices again." His voice was raspy, throaty. Her heart raced in anticipation.

She flicked her tongue inside the slit of his penis and felt him grow another inch. She loved his warm texture and earthly, masculine scent. Her head began spinning as her internal temperature ignited to near boiling.

His thickness pulled her lips apart. She sank the entire length of him down her throat.

He pumped into her with a fervid passion, and she felt the throbbing of his orgasm as it neared. "Fuck me with your mouth, baby," he growled. His voice was thick with desire and need and something else. Something she couldn't quite put her finger on. She tried to read his thoughts, but once again, there was a small part of him she couldn't reach. A part of him he purposely kept under lock and key.

"I'm going to come, sweetheart," he gasped, his breath coming in a ragged burst. He tried to ease her mouth away, but she shook her head no.

"I want to drink from you," she murmured, flicking her tongue over the slit while her hands milked his rock-hard shaft.

She felt a tremor ripple through him and knew he was close. She sucked long and hard, until hollows pulled at her cheeks. He began moving his hips, pressing against her. Then he drew a sharp breath and threw his head back.

His explosion was fast, intense, sending his liquid heat down her throat. She swallowed every delicious drop and then laved his cock clean.

She eased back on her heels and looked up at him. His chest lifted and fell with his deep, labored breathing. A deep, contented sigh curved his handsome face. He reached out and cupped her chin.

"Come here, baby," he said, his voice gentle, caring. Jace brushed her hair from her face and looked deep into her eyes. Skylar noticed something in his expression had changed. She swallowed hard. She had to be careful, otherwise the longing and wistfulness in his eyes would not only affect her body, they would affect her heart.

She had no idea that getting physical with Jace would be so emotional or so soul-stirring. Some part of her warned that this went way beyond lust. She pushed that worry to the back of her mind to mull it over later.

She slowly slid up his stomach until her mouth was only a breath away from his. His hard cock pressed against her midriff.

"Kiss me," he whispered. He bent his head down and trailed a feathery kiss over her lips. The light pressure of his mouth was both erotic and arousing.

Skylar's mouth began to tingle where the silky softness of his lips touched her. His warm tongue slipped inside. He slid his hand over her breasts and lower, until he dipped inside her panties and inched open her heated folds.

Beneath her, her legs fought for stability. Her head felt light and woozy and she couldn't seem to maintain a focused thought. She gripped his shoulders, sure she was going to black out from the pleasure. His body pushed against hers and she felt herself slacken in response. She shuddered as his exploring hands grazed her clit.

She cried out to him. "Jace..." Her pussy, burning with desire, was ready to ignite. She licked her dry lips, desperate for Jace to stoke that fire.

"I know, baby. I know." His voice was husky, deep and barely audible.

When he slipped two fingers inside her, her heart rose in her throat. She shivered as his soft, gentle hands touched her with promise. Using his knee he urged her thighs apart. A whimper escaped her lips. His fingers worked inside her, drawing out her orgasm. She shifted her body in an effort to provide him with better access.

"Yes, right there," she cried out when he touched the sensitive spot deep inside her pussy. She ground her hips against him. Her breath came in small, short gasps. At first his fingers moved slowly, and then his touch became more determined, faster and bolder, in search of its final goal.

Perspiration speckled her forehead. "Jace, please..." she gasped, her feverish longing building with every caress.

Increasing the tempo, his thumb danced over her clit and he drove another finger inside her.

A wave rippled through her cunt as her body gave in fully to his magical fingers. It felt so intimate, so right. Arching her back, she bit down on her lower lip and clenched her legs together, forcing his hand to stay deep inside her as her arousal peaked. She squirmed, squeezed her legs tighter and pressed harder against him. Her breathing turned deep and ragged as a release, powerful and intense, made her body shudder. Throwing her head back, a deep satisfied moan of pleasure rumbled in her throat as she came apart in his arms. She managed a faint smile as her sweet syrup languidly dripped over his hand.

When he slipped his hand from her panties, she immediately missed his warmth. She looked deep into his eyes.

"Shall we finish this in our room?" he asked.

She gave a little start. She'd forgotten exactly where they were. She quickly glanced around, and then presented him with a small answering smile. Closing her lips over his, she snuggled against his hard chest. She wasn't sure why, but she needed to be held by him a little longer.

Tomorrow, she vowed, tomorrow she'd get her emotions under wraps and concentrate on locating Lucas.

Tonight however, tonight was a different story entirely.

She broke the kiss and held her hand out to him. "Shall we?"

He smirked. "First I need to find my clothes."

Skylar mimicked his grin and glanced around the room. Naked bodies were sprawled across bearskin and leopard print rugs. "It's not going to be easy," she teased him.

They tiptoed through the crowd until Jace managed to find his T-shirt and jeans. His boxers, shoes and socks were long gone. Skylar didn't even want to contemplate who had them or what they were doing with them.

They quietly slipped from the room and made their way to the front counter. The clerk greeted them with a wide smile.

"Now that you've been properly initiated, I'd like to offer you a big welcome to Paradise Resort. Here are your keys, and your luggage has already been sent to your room. One more thing before you go. There's a sign-up sheet here for tomorrow's activities. Spaces fill up quickly, so be sure to get your names down early. Later in the evening a moonlight skinny-dip is scheduled."

Jace jotted his name down on the first activity sheet on the pile. Skylar glanced at it and noticed it was a scuba diving lesson. Great. Couldn't he have chosen something a little less dangerous, like napping, or sunbathing?

After they retrieved their keys, they made their way to the waiting elevator. Once inside, Jace turned to her. Skylar pressed her hand over her mouth and stifled a yawn.

"Are you tired?" he asked, stroking her bangs off her forehead.

"A little. It has been a rather *long, hard* day," she teased and reached out to stroke his cock through his jeans.

He moaned and pushed into her. The scalding look he shot her made her shiver. She loved the way he responded to her touch.

Just then, the elevator doors pinged open. Jace grabbed her hand and began escorting her down the hall. She hurried her steps to keep pace. As they neared their room, Skylar stilled, drew a deep breath and felt all the tiny hairs on the back of her neck stand up. Her head began pounding at the base of her neck. Her pulse kicked up a notch.

She swallowed her apprehension and fought to find her voice. When Jace gave her a questioning look, she nodded to the door in front of them and silently mouthed, "It's Lucas. That's his room."

* * * * *

Jace reached out and wrapped his hands around her waist. He watched her face turn ashen and feared she was about to collapse. She looked so vulnerable, so afraid. He'd had no idea just how much she feared Lucas. God, he never should have let her accompany him to the resort. This was dangerous work. She didn't belong here. What had the captain been thinking?

With the full moon only two days away, he prayed Lucas would turn fast and make his move so he could bring him down quickly. As a half-breed, Jace was able to control the beast inside him longer than a purebred. Hopefully, he'd have enough time to make the arrest and then get himself home and chained to his bed before he turned and revealed his secret to Skylar—to the world.

Skylar reached out and pressed her palms to the door. Her eyes rolled in her head and she shook all over. "He's not in there."

"Good," Jace said. "Let's go find him. Then you can keep an eye on him while I set up a surveillance camera and a listening device in his room. That way we'll be able to keep track of him from our own suite. If he tries to kill again, I'll capture him before he gets a chance."

Jace took the room key from his pocket and slipped it into their door. He took a thorough look around the room. The clerk wasn't kidding when he said they'd been booked into the Wet and Wild room. It wasn't like any other hotel room he'd ever been in. The suite was spacious yet cozy and filled with tropical palms and plants. The walls were painted in warm honey tones and plush carpeting covered the floor. On both sides of the in-wall faux fireplace, window seats offered a casual relaxing space. In the far corner he spotted a Jacuzzi. The soft hum of the jets was erotically enticing.

He walked over to the luggage cart and grabbed his suitcase. He tossed it onto the bed and unzipped it. Then he lifted his clothes out to reveal a hidden compartment underneath. He handed Skylar an earpiece and a watch then grabbed a matching set for himself.

"I didn't realize I was on a stakeout with a super-spy," Skylar teased.

Jace tossed her an easy smile. "Slip that into your ear so you can hear me, and when you need to talk to me, just press this button here." He strapped the watch to her wrist and proceeded to show her all the intricate buttons and what they were used for.

When he noticed a frown cross her features, he paused. "Are you okay with this?"

She nodded her reassurance. "Yes. I'd do anything to bring down Lucas."

"Glad to hear that." Jace strapped on his own watch and pulled a few more pieces of equipment from his suitcase and placed them into a black backpack. Then he grabbed his gun and holster.

"I'm here to help the Paranormal Task Force any way I can." Pain and hatred colored her eyes.

He flung the backpack over his shoulders and met her gaze. When she caught the questioning look in his eyes she went on to explain. "You wanted to know something about me that not many people know. Well, years ago my parents were killed by werewolves. I was injured during the attack but managed to pull through. That's how I first discovered werewolves existed and that's when my psychic abilities became enhanced. The local Federal Task Force tried to convince me it was a pack of wild dogs, but I knew better. I wouldn't let the matter rest. Then one day I was handed a card on the street. It was from your Captain. I've been helping the PTF out ever since."

Jace's expression softened. He ran his fingers over her arm as his heart reached out to her. It touched him to know she trusted him enough to share such a painful memory. "I'm sorry, Skylar. I wasn't privy to that information."

Her lips thinned. "I have a personal stake in this, Jace. I want werewolves brought to justice. Starting with Lucas."

"Then let's get started." Jace grabbed his keycard off the table. "All set?" he asked.

She nodded and walked to the door. "Let's go find him."

Staying a few feet behind her, Jace followed Skylar around the resort. He didn't want to disturb her while she concentrated on Lucas' location. Using his own superior senses, he also worked to locate him. A short while later, Skylar paused outside the door to the lounge area. She turned and gestured to him. "He's in there. You go to his room and I'll inform you of his every move." Her voice sounded shaky and Jace could tell that she was trying hard to appear calm and collected.

Fuck, he hated putting her in this position. Her unease was evident in her body language.

He fought his natural inclination to gather her in his arms and reassure her, but knew this wasn't the time or place. Instead, he whispered, "Be careful, Skylar. Remember, if you need me, I'll be here before you finish calling for help."

When she nodded, Jace reluctantly let her go. Once she was out of his line of sight, Jace hurried back to Lucas' room.

Once inside, he worked quickly to install a hidden camera and a listening device. Fortunately, Lucas didn't leave the lounge area, so he was able to complete his assignment without any interruptions.

After he was satisfied that everything had been installed properly, he slipped back into his own suite and flicked on the viewing monitors. Lucas' room flashed on the screen. "Skylar," he spoke into his watch. "All set. Come back to the room. I'll be waiting for you."

Chapter Five

ꟗ

Lucas remained seated at the bar next to a gorgeous young blonde when Skylar rose from her chair and exited the room. She wiped the perspiration from her brow and breathed a sigh of relief that Jace had managed to plant the equipment without any problems.

Skylar made her way back to their luxurious suite and used her keycard to open the door. She found Jace sitting at the table beside the faux fireplace, cleaning his gun.

He glanced her way, smiled, and then turned his attention back to his task. She watched him slip back into his professional role. Tonight she'd seen the many different facets of Agent Jace Garrett, and so far there wasn't any side to him she didn't like.

He reassembled his weapon and loaded a silver bullet into the chamber. "That should do it," he finally said and dropped his gun back into his leather holster. He glanced her way. "Thanks for keeping watch for me. I couldn't have done it without you."

She grinned and raised one brow doubtfully. "This coming from the same mouth that did nothing but complain about having me on the case."

He returned her smile. "You're growing on me."

He was growing on her, too. More than she cared to admit. Damn. She really had to gain control over her emotions and remember what was between them was just sex. Sex they needed to perform in order to fulfill a role.

Jace nodded toward the monitor and jolted her out of her thoughts. "There's not much we can do now but wait." He rose, stretched and dimmed the lights. Then he crossed the room and lowered himself onto the king-sized bed.

Skylar slipped her shoes off, rotated the kinks from her ankles and walked across the spacious room to join him. The huge mattress was cushy-soft beneath her backside. She yawned, tucked her feet under herself and watched the monitor. A comfortable silence fell over them as they waited. The only audible sound was the hot tub jets whirring in the background. The warm, scented water reached her nostrils and she inhaled. Jasmine.

After only a few short minutes they watched Lucas and the same blonde from the lounge enter the bedroom. Skylar tensed then relaxed when she felt Jace's hand close over hers.

"Don't worry, he's not going to kill until the full moon."

She smiled at him. It amazed her that he was always so damn in tune with her emotions.

Jace caught her gaze. "Do you think he knows we're here?" he questioned in a soft voice.

She grazed her teeth over her lower lip and shook her head. "I don't sense that at all. I think it was smart of the Captain to send only the two of us. Lucas likely would have sensed it if the whole task force were involved." She shrugged one shoulder. "Then again, maybe not. Back at the bar he was too caught up in drinking and fawning all over his girlfriend to notice anything."

A worried frown crossed Jace's face. His brow furrowed.

The concern in his eyes filled her with apprehension. "What is it?" she asked, squeezing his hand.

He shifted closer. "I just don't want anyone else getting hurt. That poor girl has no idea who she's with." He scrubbed a hand over his chin.

She tilted her head back to look into his eyes. "Should we warn her?" He was so close now that she could smell his spicy cologne. The dim light from the nearly full moon outside filtered through the large window and bathed the bed in a warm, silvery glow.

God, he was handsome.

Jace shook his head. "If we do then she'll leave here, and chances are Lucas will too. I don't want to lose him again, only to end up finding another dead body in some dumpster."

"Why can't we just arrest him now?"

"We have no tangible evidence and have never seen him in his wolf form. He's only a suspect right now. He's smart and cleans up behind himself. We have to wait until he changes and attempts a kill, and then we'll make our move."

He feathered his hands down her bare arm. It was hard to keep a focused thought with the warmth from his touch trailing down her body.

Skylar brushed her hand over the silky duvet beneath her and forced herself to concentrate. She considered her next idea long and hard before she spoke. She drew a heavy breath then slowly turned to face Jace. "Perhaps we could use me as bait instead of her."

Jace's eyes flashed. His jaw twitched. "Forget it, Skylar. I'm not putting you in any danger."

"But *she's* in danger." She waved her hand toward the monitor.

Jace jumped from the bed and began pacing. Skylar continued talking. "We can plant a wire on me and then you'd be able to hear and see every move he makes."

"I don't like this, Skylar." His voice was bleak.

"Why not?" She jumped up and met him in the middle of the room. His eyes were fixed on her. He pulled her closer. She exhaled a breath she hadn't realized she was holding.

He gave a quick shake of his head. "What if you find yourself in a situation like you did today and have to strip for him? He'd see the wire. Or what if you had to have sex with him? As you already discovered, this is a resort where anything goes." He drew in a deep breath then continued. "This is my investigation, Skylar. You'll follow *my* orders—and using yourself as bait isn't part of the plan."

Of course, Jace was right. He was a damn good agent who was quick to consider all scenarios. She admired that about him. She was just so worried about another innocent woman getting killed she hadn't thought matters through.

"I won't risk your safety," he added.

The knowledge that he worried about her warmed her. Her heart began pounding in her chest. They remained pressed up against one another for the longest time. Until a sound from the monitor drew their attention.

"Looks like they're going to bed," Jace said when the lights in Lucas' room flicked off. "At least we can still hear what's going on. And you can feel his presence, so we'll know if he leaves the room."

Once again, Skylar stretched and yawned. "Since we don't have to worry about him changing form or killing until the full moon, we should probably get some sleep, too. We'll want to be fresh for our scuba diving lessons." She rolled her eyes heavenward. "Why on earth did you pick scuba lessons?"

"I spotted Lucas' name on the list."

"I should have known." Skylar admired his dedication. No matter what the circumstance, Agent Jace Garrett was always on the job.

"Plus, I wanted to see you in your swimsuit." His gaze was drowsy, sexy and the fire smoldering in his eyes licked her from head to toe.

The heat rising in her body warmed her skin.

When he stepped away from her, she immediately missed his touch. In three long strides, he crossed the room. He gestured toward the complimentary bottle of champagne. With a suggestive edge to his smile, he said, "Perhaps a nightcap before bed." The deep timbre of his voice stroked her flesh. Goose bumps pebbled her arms.

Skylar nodded as a surge of desire twisted her insides.

He uncorked a bottle of champagne, poured two glasses and handed her one.

"I hope this one is different from the glass I had earlier. I don't know what was in that, but it made me do things I wouldn't do under normal circumstances."

He brushed his thumb over her lips. His eyes darkened. "There was nothing in that champagne, Skylar," he said, his voice a low, intimate whisper.

She tossed him a perplexed frown. "What do you mean?" She took a small sip and felt the bubbles tingle all the way to her toes. "I felt lightheaded."

"I drank from your glass, too, and I'm fine. You did what you did earlier because you *wanted* to, not because you were drugged." He pulled her in close and she melted against him. He gave a lusty groan when her body molded against his.

Skylar sucked in a tight breath and felt herself blush from head to toe. Jace was right. She'd done it because she *wanted* to. She'd enjoyed performing in front of all those people and had discovered a side to herself that she hadn't known existed.

"About earlier," he murmured into her ear. "We never did finish what we started." He nodded toward the hot tub. "Shall we?" He leaned in close, his breath hot on her neck. She felt her whole body quiver in delight.

Without waiting for an answer, he slowly began to remove her sweater. She reveled in the feel of his warm hands against her skin. She watched, transfixed by the heat in his eyes as he peeled her top free and let it fall to the floor. He ran his palms over her cleavage.

"So soft," he murmured. "So very nice." The warmth and sincerity in his voice made her breath catch.

Skylar felt her legs weaken beneath her. When Jace licked his lips, her nipples hardened under his hungry gaze. She grew impatient as he took his time undressing her. The agony of waiting for him to make love to her was almost unbearable.

She arched into him and felt his cock through his jeans. Her fingers tingled, anticipating the touch of his engorged phallus. She reached out and found him throbbing.

"You're overdressed," she murmured. It frightened her to think she wanted him more than she wanted her next breath.

In one fluid motion, he unzipped his pants and kicked them aside. He yanked his shirt off and let it drop from his fingers. A tremor rippled through her as she listened to the soft rustle of his clothes falling to the floor where they mingled with hers. When her gaze dropped to his cock, her juices began to flow.

He turned his attention back to her. He unsnapped her pants and slid them down her legs. She felt her pussy lips swell. Every nerve ending in her clit screamed for attention. He slipped his hand between her thighs. His nostrils flared when he felt her dampness.

She stood before him nearly naked, covered only by a flimsy pair of panties. He grabbed the small scrap of material, snapped the thin elastic, and tossed them aside.

"Come with me." His voice was a low, rusty growl.

He slid one arm around her shoulder and the other under her legs as he scooped her up and carried her to the Jacuzzi. After they slipped into the warm, scented water, Jace disappeared as he dipped himself beneath the surface. A moment later he reappeared directly in front of her. Water dripped down his face as he palmed her cheeks and stared deep into her eyes.

"You're beautiful." He urged her thighs apart and nestled himself in between. She felt her whole body warm from the inside out. His hands began an unhurried exploration of her curves. The pure desire growing in his dark eyes made her whole body succumb to her needs.

"I want you, baby," he whispered, stroking his lips over her earlobe.

He dipped his hand between her thighs. The roughness of his hands connecting with the softness of her skin made her whole body come undone. She quivered as her heart skipped a beat. His hands skimmed her curves, leaving a trail of fire in their wake. A fire burning so hot, so out of control, that even the water surrounding her was incapable of extinguishing it.

Her whole body tightened when his fingers caressed her swollen clit.

She couldn't understand this kind of desire. It was powerful. Raw. Unstoppable. With a simple touch, he was able to turn her inside out.

He moved in for a kiss.

She savored the satin warmth of his tongue caressing hers. She watched his gaze darken as they dropped from her eyes to her lips to her large breasts floating on the surface of the water.

"Magnificent," he breathed heavily. He groaned and pressed his cock against her thigh. Her whole body went up in flames. He kissed the hollow of her throat and tracked downward until he drew one hard nipple into his mouth. Skylar threw her head back and gasped. When she writhed against his mouth, she felt his teeth close over her almost painfully.

Heat coursed through her, and she couldn't believe how close she was to finding release—simply from the erotic sensations evoked by his ravishing mouth.

Skylar cupped her other breast and offered it to him. He treated it to the same pleasure as the first, greedily drawing it into his mouth and relishing her hard nipple.

"Come here." He lifted her from the water. A rush of cool air kissed her skin. A sensation that was quickly forgotten as Jace positioned her in front of the pulsating jets. She cried out as the hard spray stimulated her clit. She closed her eyes to savor the stinging sensation on her most delicate flesh.

Turning her around to face him, Jace dragged her back into the water, immersing her. Perhaps it was the way he looked at her, like no man had ever done before, that made her feel so desirable. The way his tender hands touched her, like she was a delicate treasure to be treated with the utmost care, flooded her with unfamiliar feelings. She hadn't expected that his warm touch and gentle hands would be so emotionally moving. She hadn't realized how dangerously close she was to feeling more than simple lust for him.

His mouth found hers again as he pushed one thick finger into her slick core. The exquisite pleasure made her cry out and arch her hips forward. Her muscles contracted in bliss with the rippling approach of an orgasm. She heard a low growl beneath his warm breath. His lids slid shut, as though the sensations were too much for him to bear.

Once again he lifted her from the water. He gently set her on the edge of the hot tub and eased her thighs apart. Cool air rushed over her, but its effect was lost as her rising internal temperature kept her burning hotter than a raging inferno.

His gaze caressed the damp curly hair between her thighs. He trailed his hands over her flesh and his tongue followed the motion higher and higher until his warm breath tickled her moist clit, making it tighten in anticipation. His teasing stirred her libido and fired her passion until she pushed her pelvis forward in provocative invitation.

"That's a girl," he murmured from somewhere deep between her legs.

He dipped his tongue into her cunt, and then feathered it over her swollen folds. Her skin swelled with the evocative sensations. He matched her soft moans of delight as his mouth and tongue stimulated her entire body.

She rocked back and forth in silent encouragement. His tongue danced and indulged, suckled and nibbled, bringing her so close to the edge she felt dizzy. She needed it now. Hard and fast to take her over the edge.

"Please, Jace," she whispered.

He pulled back and looked at her. "Please, what?" The sincerity in his voice filled her with warmth. His tone was so soft, so soothing. "Tell me what you want."

His words, his gaze and his touch all had a profound effect on her. She felt so close to him—a part of him. As though she'd known him her entire life. Yet, she didn't really know him at all. And there was still that small part of him that he'd kept closed off to her.

She looked deep into his eyes and knew how desperately she wanted to lose herself in him again. "Make love to me," she urged.

He willingly obliged.

He pulled her back into the water and pressed his lips over hers. He eased his cock inside her while his thumb rubbed the spot that needed it the most. Her folds swelled open as he applied just the right amount of pressure.

"That's it," she cried out. She intertwined her hands in his hair and dragged him closer as a storm began brewing in her body. His cock thrust inside her until she came apart in his arms. As her orgasm racked her body, she felt her muscles spasm, squeezing his erection, forcing him to remain deep inside her. Her body shuddered with such intensity she gripped his shoulders to avoid blacking out.

She clung to him and he held her tight as her breathing slowly returned to normal. Pulling back, she eyed the man who'd brought her to such heights of ecstasy. She knew they had no future, but the night belonged to them. Tomorrow everything would be back to normal. The circumstances for them being together would still be the same. They'd still be using each other to capture Lucas.

She understood that Jace was like most men, he wanted her in his bed and nothing more.

* * * * *

Fingers of warm, golden light sliced through the crack in the dark curtains as the sun began its ascent. Not wanting to wake Skylar, Jace quietly slipped from the bed. He padded softly over to the window and drew back the heavy fabric draperies. He winced and used his hand to shade the sun from his eyes. In the early morning hours the resort lay in utter stillness. A few gulls cried over the cool waters of the Atlantic Ocean as they began their daily ritual search for food.

Jace inched open the glass pane and inhaled the salty sea air. He glanced at the long stretches of pristine white sand that surrounded the luxurious resort.

He stole a quick look at the monitor resting on top of his bureau and watched Lucas and his lady friend sleep. Only one more night before the full moon. He could already feel the beast within him stirring to life. He just hoped Lucas turned at the first sign of the full moon, so he could get the hell out of there and chain himself to his bed before he turned completely. He could only control the beast for so long.

His attention drifted back to Skylar and he sighed. What was it about her that made him feel things he'd never felt before? Perhaps it was the amazing strength of character that he'd rarely found in others. Or perhaps it was her willingness to put other people's safety before her own, her willingness to do whatever it took to get the job done. Or that like himself, she was a loner and felt like an outcast.

Suddenly he wished he'd never met her. Now it would be twice as hard going home to his empty apartment every night, knowing that he couldn't have a family of his own. He could never risk hurting someone he cared for.

He was starting to have deeper feelings for her, making it harder and harder to separate emotions and sex. But he had to control that. She was a threat to him. If she ever managed to read that small, hidden part of him, she'd be a threat to his identity and perhaps to his life.

Skylar stirred and opened her eyes. She quickly shut them again. "Don't you ever sleep?" she whispered and turned over, taking all the blankets with her.

"I had to be awake before Lucas, to make sure he didn't ditch us before we woke."

He watched her open one eye and then frown in concentration. "He's still here," she said matter-of-factly.

Jace walked over to the bed and sat beside her. "I know. Everything is going according to plan. You can get a few more hours sleep if you'd like. I'll keep my eye on things."

"No. I'll sleep when I'm dead," she teased, mimicking his earlier words. "How about some coffee?"

"I'll call room service."

She reached out and touched his arm. His nerve ending immediately responded to her warm, gentle hands. "It's probably too early for that," she said.

He took a quick glance at the clock. Ten minutes past six. "Breakfast is served between six and nine, so we're fine." He watched her eyes darken with desire as she trailed her nails lightly over his forearm. Jace flinched and eased away.

He couldn't do this. He couldn't continue to be intimate with her. Not with the emotions that were brewing in him. It would be too hard, too painful to walk away from her when the investigation was over. He could lose himself in her—body and soul—and that was the one thing he couldn't afford to do. He needed to stay away to protect his own heart. And to protect her.

She must have sensed his emotional retreat. She sat up straighter in the bed and assumed an air of professionalism.

"Do you think Lucas will make his move today?" Jace heard the slight waver in her voice.

He gave a quick shake of his head. "No, he's not going to try anything until the full moon. So we just need to keep an eye on him until then, to make sure he doesn't leave the resort."

Damn, he didn't want to hurt her like this, but he was beginning to fall for her. And he knew there could never be anything more between them than just sex. For one, it could cost him more than his job if she discovered he was a werewolf, and two, if they did get emotionally involved, what would happen during a full moon? His memories during the change were scattered and violent. What if she got too close? Would he kill her? He did, after all, have the blood of a werewolf running through his veins.

Turning his back to her, he walked over to the phone. He dialed room service and ordered coffee along with two breakfast platters. After he hung the phone up, he turned back to Skylar. With a sheet wrapped around her body, she climbed from the bed.

Her eyes were sad. "I need a shower," she said and he could hear the emotion in her voice.

Jace watched her cross the suite. A moment later he listened to the soft rush of water. Needing something to take his mind off his own emotions, he turned his attention to the monitor and the job at hand. He needed to get himself under control before he blew this assignment. While he waited for their breakfast to arrive, he sat in a recliner and stared blankly at Lucas' room.

The bathroom door creaked open and Skylar came out just as room service arrived. Jace wheeled their cart to the table and lifted the silver lids to reveal a delicious looking and smelling breakfast of bacon, eggs, toast and hash browns. Too bad his appetite was gone.

"Come sit with me." He pulled a chair out for Skylar and motioned for her to join him.

She pulled on a robe, crossed the room and graciously accepted her seat. "Thanks. Mmm, smells great," she said, plastering on a fabricated smile.

"Coffee?"

Skylar nodded and held out her cup.

Jace watched her take a small sip of the hot brew and began to wonder how someone as beautiful, fun and spirited as herself wasn't married.

Suddenly, thoughts of her with another man sent fire pitching through his blood. The wolf inside him howled with rage.

"Skylar?" The serious edge to his voice must have startled her.

Her eyes opened wide. "Yes?"

"I was just wondering why you're still single."

He watched emotions play across her eyes. She looked troubled. She bit down on her lower lip and exhaled a deep, heavy sigh. "Because I'm psychic."

"What does that have to do anything with anything?" He picked up his fork and moved his eggs around on his plate.

She looked at him like he already knew, then she gave a slight shrug of her shoulders. "My abilities don't just scare women, it scares guys off too. But you already know that, don't you?" Skylar popped a piece of bacon into her mouth and then wiped her lips with a cloth napkin.

He tossed her a bewildered look. "Why would you say that?" He sipped his coffee and stared at her.

She reached out and placed her hand over his. "There is a part of you that remains closed off to me, Jace. You may not realize it, but I do." She lifted one perfect eyebrow as though daring him to deny it.

Anxiety gnawed at his stomach. He opened his mouth to protest but stopped himself. Shit. What in the hell was he supposed to say? *That the small part of me that I keep closed off is the werewolf side of me? The side that would probably rip you in two if given the chance.*

"It's my job," he lied. "It keeps me from getting too close to someone. I wouldn't want to put a wife and kids in jeopardy." It was as good an excuse as any.

"It's okay, Jace. You don't have to explain. I understand that men get scared off when they find out. I learned long ago to accept that." She blinked back the dampness in her eyes.

His stomach did a nosedive. He reached out and traced the outline of her face. He feathered his fingers over her jaw. "Skylar, you're wrong…"

She bit down on her lip, smiled, and let out a humorless chuckle. "Really, Jace, it's okay." She raised her hand to cut him off. "I felt your retreat this morning. Let me just make things easier on you by telling you I'm not interested in anything more either."

His heart tightened in his chest. "You're not?" God, he hated that she believed he wanted her for sex only.

She shook her head. "We can enjoy what we have here and then both walk away in the end with no complications, no strings. Okay?" Her voice was a hesitant whisper.

Even though it wasn't okay, he nodded his agreement. He swallowed, unable to stomach the thought that she believed he was no different from any other man she'd been with. Then again, he wasn't giving her any reason to believe otherwise.

He tightened his hand over hers. "If that's the way you want it." And he knew deep down, that that was the way it had to be.

She nodded, lifted her mug and saluted him. "To sex and nothing more."

He lifted his mug and clinked it with hers while he tried to push his growing feelings for her to the far corners of his heart.

Chapter Six

Ꟗꟗ

By the time Lucas crawled out of bed and finished breakfast it was nearing ten o'clock. In less than one hour they were to begin their scuba lessons. They followed him through the resort, being careful not to arouse his suspicion.

When he stepped out into the bright sunshine and took a seat on a cushioned lounge chair near the crystal-clear pool, Skylar and Jace did the same. Skylar peeled off her sarong skirt. Dressed only in her bikini, she stretched out in her seat and lifted her face to the sun, drinking in its warmth.

Without a cloud in the pale blue sky, the bright rays immediately began to warm her body. She slipped her straps from her shoulders to avoid tan lines.

She noticed how Jace's eyes smoldered as he watched her every movement. She studied him as he peeled off his T-shirt and pulled his lounger closer to her. His skin looked pale in comparison to hers.

A bartender stopped by with a tray of cool fruity drinks topped with colorful little umbrellas. Skylar wiped the perspiration from her brow and accepted one. She took a sip of the icy concoction and moaned in pleasure. "This is delicious." She placed it on the side table next to her.

She turned her attention back to Jace and eyed his broad chest. "You'd better get some lotion on or you're going to burn."

His eyes darkened with heat. He grabbed a complimentary bottle off a nearby table. "Let me do you first."

Skylar flipped over onto her stomach. Jace splattered on entirely too much of the thick, creamy sunblock. He began massaging it into her skin. A moment later she felt him unhook the back clip of her bikini top and stroke his large hands seductively over her bare flesh. His hands trailed down, lingering near the crest of her buttocks.

The smell of the rich coconut lotion mingling with Jace's earthy scent filled the air and aroused her senses. She inhaled deeply, and relaxed her tense body. The rough texture of his powerful hands felt good as they kneaded her tight muscles.

In no time at all, his touch changed to a feathery enticing caress, gently brushing along her sides, going higher and higher until he stroked the outer edge of her breasts. Her nipples immediately responded, growing hard as they anticipated his touch.

When she heard his breathing change, she twisted around to look at him, but he gently eased her back down. He worked his hands lower over her buttocks. He stroked her thighs and inched her legs open. He leaned closer and she felt his hot breath whisper across her ass.

He pulled the thin scrap of fabric away from her pussy. When his hand nudged her clit her body went up in flames. She shivered with excitement. The pleasure made her insides contract and shudder.

She could barely speak, barely whisper. "Jace..." she croaked and started to twist around, but before she could protest further, he gently pinned her shoulders to the chair. She felt his long, warm fingers inch open her vulva and sucked in a tight breath. When he dipped one finger deep inside her cunt, she slipped into a euphoric haze and gave a little whimper. A surge of warmth flooded her veins.

Her silken pussy lips closed over his fingers like a glove. She could no longer think, she could only feel. Her muscles spasmed and sucked his fingers in deeper.

God, it felt so damn good. So much pleasure. His touch overpowered her senses and all she could think about was having his cock rammed inside her. That delicious thought started her feminine juices flowing. She craved the feel of his hot, naked flesh against her own.

This man aroused a sensual hunger in her that was beyond her wildest dreams. A hunger she had absolutely no control over.

She struggled just to whisper. "Everyone will see us." She wondered why she was worried about such a thing when only last night she'd given Jace a blowjob in full view of everyone.

"Only if you move," he murmured into her ear.

His thumb rubbed her clit, applying just the right amount of delicious pressure until it poked out from beneath its fleshy hood. Her composure vanished and she melted all over him.

"Do you want to move, Skylar?" His voice was a ragged whisper.

She swallowed hard. Her whole body began to shake and quiver from his intimate touch. She began rocking her hips, and then suddenly she realized something that Jace seemed to have already known. She liked people watching her.

She moaned, flipped over onto her back and arched into him. He grasped her ankles and spread her legs as wide as possible.

His smile was smug. "That's my girl." His voice covered her like a warm blanket. "Let everyone know you're wet and hot and getting finger-fucked."

She reached out and cupped her breasts, running her warm fingers over her pebbled nipples. Her hunger was so carnal, so raw. A soft moan gathered in her throat. When she noticed the smoldering look in Jace's eyes, she moaned louder.

"Do you like that, Jace?" She writhed beneath him. "Do you like me touching myself?"

His low pleasured growl rumbled like distant thunder. He thrust another finger deep inside her. She gyrated against him and began to pant as he pulled open her labia with his other hand. "I love the way your body reacts to my touch, sweetheart," he whispered, curling his fingers deep inside her. "You're always so hot and wet for me. You have no idea what that does to me."

She stole a quick look at the huge bulge in his swim shorts. "I have a pretty good idea."

He rewarded her with another thick finger. She twisted and bore down on his hand, begging for more.

"Do my fingers fill you, Skylar?" His eyes burned with desire.

"Not enough. I want your cock," she pleaded shamelessly. "I want you to fuck me."

He grinned. "Here?" With a tip of his head, he gestured toward the crowd that had begun to gather. "In front of all these people?"

Before she knew it what was happening, the couples around them began to strip. That didn't surprise her. They were, after all, at a resort where such activities were expected to happen. What did surprise her, however, was how much she enjoyed that.

In no time at all, hot, lusty bodies were sprawled everywhere. One woman reached out and ran her hands over Jace's chest. He groaned and leaned into her.

When those same hands touched Skylar's breasts, she watched Jace's eyes darken with lust. He gave a sexy moan, stared at her mouth and licked his lips. He sidled closer and pressed his sweet mouth over hers. His hard, possessive kiss was full of passion and promise. His tongue swept through her mouth and she reveled in the taste of him. She luxuriated in the heat radiating from his body. After he broke the kiss, he leaned back and watched their new playmate touch Skylar.

Skylar cocked one brow and placed her hand over the other woman's fingers as they roamed her body. She arched into her touch. "You like this," Skylar said. It was more of a statement than a question. "You like it when she touches me."

She felt Jace's body vibrate with excitement. He took several deep breaths.

"Yes," he admitted, his voice thinned to a whisper.

The woman reached down to caress Skylar's nether lips and Jace growled with the ferocity of a wild beast. Skylar watched his cock push against the thin fabric of his shorts. He wiggled his fingers deep inside her while a pair of feminine fingers stroked Skylar's clit.

Each long stroke and swirl of their fingers brought her closer and closer, until she felt her body explode into a thousand pieces. Her mind started spinning, she felt weak, dizzy. Her warm syrupy heat began dripping down her thighs. It took a long moment for her to find her breath and come back down to earth.

She caught Jace's lustful gaze and he gave her an intimate, sexy smile. She knew what he wanted, what his eyes were asking for.

When she reached out to stroke his cock, she felt the hands of another man touch her breasts. She watched Jace's gaze change. He didn't like it. His eyes turned hard, threatening. Possessive.

For a brief moment she thought she saw a flash into that dark area of his mind that he'd kept closed off to her. She saw rage, anger and ferociousness. Little alarm bells jangled in her head. A tingle of apprehension worked its way through her body—a tingle that warned her to be careful. Before she had a chance to look deeper he quickly shut his mind to her probing.

She pushed her fears aside. Deep down, she knew Jace would never purposely hurt her. She instinctively trusted him, and trust was something that didn't come easily to her.

The other man's hands roamed over her body. Jace flinched and opened his mouth. Skylar assumed he was about to protest. Such an action could blow their cover and with Lucas watching she couldn't let that happen.

She pressed her fingers to his lips and looked deep into his eyes. "I'm with you, Jace. Only you."

His features softened. When he leaned into her she breathed in his evocative, manly scent.

The man and woman who'd been touching them suddenly found each other, leaving Jace and Skylar alone once again.

He slid his thumb up and down her soaked slit. "I believe you're ready to be fucked."

Just then a man cleared his throat. His voice cut through her thoughts. "Excuse me. I hate to break up this little gathering, but we're beginning the scuba lessons. Will those of you who signed up please gather around the pool? We'll begin our lessons here before we attempt the ocean." He stood with a clipboard and checked people's names off as they approached.

Jace eased himself off the chair and pulled Skylar along with him. He helped her retie her top and adjust her bikini bottoms.

He brushed her hair from her face and leaned into her. "We'll finish this later," he whispered in her ear. "When we're alone and I don't have to share you with *anyone*." His voice was thick with emotion and Skylar looked at him in surprise. He almost sounded possessive, jealous. Surely she was mistaken. Over breakfast, he'd made it clear he only wanted her for sex. Why would if bother him if she was with someone else? And why had jealously burned in his eyes when another man touched her?

She remained close to Jace as they positioned themselves around the pool. Lucas stood alone, without his lady friend, far away from them. For the first time, Skylar really studied Lucas' features. His eyes were the same rich chocolate color as Jace's. Interesting. Although similar in color, Jace's were warm, soft and full of emotion, while Lucas' eyes were cold, bleak and devoid of feeling. An involuntary shudder overcame her.

Jace must have felt it. He circled his arm around her waist and pulled her in tighter against himself.

Skylar leaned into Jace's comforting embrace and when she stole a quick look at him, her heart rose to her throat. They'd agreed to be lovers for the weekend and nothing more. Surely she could handle that.

Suddenly a knot began tightening in her stomach. None of the men she'd been intimate with in the past had affected her the way Jace had. What was it about him that made her common sense pack up and take a vacation?

When this little fantasy weekend was over, she'd simply have to learn to forget about Jace Garret and move on. Easy.

He caught her staring at him and smiled. Butterflies erupted in her stomach. Then again, maybe it wouldn't be quite so easy to forget him.

The sound of the instructor's voice pulled her thoughts back to the present. "Skylar, perhaps you could step over here and help me out."

She moved away from Jace and took a position near the instructor. After he placed the tank on her back and breathing apparatus around her mouth, she noted that his hands lingered on her body longer than necessary.

When she glanced over at Jace, a splinter of fear crawled over her skin.

She felt a darkness dwelling deep within him.

* * * * *

Jealously roared inside Jace's veins as the beast within him stirred. He hated that another man touched Skylar in such a familiar way. He should be the only man allowed to caress her so intimately. He fisted his hands to stop them from trembling.

He knew he should have pulled back physically before he was in too deep emotionally and couldn't find his way out, but when it came to her he was too damn weak to resist the temptation. He wasn't even sure the reinforced holding cell down at the precinct was enough of a restraint to keep him away from her.

He glanced over at Lucas and noticed that he was giving him a quizzical look.

Could he sense the wolf within him? Being a half-breed, Jace was gifted with the ability to hide his true nature. That's what made him such a great hunter. The werewolves couldn't sense his approach. Jace looked back at Skylar and knew he'd have to regain his control, because if he acted out of character it could risk blowing the whole operation.

"Now if you will all pair up, I'd be happy to assist you while in the pool," the instructor said.

Before he had a chance to gather up Skylar, he watched her saunter over to the other side of the pool and strike up a conversation with Lucas. Fire pitched though his blood. He was damn well going to kill her. How dare she move forward with her plan after he had already vetoed it. What if she got hurt? Lucas was a killer who would think nothing of tearing her throat open at the first opportunity.

He forced himself to look away and tried desperately to slow the blood pounding through his veins. He reached up and began a slow massage of his temples. If he didn't cool it, Lucas would surely sense something was amiss.

A moment later, a pretty young woman cuddled up beside him. "Seems neither one of us has a partner." She tossed him a bright-eyed, innocent smile.

Jace huffed and shook his head. "Guess not." Any other time, he'd definitely be interested, but right now only one woman consumed his thoughts.

A woman he was ready to strangle!

She leaned into him and pressed her huge breasts against his chest. "Would you like some help with your equipment?"

she purred. She licked her lips suggestively and let her gaze roam over his body.

"I'm good, thanks," he said, and scooped his tank off the ground and tossed it over his back.

"Then perhaps you could help me with mine," she cooed. Jace gathered her tank and adjusted it over her shoulders. He stole a quick glance at Skylar. She was watching him carefully. When he scowled at her, her attention drifted back to Lucas. The instructor motioned for them all to climb into the water.

After an hour of having Mandy, his new friend, bump and grind against him, Jace was ready for a break. He was totally distracted and couldn't even seem to follow the instructor's simplest directions. Mandy didn't seem to mind his inattentiveness. She continued pawing him, touching him in areas that were a little too intimate for his liking. It wasn't like he could easily put a stop to it without rousing everyone's suspicions. He had no choice but to play along.

When the instructor finally signaled that the pool lesson was over, Jace was the first to make his escape.

"We'll all be heading down to the ocean after a long lunch break," he said. "Please assemble back here around two. I'm sure many of you, along with your new friends—" he gave Jace a conspiratorial wink, "—will find something to do to keep yourselves occupied until then."

Jace grunted. Two hours was ample time to strangle Skylar.

After the crowd fell away in pairs, Jace caught Skylar's attention and jerked his head toward the bar. She excused herself from Lucas and made her way inside. Jace followed. Once out of Lucas' view, he grabbed her arm and twisted her around.

"What the hell do you think you're doing?" he growled into her ear.

She pulled away. "My job," she replied.

He narrowed his gaze and glared at her. "It's *my* job, not yours. And I didn't agree to use you as bait."

She drew a long breath. "Look behind me, Jace." She motioned over her right shoulder.

He looked beyond her shoulder and spotted Lucas' girlfriend cuddled in the arms of another man. He turned his attention back to Skylar. "Your point?"

"Lucas has grown tired of her. He's also growing antsy. I sensed he was playing with the idea of leaving. I needed to give him a reason to stick around and I needed to do it fast. I didn't have time to consult with you."

Jace shrugged and shook his head. "All the couples here are sharing, Skylar. That's what this resort is all about. Lucas is just as likely to find someone else."

"That someone else was me. I felt it with every fiber of my being when he looked at me."

Jace stalked back and forth and cursed under his breath. If Lucas so much as hurt one tiny hair on her head…

"We won't let it come to that. We can control the situation, Jace. Besides, you said he won't kill until the full moon. My goal is to keep him here until then."

"You sure about this?" He gave a weary, resigned sigh.

She nodded. "Absolutely."

Jace scrubbed his hand over his chin and eyed her carefully. "Tell me, do you sense he's going to stick around now?"

Her lips curled up in distaste. "I told him I'd see him at the midnight swim." He felt her body shiver in disgust.

He stepped closer and rubbed the gooseflesh on her bare arms. "I don't want you to do this. I won't let him touch you."

She looked directly into his eyes and said, "I know."

He pulled her into his arms. "I don't want you to get hurt."

"I won't, as long as you're with me. Working together, we'll be able to control the situation."

Jace grunted and held her tighter. This assignment had just become a hell of a lot more complicated.

Chapter Seven

ꝏ

Darkness had descended over the resort. Skylar slipped her hand into Jace's and hurried her steps to keep pace as he guided her down a long, planked walkway that led to the ocean. The tangy smell of salt and sea filled the night air.

Skylar scanned the rippling water shimmering beneath the nearly full moon overhead. A lovers' moon. Looking out over the vast Atlantic Ocean, not a trace of civilization could be found. It was such a beautiful, romantic spot.

As they drew nearer to the ocean, they heard the murmur of voices and saw the silhouette of couples strolling along the pristine white sand. She squeezed the soft sand through her toes and reveled in the sensation.

Waves lapped gently against the hull of a speedboat tied to the dock. How she'd love to have sex with Jace out in the open water with sea spray dusting and cooling their heated bodies. She swallowed and quickly reminded herself that this was not the time to be dwelling in fantasy—she had to concentrate on the dangerous mission ahead.

She took a deep breath, knowing that tonight she'd be meeting Lucas for the scheduled moonlight skinny-dip. The thought of being close to him again and having him touch her skin repulsed her, but it was the only way to keep Lucas at the resort and keep an eye on him until the change occurred tomorrow night. Although her life wasn't in danger at the moment, Jace had assured her that if Lucas so much as threatened her life in any way tonight, he'd be on him in seconds.

Skylar caught Jace's glance. Lit only by the glow of the moon, his captivating eyes distracted her from the alluring, romantic ocean view. Moonbeams danced on his long, silky, black locks. She crossed her arms over her chest and shivered. She was sure the shiver had nothing to do with the cool ocean spray and everything to do with the handsome man beside her.

She leaned into his warm body and fought the evocative sensations that washed over her. In that instant she knew there'd be consequences to engaging in a purely physical weekend with him. He wasn't like the other men she'd been with. Jace Garrett was affecting her heart.

She forced herself to remember that Jace was offering physical pleasure, not his heart. And he wasn't asking for anything more from her. She'd have to deal with the repercussions of getting too close to him emotionally when the weekend was over.

"Just try to stay close to me. Don't get out of my sight," Jace said. "And remember the signal. If things get out of hand I'll casually interfere. When you need me, start running your fingers through your hair."

She bit down on her bottom lip as the hair on the back of her neck once again began to tingle with foreboding. "Jace?"

He stopped walking and looked directly at her. "What is it?"

"Something is going on." She squeezed her eyes tight and then opened them again.

He brushed a wayward strand of hair from her face and looked at her carefully. "Is everything okay?"

She shook her head, rubbed her fingers over her temples, and concentrated. "I'm not sure. I'm getting a strong sense that Lucas isn't the only werewolf here." She opened her eyes wide and drew a sharp breath. "I feel it, Jace. I feel another beast stirring nearby, but I can't seem to pinpoint the location."

Jace took a tentative step backwards, his nostrils flaring. She noticed the apprehensive look in his eyes. Was he afraid that they were up against more than they could handle?

"Do you think we should call in reinforcements? Maybe the Captain should be informed of this?" She began wringing her hands together.

"No," he said quickly. "He'll want to send in a team, and that might arouse Lucas' suspicions. If that happens, we'll lose track of him for sure." He took another distancing step back. "Maybe you're just tired. You didn't get much sleep last night."

Why didn't Jace believe her? Anger welled up inside her. Did he not trust her psychic abilities? He was acting so strange, like he had something to hide. Skylar looked at him hard and tried to probe that small closed off area of his mind. Nothing.

She pinched her lips in irritation. "Do you know something I don't know?" she asked, her eyes narrowing.

"No. Of course not. Let's just concentrate on Lucas. That's what we're here for. Forget about everything else." His voice was gruff and impatient.

She nodded and straightened her spine. "Fine," she said, and gestured for him to lead the way to the water. He turned his back to her and quickly walked along the sandy shore.

Skylar had no intention of forgetting about it. She'd focus on the location of the second werewolf with or without his help.

A short while later, she scanned the beach looking for Lucas. He was busy chatting with a woman Skylar didn't recognize. Was she a new member? Skylar's skin began to crawl as she touched the woman's mind. Unfortunately the connection was broken before she could assess it further. It was as thought the woman had felt her probing and put up a shield. She'd have to mention this woman to Jace and have him look into her identity. Something just wasn't right about her.

When Lucas spotted Skylar, he waved. Just before she made her way over, she caught Jace's glance from a distance.

In the split second it took her to turn and nod to him, the other woman had slipped away.

Lucas' dark haunting eyes scrolled the length of her body as she approached. There was a hungry gleam in his gaze. A sly smile turned up his lips. She forced herself not to tremble while her stomach took a nosedive. How could she go through with this? She summoned all her strength and courage and returned his smile.

She felt Jace's eyes on her back and relaxed a little. It was time to find out more about Lucas. Find out exactly what his plans were. She'd do whatever it took to bring him to justice. For every person that had been a victim of a werewolf attack.

Her thoughts strayed to her parents. God, how she missed them. She longed for a family of her own. How she'd love to have a house full of children and a man to cuddle up to at night. A warm, caring, sensitive man. A man with integrity and a love for children. A man like Jace Garrett. She gave a heavy sigh. She'd given up hoping for that long ago.

The sound of Lucas' voice pulled her back to the matter at hand.

"Going in?" he asked with a wave of his hand.

Skylar turned in the direction of the water. A few daring couples had stripped naked and braved the cool ocean. She knew if she joined Lucas in the water, Jace would lose track of her exact location. She plastered what she hoped was an inviting smile and fought to find her voice. "Soon. I just thought I'd sit and watch for a while. Would you like to join me?"

Lucas followed her to the dock. She sat down on the hard boards, letting her feet dangle in the cool water. A wave rushed up over her legs.

Sitting so close to him, she could feel his pent-up energy, his restlessness. She could also sense his urge to kill again. In one more day, the moon would be full and he'd make his move. She had to find a way to give him a reason to stick around that long.

"Who's the guy you're with?" he asked darkly, jerking his thumb down the beach.

Anxiety gnawed at her gut. She followed his gaze until she spotted Jace. "My husband," she said matter-of-factly, hoping her voice didn't sound as shaky as she felt.

He grunted as though he didn't believe her. "Yeah, and the girl I was with earlier is my wife." He leaned back on his hands and stared at the night sky.

He was very astute. She'd have to be careful. "Why do you ask?" She mimicked his position and gazed up at the stars dotting the black, velvety canvas.

He twisted sideways and caught her glance. "He looks familiar." He sidled closer, until his body was only a breath away from her. She sat up straighter and looked at him. Unbridled desire burned in his eyes. She shuddered involuntarily.

God, she hated the way he stared at her. Like he could see into the depths of her mind, read her every thought, feel her every emotion.

A heavy cold penetrated her bones. She swallowed past the knot in her throat. "Familiar in what way?" She schooled her expression to polite interest.

"I feel like I know him from somewhere." Lucas whirled around and stared down the long stretch of sandy white beach. "I've noticed him watching me a few times. You sure he doesn't know me?" He shot her a sidelong glance.

"I'm sure," she said trying to keep her voice level.

He seemed to be asking an awful lot of questions. Skylar was uncomfortable with his prying. She was sure her body had grown stiff enough to use as a surfboard on the moonlit ocean. She had to be careful not to show her fear. He was a werewolf and could probably sense anxiety.

She had to change the subject, but what could she possibly talk to him about? The cry of seagulls overhead drew her attention. She stared at a lone gull playing in the light breeze as her mind whirled for something to say. She watched the large bird soar across the sky. She was suddenly overcome by the sensation that someone besides Jace was watching her. She twisted around but saw no one.

"I have the strangest feeling that I know him." His breath was hot on her neck.

Her pulse leapt in her throat. Damn, did Lucas know Jace? Did he know why they were there? That thought unnerved her. A shiver of unease slithered down her spine but she pushed it away. She took a deep breath, willing herself to be calm. To be brave.

He gave her a wolfish smile. "He seems to watch you awfully closely, too," he added, his voice traveling into the still of the night.

She toyed with the spaghetti straps on her bikini top, hoping to draw his attention away from Jace. "He just worries about me," she said breezily, trying to ease Lucas' suspicions. "He just wants to make sure I'm happy and having fun."

That action piqued his interest. Lucas leaned in close, the curtain of his hair covering the darkness in his brown eyes. "You're with the right guy for that." A deep growl rumbled beneath his voice as his eyes shifted downward to examine the creamy swell of her cleavage. Her stomach plummeted. His smile was smug, dangerous. A shiver skipped down her spine as she battled her nerves.

"Come play with me and I'll guarantee you'll be *more* than happy." His voice held a trace of arrogance.

He closed the small gap between them, reached out and pulled her flimsy strap all the way down her shoulder. When his bare hand touched her naked flesh, visions of his crimes screamed into her mind, warning her to tread lightly. A chill ran through her body and she felt her blood run cold. She struggled not to faint, frightened by the disturbing images his memories evoked. She had to block her mind to his visions of darkness, destruction and chaos.

She wanted to extricate herself and run, but she'd come too far to turn back now.

"Come play with me, Skylar."

There was something about his voice. Something hypnotizing, something that drew her in, something that could, against her own best judgment, make her follow him anywhere.

And that scared the hell out of her.

* * * * *

God dammit, Lucas was touching her. He'd hoped it wouldn't get that far. She was only supposed to lure him in and then set up another date for tomorrow evening, enticing him to stay at the resort until he transformed.

He clenched his hands and stalked back and forth. Then he stilled his steps and sank onto the sand. He had to cool it. To back off. And to trust that Skylar knew what she was doing. Surely if she were in trouble she'd signal him.

He never should have agreed to use her as bait. Although he desperately wanted to capture Lucas, there was nothing more important to him at the moment than her safety. He gazed across the long stretch of sand, being careful to keep her in his sight.

He took a minute to recall their earlier conversation. Could the werewolf she sensed be him? He didn't even want to consider that possibility. He'd kept that part of his mind shut off for years… Was she really that skilled? Perhaps there *was* another werewolf nearby. Neither option appealed to him. He stole a quick look around and sniffed the air but nothing seemed out of the ordinary.

He focused his attention on Skylar. She was so brave to do what she was doing. He admired and respected her for being so courageous. It had to be difficult for her to get so close to Lucas. To have him touch her.

He gritted his teeth and raked his fingers through his hair. He should be the only man allowed to touch her. If only things were different… If only he didn't have the blood of a werewolf running through his veins. He gave a heavy, resigned sigh. But things *weren't* different. He could never have what other men took for granted. A wife, a family. He might hurt Skylar. If he did, he'd never be able to live with himself.

"There you are. I've been looking everywhere for you." The sound of a female's voice drew his attention.

He twisted around and spotted Mandy slinking up behind him. "Hi, Mandy." He nodded his greeting to the pretty redhead giggling beside her. Oh boy. He resisted the urge to roll his eyes.

She touched her tongue to her bottom lip. "Are you going for a swim?" Mandy asked, her smile stretched wickedly as she thrust her heavy breasts forward.

"Maybe later. I'm just watching right now." He folded his arms across his chest and stared off down the beach.

"Ooh, so you like to watch, do you?" She made a sexy noise and shifted closer. "I didn't know you were such a bad boy, Jace," Mandy murmured seductively.

He snorted and shook his head in exasperation. He didn't have time for this.

"Good thing Cindy and I like bad boys." She reached out and stroked Cindy's long strawberry-colored hair then winked at her. "Don't we, Cindy?"

Cindy giggled her response and sank down onto the sand next to Jace. "If you like to watch, maybe you'd like to watch us for a while," she whispered into his ear, her crimson-colored lips brushing his cheeks. "And then later, if you'd like, you can join in."

She pulled on Mandy's arm until the two of them were cuddled up together beside Jace. Holy shit. They weren't going to do what he thought they were going to do, were they?

The two began to peel each other's flimsy bathing suits off. Guess so. Milky-white breasts pressed against one another. Their nipples tightened and hardened under his gaze. Their lips met in a sensual, seductive kiss. Tongues snaked out to join in a mating dance. Their hands greedily stroking each other's creamy skin.

In spite of himself, he felt his body respond to their seduction. He swallowed hard and forced himself to look away. The last thing he should be doing was enjoying the erotic show while the woman he loved was risking her life. *Love?!?* Where in the hell had that come from? Was it love he felt for her? He wasn't sure. All he knew was that what he was experiencing with her was unique. Something special. Something he'd never felt with another woman before.

Something that gave him an unfamiliar fullness in his heart.

His heart rose in his throat when he spotted Lucas and Skylar walking into the water. Every nerve ending tingled, and every animal instinct he possessed warned him of danger. Even though she didn't signal him, he sensed she was in danger with every fiber of his being. He may not be psychic, but he'd been a paranormal task force agent for a long time and had great gut instincts.

"Excuse me, ladies, I'll be right back. I think I'll find us some more people for this party." He climbed to his feet.

They both giggled excitedly. "Hurry back," they murmured in unison.

With long, hurried steps, he crossed the beach. Skylar and Lucas were up to their waists in seawater. She was gazing up at Lucas. From his distance he couldn't see her face, her eyes, or her expression, but she almost seemed mesmerized by him. What kind of power did he wield over her?

His pulse drummed in his throat as he quickened his pace. At this point he didn't care if he blew the operation or not, he just had to make sure Skylar was safe.

Cool water splashed over his body as he pushed through the waves to meet them. He tried to remain calm, but his heart pounded erratically in his chest. Lucas glared at him as he approached, his eyes dark, his nostrils flared. Jace noticed the dazed expression on Skylar's face.

Jace kept his voice steady and deep. "There's a party going on down the beach." He pointed to the spot where Mandy and Cindy were. They waved back. "We were wondering if you two would like to join in?"

A wide smile crossed Lucas' face. He seemed intrigued. "Sounds like a great idea."

When Lucas turned his attention away from Skylar, she shook her head and blinked her eyes back into focus. Jace watched her look around, as though confused as to where she was. She seemed to be surprised that she was in the water.

"I'm in the mood for a party," Lucas said to Skylar. He took her hand. "Let's go."

"I'm going to have a quick swim." Her voice crackled like brittle bone, but she quickly recovered her composure. "I'll meet you when I'm finished."

"I don't think so," Lucas bit out abruptly, his eyes burning into her like hot coals. There was a low growl beneath his harsh voice.

Jace felt rage well up inside him. The beast within him stirred. He was about to grab Lucas and slam his fist into his face. Just as he took a small step closer, Skylar flinched and cried out. Her face turned ashen.

"What is it?" Jace asked, grabbing her before she collapsed into the water.

"My leg, it hurts. I think I've just been stung by a jellyfish." She bit down on her lower lip and moaned.

"Come join us when you're feeling better," Lucas said. Promise lingered in his gaze. He turned his back to them and made his way over to Mandy's party.

"Come here." Jace gathered her into his arms and carried her from the water. "How bad is the pain?"

"It burns." She twined her arms around his neck and hugged him.

"Let me see it." He sat her down on the sand and took a closer look. "The tentacles are still embedded. Squeeze my hand. This is going to sting." He scooped up a handful of sand and brushed it over the fleshy red spot on her leg.

She made a hissing noise and tightened her hand over his. "Ow!"

He looked deep into her eyes. "I need to get you inside to put some sugar on this."

She looked at him quizzically. "Sugar?"

"Yeah, it helps lessen the pain." He scooped her into his arms.

"How do you know that?" She nuzzled her mouth against his neck.

"I was stung as a child."

"How lucky for me," she teased.

He smiled and exhaled a slow, calming breath. He was so damn relieved she wasn't hurt worse.

Her arms closed around his neck as he hurried back to the lobby.

Skylar glanced over his shoulder. "What about him?"

Jace huffed. "He's going to be occupied for hours. Do you still sense he's going to leave?"

"No, I sense his need to hunt. He feels he's got plenty of bait here. He's not going anywhere."

"Good. We'll fix you up and then get back to work."

"Now that you've removed the tentacles it's starting to feel better," she said. "Thanks. You're my hero."

"Yeah, that's me, a real hero." He rolled his eyes heavenward. "If I were a hero I never would have let you risk your life." He carried her along the planked walkway that led back to the resort.

"As long as you were near, my life was never in any danger." She got quiet, almost thoughtful for a moment.

"What happened down there, Skylar?"

She shook her head in bewilderment and bit down on her bottom lip. "I don't know."

He furrowed his brows as he adjusted her weight in his arms and pulled open the main lobby doors.

She brushed her hair from her face. "It was like Lucas had this power over me. It was scary. I don't even remember walking into the water with him."

Jace cursed and carried her to the lobby counter. "Can you please send some sugar to our suite?" he asked the night clerk. Before the man had a chance to respond, Jace carried her to the waiting elevator.

"I guess it's a good thing I got stung when I did." Skylar stroked her hand over his face, and lower, until she touched his naked flesh. She splayed her fingers over his chest. Her silky, intimate caress felt so good.

When she moistened her lips, all he could think about was pillaging her sweet mouth. He cleared his throat. "Why do you say that?"

She cocked a brow. "You were two seconds away from blowing our cover." Her warm breath washed over his face. Her lips hovered enticingly close to his.

"I didn't care about our cover. All I cared about was you and your safety. We never should have used you as bait. When

Lucas looked at you like you were lunch, all I wanted to do was kill him," he growled.

"I know, and as much as I would have enjoyed watching that, I'm glad you didn't do anything foolish."

He stared into her emerald-green eyes. A languorous warmth stole through him. "I guess I owe you my thanks."

She made a sexy noise and shifted. "I'm waiting." She brushed her lips over his and moaned into his mouth. Desire moved over and through him. Every nerve ending in his body came alive.

He became acutely aware how much his body ached for her. "How about if I show you how grateful I am, instead?"

Chapter Eight

༄

Skylar remained snuggled in Jace's arms as he carried her to their suite. She couldn't believe how caring and nurturing he was. The fact that he'd been so concerned about her safety when she'd been with Lucas, so gentle with her after she'd been stung, warmed her deep inside. Her heart did somersaults in her chest. She felt so close to him. Not just physically, but emotionally as well. She tightened her arms around his shoulders and nuzzled her face into his neck. As she inhaled his scent, her libido stirred to life. A restless ache gathered between her thighs.

Jace pushed open the door to the suite and carried her inside. He laid her across the satin bed sheets. "Are you feeling okay?" There was so much emotion in his voice, it made her breath catch. He brushed her damp bangs from her forehead.

She leaned into his touch. "I am now," she said, her voice filled with a longing for something she knew she would never have—the love of this wonderful man.

A moment later someone knocked on the door. They both turned in the direction of the sound. "Must be our sugar," Jace said.

She watched him walk across the room. Her whole body shuddered with need. A second later he came back carrying a silver bowl full of white granules.

"Maybe I should have a bath first, I'm still covered in sand."

Jace nodded his agreement. "You wait here, and I'll run it for you. I don't want you walking on that leg just yet."

As she listened to the rush of water from the other room, her heart twisted in her chest. She was falling for this guy. This tough detective who had a sensitive, nurturing, caring side that made her feel things she'd never felt before. A guy who'd made it perfectly clear that all he wanted from her was sex.

If only she weren't a psychic, if only she were normal like other women, then perhaps there could be more between them. The thought of leaving the resort, never to see him again, sent cold chills down her spine. A heaviness fell over her and she blinked back the moisture gathering on her lashes.

He came from the bathroom and scooped her up. "All ready," he said. His gentle touch chased the chill from her body.

Before he eased her into the hot water, he stripped her skimpy bathing suit from her body. After he helped her into the bath, he grabbed a cloth and began to wash the gritty sand from her skin. The warm, scented water and soft washcloth felt exquisite against her naked flesh.

Moaning in pleasure, she breathed in the aroma of the flowery bubble bath and let her eyes slip shut. She relaxed and let her head fall to the side. The porcelain tub felt cool against her heated cheeks. Nice.

Jace worked the cloth over her entire body, taking care to cleanse every inch of her skin, until the last specks of sand were washed away.

"I love the way you touch me."

"That's good, because I love touching you." When Jace dragged the rough cloth across her nipples they tightened and hardened in response. A rush of warmth spread through her veins and settled low in her stomach.

"Mmm, so good," she whispered, tossing her head to the side.

Using his elbow, Jace spread her legs and dipped the soapy cloth in between her thighs, rubbing it gently over her most tender flesh. She drew a breath and reveled in the soft caress. He pushed the cloth deeper. As the fabric grazed her nether lips, her labia yawned open and her clitoris sprang to life. She inched her legs further apart to provide him with better access to her eager pussy.

When she heard his breathing change, her lids fluttered open and she stole a look at him. His dark, sexy eyes caressed her with sultry heat. She felt the cloth slip away and fall to the bottom of the tub. His long fingers replaced the cloth and surfed over her sex. He stroked the full length of her, from front to back, his fingers probing, thrusting into her tight opening.

She moaned and arched into his touch, offering herself up to him. "Yes, Jace, that feels wonderful."

"Just relax, Skylar, and let me take care of you." His voice was a soft, intimate whisper.

He stretched her wet lips open, while his thumb put pressure on the spot that needed it the most. A wave of passion overcame her and her body quivered in delight. Jace groaned when he felt her evocative responses. He leaned in closer and feathered his lips over hers. She loved the taste of him, the light pressure of his mouth moving over hers.

When he dipped another finger inside her, blood screamed through her veins with the sudden onslaught of pleasure. He ran his thumb back and forth over her swollen clit, pushing his fingers higher into her pussy. A storm began brewing deep in her body. She cried and bucked against him. He pumped into her, changing the rhythm and tempo, drawing out her response. A fine tremor burned through her skin, leaving her feeling breathless.

His fingers impaled her again and again, until her skin came alive. She tried to concentrate on the wonderful sensations as her mind whirred. A moment later her muscles undulated as a powerful, earth-shattering orgasm swept through her. Her release was swift, intense. Her breath came in a ragged burst as her muscles clenched around his fingers.

She twined her arms around his neck and held on to him tightly as the world around her began spinning on its axis. She called on every ounce of strength not to black out from the all-consuming pleasure.

After she came down from her climax, he gathered her into his arms. "Come with me, Skylar. My mouth craves a taste of your sweet pussy." The deep rawness of his voice shot through her.

As he carried her to the bed, she spotted his open suitcase. A pair of shiny handcuffs caught her eye. She bit down on her bottom lip and felt herself flush. Jace's gaze followed hers.

"You want to play?" he asked, lust darkening his eyes.

She nodded. "I've never..."

"Then it's time you did," he said, cutting her off.

He laid her across the splash of satin and grabbed his cuffs. "Do you trust me?" Silence enveloped them as she stared deep into his eyes. "You have to trust me if you're going to let me cuff your hands." A light sheen of perspiration speckled his forehead. She reached out and wiped it away.

"Yes," she whispered, and knew she'd never trusted anyone quite so much.

"Good," he said, grabbing a silk scarf from her bag.

Her body tingled in anticipation. "What are you going to do?" she asked as he draped the scarf over her eyes.

"We're going to play a game using your psychic abilities." The deep timbre of his voice caressed her body. Desire ran through her and she took a sharp breath.

"Are you up for it?" His warm breath fanned her face.

Speech was beyond her current capabilities. She nodded and swallowed the sudden dryness in her mouth. He tied the cool silk over her eyes, blocking her vision.

After he shackled her wrists in the handcuffs, securing her hands to the bedpost, she felt his body close to hers but never making contact. She could feel his heat, his energy and his untamed passion. She hungered for his touch, his tongue. She ached for him to make sweet, passionate love to her.

His mouth was close to her ear. "Tell me where I'm going to kiss you first, Skylar." His deep, rich voice seeped into her skin filling her with need.

Her heart began to pound in her chest. She exhaled slowly. "My neck."

She was right. That first delicious flick over her throat made her body convulse. This was amazing. *He* was amazing. Forever after, she'd be spoiled for any other man. He knew just what to do, just how to touch and stroke to prolong the exquisite agony. No one could ever live up to Jace Garret's skill. She couldn't believe how dangerously close she was to falling for him. If she hadn't already.

"Very good. Now tell me where I'm going to kiss next." She felt him move down her body, his hands tracing the pattern of her curves.

"My breasts," she murmured, writhing beneath him as she waited for that next seductive kiss.

She reveled in the silky sweep of his hair against her damp, naked skin. His lashes tickled the swells of her cleavage. She listened to his labored breathing and knew he was enjoying this as much as she was.

His hot tongue flicked her nipples with the utmost skill and they hardened almost painfully. It felt so good. So damn good. He knew exactly what she wanted, what she needed.

He growled. "You taste like heaven." He drew one pebbled nipple into his mouth, grazed his teeth over it and gently bit down until she screamed in delight. His hungry touch played havoc with her senses. She squirmed beneath him as primitive lust exploded through her body.

"Skylar, that's two for two. Where do you think I'm going to kiss you next?" His voice came out in a rough whisper.

She fought to find her own voice. "My pussy," she murmured, her sex muscles throbbing in anticipation. "Please kiss my pussy." Writhing on the bed, she gyrated her hips, begging for the feel of his tongue on her wet cunt.

He pushed her legs open as far as they would go. Parting her silky wet curls, he displayed her passion-drenched pussy. She heard him draw in a sharp breath before she felt the rough velvet of his tongue on her inner thighs. His breath was hot, his breathing was labored. Her entire body vibrated with need and desire. His tongue trailed higher until he breathed a kiss over her moist crevice, parting her labia with his tongue.

She began panting heavily. "God, yes!" she cried out, bucking against him. Her whole body moistened as raw need seared her insides. The pleasure was exquisite. She whimpered and thrust her hips forward in search of his mouth.

She sucked in a tight breath when he flicked his tongue over her clit. The stubble shadowing his jaw rubbed her inner thighs—both pain and pleasure mingled into one.

A feverish longing built with his every delicious caress. His hands began a lazy journey over her stomach and higher until he stroked her heavy breasts. A maelstrom of sensations ran through her. She craved the feel of his skin, to touch his sinewy muscles, but with her arms pinned above her head she couldn't budge. It surprised her to discover how much she like being bound to the bed. Jace was helping her learn so much about her needs and her sexual desires. He seemed to know what she liked even before she knew it herself.

He pushed his tongue deep inside her moist pussy, and she could feel the tension of an impending orgasm. Every nerve ending in her body was alive, on fire. He drew her clit into his mouth and suckled until her release was only a stroke away.

"Please, Jace. I want your cock. I want to feel you inside me when I come." Her voice was rough, shaky.

Jace gave a lusty moan as he tore the scarf from her face. His dark eyes blazed as he gazed at her with pure desire. There was so much emotion in his gaze. "I want to see the look in your eyes when you come for me."

Her breathing deepened in time to his.

He slid along her body and spread her folds with the tip of his cock, scraping it over her clit before he plunged inside her silken sheath. A deep growl rumbled from the depths of his throat.

"You're so hot and tight," he breathed into her mouth.

She opened her lips. "Kiss me."

Jace threaded his fingers through her hair. His lips closed over her, branding her with his heat. His tongue joined hers in a sensual mating dance. The exquisite texture of his silky mouth filled her with warmth. Emotions swept through her, flooding her chest with an unfamiliar fullness.

"Sweetheart, you're amazing." The depth of emotion in his voice surprised her.

He kissed her hard, possessively, until every coherent thought was wiped from her mind.

* * * * *

Jace pumped his cock in and out of her and thought about how he difficult it would be to be with any other woman without comparing her to Skylar. She touched something deep inside him. His heart ached for her in ways that were unfamiliar to him. He'd spent years longing for a woman like her, for a family, for someone to share laughter and heartache with. Now that he had a taste of what heaven was like, how could he possibly go on without her?

Perspiration trickled down her breasts and he leaned his head down and traced it with his tongue. She wrapped her legs around his back and cried out in ecstasy. He watched her eyes glaze over as she tumbled into orgasm.

The pressure building in his cock reached a fiery explosion as he released deep inside her tight sheath. Their cries of pleasure merged and they clung to each other as if their very lives depended on it.

He remained inside her, basking in her heat and warmth. He couldn't believe how much he wanted this woman—inside the bedroom and out. Somewhere along the way, in their quest to capture a bloodthirsty werewolf, they'd made a connection—a tender, emotional connection that made him feel closer to her than he'd ever felt to anyone else. He hadn't planned for this to happen. He hadn't planned on falling for the psychic who could, at any time, discover his secret and destroy his future. Especially when he gave in to his emotions.

He eased back and looked at her. Moisture shimmered on her bottom lip and once again he felt himself harden. He could never seem to satisfy his thirst for her.

He felt himself reach out to her, heart and soul. "Do you want me to uncuff you?"

"Yes. I want to touch you," she murmured.

He grabbed the key off the nightstand and released her hands. "Thank you for this, Skylar." When their eyes connected something special passed between them.

She reached out and stroked his cheek, her eyes drowsy, sexy, sated. "The pleasure was *all* mine." Her warm smile touched his heart and made him want to tell her how special this was for him, how special she was. But if he did, then what? They couldn't possible go any further with their relationship.

Just then a sound from the monitor drew their attention. They both turned.

Jace spotted Lucas' girlfriend along with another man enter the suite. Panic ran through him. "Where's Lucas?" He jolted upright.

Skylar touched his arm and pulled him back. "Don't worry, he's still at the resort. I can sense it. He's likely still partying with those two girls."

He felt the wolf within him shift. As the full moon crept closer, every nerve ending began to tingle, anticipating the change. He needed air, to clear his head and help control the beast. "Maybe we should go check. Just to make sure."

She nodded. "Sure. Or you could just trust me, and we can sit back, order room service and enjoy the show." She nodded toward the monitor.

Jace followed her gaze in time to see Lucas' girlfriend slowly peel off her shirt. Her large breasts fell forward and the man reached out to stroke them. He tweaked her nipples before pulling one swollen peak into his mouth. Jace felt his cock thicken as he watched the erotic show.

"Perhaps you're right," he said, his tongue struggling to work. "Maybe I should trust your abilities and just enjoy the show."

"I have a better idea," Skylar said. "How about whatever she does to him, I'll do to you?" His heart pulsed in his throat as he watched the other woman get down on her knees and pull the man's pants to his ankles. A second later he felt Skylar's mouth close over his cock. Her warm mouth slid down the length of him.

He groaned and grabbed a fistful of her hair. "I believe you were correct back at the precinct when you said I should leave all the thinking to you."

* * * * *

Birds chirped a melodic song outside their bedroom window as daylight arrived. Skylar stretched out across the bed and stole a quick look at the clock. It was well past eight in the morning. Her hand automatically reached across the bed, looking for the caring, considerate man who had brought her to heights of pleasure she'd never before experienced. A man who did things to her senses, her body. A man who filled the ache deep inside her.

Last night when she'd fallen asleep locked in his embrace, she'd felt so wanted, so desirable. A smile touched her mouth when her hand connected with his broad, muscular chest. She was actually quite surprised to find Jace sound asleep beside her. Surprised that he wasn't up already, staring at the monitor, waiting for signs of Lucas' return.

As she lay there looking at Jace, warmth and comfort pooled inside her. He'd come to mean so much to her in such a short time. Throughout the night, his tender lovemaking had touched the part of her soul that hungered to be wanted, to be loved.

Biting down on her bottom lip, she wondered what she'd gotten herself into. What had happened to the no-nonsense, non-romantic, career-oriented woman that had started this investigation? When Jace had been deep inside her, she knew they'd crossed all boundaries—emotional and physical. Hadn't she sworn she'd never let this man get under her skin?

But Jace wasn't just any man.

He was so different from the others, so caring, so gentle and tender. She breathed a heavy sigh. How could she ever walk away from him with her heart intact?

She wanted to touch him again, to find safety and comfort in his arms one more time. Her eyes scrolled the length of him and she resisted the urge to caress his flesh for fear of waking him. After last night, he needed his sleep. She grinned wickedly. She knew he hadn't been getting much rest lately, thanks to her.

Sometime throughout the night, he'd kicked off the sheets. They lay in a rumpled heap at the foot of the mattress. His long, dark hair was a tangled mess. Her gaze dropped from his face to his chest, then wandered lower to examine the rows of muscles rippling down his stomach. A cluster of dark curly hair flirted with his belly button then tapered to a thin line. She followed that line until it mingled with the tuft of hair at the base of his cock. She licked her suddenly dry lips. Her pulse leapt in her throat as she took in the sight of his masculinity.

She drew a sharp breath when his cock twitched under her hungry eyes. Her gaze quickly traveled back to his face.

"Good morning," he said, a huge smirk on his face. Reaching out to her, he brushed his hands over her puckered nipples. "Sleep well?" His voice was a warm, intimate whisper.

Caught in the act of gazing at his cock, she felt herself blush. A tremor shimmered through her body as his hands closed over her breasts with gentle softness. "For what little sleep I actually got, I guess so."

His eyes twinkled as his smirk widened. He feathered his fingertips over her naked flesh. She closed her eyes and absorbed the warmth from his silky touch.

"How's your leg? We never did put any sugar on it."

"It's just fine," she assured, and drew in a contented sigh as she leaned into him. Her lids fluttered open and their eyes locked. "Thanks for last night," she whispered and brushed her lips over his.

"Anytime," he replied, circling his arms around her waist, pinning her body to his.

"Really?" she questioned. She just couldn't help herself from asking, from wanting more. "Do you mean that?" Hope welled up inside her. Was it possible that he wanted to take their relationship to another level?

He flinched and began to look a little uncomfortable, weariness in his eyes. She looked away, regretting that she'd said anything. His hands dropped to his sides as he released her from his embrace. She pulled away from his body and drew her bottom lip into her mouth. She resisted the urge to slap herself for asking such a stupid question. *Of course* he hadn't meant that. Why did she constantly have to remind herself that he only wanted her for sex?

They had one more day until they left the resort. Once they closed the investigation and parted ways she'd have no reason to ever set eyes on him again. A slice of pain cut through her and she tried to fight it off. She never should have let her feelings get so out of hand.

Jace climbed from the bed and walked over to the window. What was he thinking? Was he sorry he couldn't offer her more?

Skylar's senses told her that Jace, unlike the other men from her past, didn't fear her psychic abilities. Surely he never would have played such a seductive game using her skills if he'd been uncomfortable. If that was the case, then what was holding him back from wanting a relationship with her? She believed he cared for her. She could see it in his eyes when they made love. She could feel it in his every touch, his every kiss.

So what exactly was behind that small area of his mind he'd closed off to her? Maybe it was time for her to find out what Jace Garrett was afraid of.

Jace pulled back the paneled curtains. When he eased open the window the fragrant smell of rain and jasmine filled the suite. Thunder growled in the distance.

"Looks like a storm is brewing," he said, turning back to her.

She glanced over his shoulder. The sun had disappeared behind a wall of dark, threatening clouds. Her body chilled as a cool breeze washed over her.

He noticed her tremble. "Are you okay?"

"Just a little cold."

He shut the window and walked over to her. Grabbing her by the hand he pulled her to her feet. Their naked bodies collided.

"Let me warm you." His soft words dripped over her like warm butter. He smoothed her hair back and dropped a kiss onto her forehead.

Snuggled against his chest, she breathed in his scent and ran her fingers over the hard contours of his body. He ran his hands up and down her arms. The sweet friction created heat and warmed her body.

His touch quickly turned into something more. Something erotic, something that kicked her libido into overdrive. It didn't take much for her to want him again. One simple touch, one simple look, and she was putty in his arms. She was helpless to resist him. She pulled his mouth down to hers for a hot, fiery kiss. His tongue delved deep and she moaned as heated desire coiled through her. The kiss left them both shaking. Sexual tension crackled in the air as she sank into the plush softness of his mouth.

He reached down and massaged the damp curls at the apex of her legs. Her body melted beneath his when he stroked her petal-soft pussy and urged her thighs apart. A whimper escaped her lips as she shuddered her surrender.

"I want you again, sweetheart. I can't seem to get enough of you." Need made his voice husky. He feathered his lips over her shoulder, and then nipped at her with his teeth. When he kissed the erogenous zone at the hollow of her throat, her body went up in flames.

Skylar closed her eyes and reveled in the sensations. She arched into him, his wet tongue warm against her cooled skin.

She focused her attention on his engorged cock as it strained against her thighs. Swallowing deeply, she reached out and squeezed it. It felt like granite. It pulsed with arousal as liquid dripped from the slit. He gave a low moan and circled his arms around her, beginning to rock his hips, sliding his cock in and out of her hand. She slid her other hand lower and cupped his balls, her fingers playing with his silken curls. She milked his heavy sac, drawing out more of his tangy male juice. She gathered his salty fluid on her fingertip and slowly drew it in her moth.

"Mmm, I love the taste of your come," she murmured. He liked that—his sexy moan told her so. A fiery glow began gathering deep in her pussy.

Jace threw his head back and growled. They were suddenly so impatient, so hungry for each other again. In one smooth motion he pushed her against the wall.

His dark eyes were blazing. His gaze devoured her. "I want to fuck you, Skylar." His mouth curved enticingly as his warm breath caressed her face.

His gaze dropped from her eyes, to her lips, her breasts. Need reverberated through her blood. They were both so wild, so out of control.

Her eyes slid closed as her sex juices began to flow. "*Yes.* Please fuck me."

He pinned her arms above her head and widened her legs with his knees. He trailed damp kisses over her jaw before he gently sank his teeth into her neck.

In one fast motion he drove his cock into her. She yelped as his body crushed hers against the wall. Her breath caught. She felt his restraint as he waited for her to catch up.

She squeezed her pussy around his cock, letting him know she was ready—ready for him to fuck her. He drove his cock in as deep as he could.

There was nothing gentle about this encounter. They were both taking what they needed. And she needed him. Needed to be one with him again. Jace was offering her his body, not his heart, and right now that was enough for her.

Growling into her ear, he took her fast and hard, stoking the fire inside her with his cock. Her mind exploded with the onslaught of pleasure. His fingers bit into her hips as he pulled her up and down on his cock. Her entire body arched and her breath caught sharply.

Grinding against him, she met and welcomed his every thrust. "You feel so good," she cried. "So good." She shuddered violently.

Her words drove him on. He plunged harder and deeper, slamming her back into the wall. She listened to his shallow pants and knew he was close.

Hot pressure began building inside her as need consumed them both. When he slipped his hand between their bodies and stroked her clit, she came in a swift, glorious release. For a moment she felt as though she'd lost consciousness. Jace cried out her name and shared in the ecstasy as his come flooded into her body.

Chapter Nine

ꙮ

The remainder of the day passed without incident. They'd spent the entire afternoon following Lucas, being sure to keep out of sight while keeping him and his whereabouts known at all times.

Skylar glanced out the large bay window of the main lobby. The full moon was only a few hours away. A shiver of fear tingled all the way to her toes. Jace must have felt her nervousness. He slipped his arm around her waist and pulled her closer. It always surprised her how safe she felt in his arms.

When she looked up at him with a tremulous smile on her face, he smiled back. His dark eyes gleamed with the same emotion she'd glimpsed earlier during their lovemaking. He reached out and tucked a wispy strand of hair behind her ear. Warmth moved through her.

She furrowed her brow and studied him as he scrubbed a hand over his chin. As the day progressed, she'd noticed a radical change in Jace's behavior. Calm and control gave way to restlessness and agitation. Skylar tried to convince herself that he was simply concerned about how the night would unfold. But some inner instinct told her she was wrong. Something else was going on with him.

But what?

Shortly after dinner, they found themselves standing outside the doors of the lounge where only two nights previous, she'd performed oral sex on Jace. A small group had gathered for another initiation ritual that was to take place in a few minutes.

Lucas leaned against the back wall of the long hallway. Skylar felt his hot gaze on her back. A knot tightened in her stomach, warning her of the danger ahead. The same eerie feeling that she'd had last night at the beach washed over her. She sensed it with every fiber of her being—there was another werewolf in the vicinity.

She chanced a glance at Lucas. He tilted his head, as though scrutinizing her. His piercing gaze was disturbing. It was as if he could see into the depths of her soul. She shook off the uneasy feeling creeping down her spine.

When the concierge opened the lounge doors, she stepped inside. Soft light pooled on the floor and bathed the room in a sensual, romantic glow. The fresh smell of lilac perfumed the air. The concierge gestured to the party host who then made his way to the podium at center stage.

She felt Jace's hand close over hers as he guided her to a table in the far corner. Welcoming his comforting touch, she leaned into him. She accepted a glass of champagne from a nearby waiter and took a seat beside Jace. Absently, she ran her finger around the perimeter of her glass as she scanned the room.

The host's voice drew her attention. A hush fell over the crowd. "It seems we have a new guest. She registered late last night." He waved his hand, summoning her to come forward. "Everyone please give a warm welcome to Tamara."

Skylar's whole body stiffened when she caught sight of the new member. It was the same woman who'd been talking to Lucas down at the beach. Was she there with Lucas? Or had she simply met him during the moonlight skinny-dip?

Last night, after the jellyfish incident and the commotion between Jace and Lucas she'd forgotten to mention the woman to Jace. She leaned in to tell Jace that she recognized Tamara from last night, but before she had a chance to speak, the host called for all the men to come forth. She didn't want Jace to go, but knew she had little choice in the matter. She didn't want to blow their cover when they were so close to bringing Lucas down.

The men stripped and formed a circle around Tamara. Skylar watched, her heart beating erratically, as Tamara brushed her long brown locks from her shoulders and narrowed her blue eyes as she circled the men. The women in the crowd began their tribal chanting.

A knot formed in Skylar's throat as nausea welled up inside her. What if Tamara picked Jace? What if she had to sit and watch Jace become intimate with her in full view of everyone?

She sat there staring at him. Her heart did a backflip in her chest as she wondered exactly when it was that she'd first fallen in love with him. Was it the first moment their eyes met? Or was it the first time he held her in his arms and kissed her? She felt so connected to him. He seemed to know her better than she knew herself.

Hour by hour she'd fallen deeper and deeper in love with him. She felt almost dizzy when she realized the extent of her feelings for him and how deep they ran. She had no idea what she'd been craving, what she'd been missing, until she'd met him. She gripped the table for support and drew in a sharp breath. How could she ever walk away without exploring and nurturing the emotions between them? She had to talk to him, to tell him her feelings. She couldn't let thing end between them, she just couldn't.

Maybe it was time to show him that there could be more to their relationship. Some things were worth fighting for. Jace Garrett was one of those things. Somehow she had to find a way to show him that they could move beyond a purely physical relationship.

The chanting crowd grew louder pulling her attention back to the present. To the initiation taking place on center stage.

When Tamara reached out and stroked Jace's thick cock, a wave of white-hot jealousy ran through Skylar. She was surprised at the depths of its power.

Unable to stomach watching her touch Jace, Skylar turned her head away and bit down on her bottom lip. That was when she noticed Lucas staring at her. A smirk played on his face. Skylar had the distinct impression that he knew everything. That he knew who she was and why she was there. But how was that possible? They'd been so careful to play along and keep their identities hidden.

She turned back to face Jace. He caught her gaze and mouthed the same reassuring words she'd said to him down by the pool. *Only you.*

The tenderness in his expression brought tears to her eyes. Her heart reached out to him, and she ached to tell him how much she loved him.

He obviously knew her well enough to know how disturbed she was by the situation. How much it bothered her to watch another woman touch him. The same way it had bothered him to watch another man touch her.

Surely he wouldn't have acted so jealous if he didn't have deeper feelings for her. The soft way he looked at her, the gentle way he touched her and made love to her told her that his feelings for her were more than physical.

Then why had he retreated emotionally this morning? And why did he keep a part of himself closed off to her? Had he been burned by a woman in the past? Was he too afraid to try again?

She was suddenly desperate to talk to him, to better understand his doubts and his fears, but she knew that would have to wait. Right now they needed to concentrate on capturing Lucas.

"This is the man I choose," the woman said, standing in front of Lucas. Tamara's gaze sifted through the crowd and settled on Skylar. When their eyes met and locked, a tingle of foreboding made all the tiny hairs on the back of Skylar's neck stand up. She could feel the blood drain from her face. She had the distinct impression that Tamara was the other werewolf she'd sensed.

When Tamara and Lucas walked hand in hand toward the stage, Jace grabbed his clothes off the floor and backed away.

He tiptoed through the lusty couples already engaged in sex on the bearskin rugs and came back to the table to reclaim his chair.

Fighting down her rising panic, Skylar grabbed his arm. "Jace, it's her. She's the werewolf I sensed last night."

He flinched and pulled away. "I know." His gruff voice took her by surprise.

"You do? How?"

"I just do," he said and she knew he wasn't about to give further explanation. A low growl sounded deep in his throat.

"Are you okay?" she asked, once again reaching for his arm.

He moved out of her reach and hastily pulled his clothes on. "No," he bit out then turned to her.

When she drew back in surprise at his harshness, he reached for her hand. His eyes softened. "Sorry, Skylar. I'm just not feeling myself. I want this over with." She noticed the texture of his hand felt somewhat rougher against her soft skin. Like he'd been running it over gritty sandpaper.

"Look," he whispered, nodding to the side doors.

Skylar glanced up in time to spot Lucas and Tamara slip out without anyone noticing. At this point all the couples were too busy engaging in their own little party and were oblivious to anyone else.

Jace touched her arm and she turned to face him. "It's time to go. Do you still have my gun?"

She patted her purse and nodded. After drawing a calming breath she said, "Let's go find them."

Keeping their distance, they exited through the same door as Lucas and Tamara. Skylar caught a flash of Tamara's shirt before the elevator doors shut tight.

"They're heading upstairs," she said, swallowing the knot forming in her throat. She wrung her hands together and hurried her steps to keep pace with Jace as he bolted for the staircase.

"They must be heading back to Lucas' room," he said breathlessly as he reached their floor. He turned and waited for her to catch up. When she reached him, he pulled the door open and, after checking to make sure the hallway was clear, he slipped through and motioned for her to keep close to his back. Silence enveloped them as she quietly followed him down the long hall.

When they passed Lucas' suite, she nodded, letting Jace know they were in there, but oddly enough he seemed to already know. Already sense it.

They moved to their suite. Jace slipped the card into the electronic lock and whispered, "We have to check the surveillance monitor to see what they're up to. They must be hunting together, searching for their next victim."

He nodded toward the monitor. "They're pacing. They'll change soon."

Skylar eased herself down on the bed and stared at them as they moved restlessly around the room. She knew they were waiting to change, but she sensed they were also waiting for something else. But for what, she didn't know. "What do we do, Jace?" she asked nervously. Her fingers shook as she took Jace's gun from her purse and handed it to him.

"We wait for him to make a move." Jace grabbed his holster and hooked it over his shoulder. When he did, his wallet fell to the floor, unnoticed. "I have to run to the bathroom. I have more silver bullets in a hidden compartment in my shaving kit. Keep an eye on them for me."

Skylar stared at his back as he made his way across the room. Feeling too anxious to remain seated, she stood up and began pacing. Her foot kicked Jace's wallet and sent it flying across the floor. She crossed the room and bent down to pick it up. Before she placed it on the nightstand, curiosity got the better of her, and she took a quick peek inside. A clear plastic sleeve filled with pictures caught her attention. She pulled it free and studied the photo of Captain Sanders' twins. She smiled. Jace really did love those kids. Tucked in the back she found a picture of his mother. It was a duplicate of the one she'd seen in Jace's apartment. She pulled it out and ran her finger over the image.

Suddenly, the room started spinning. Nausea began welling up inside her and she knew a vision was coming. She grasped the picture tighter and sank onto the bed as memories began to infiltrate her mind.

Violence and pain descended upon her like a storm. Skylar was no longer in the hotel suite. Instead, she found herself standing in a dark, isolated alleyway watching as a ferocious werewolf sexually assaulted Jace's mother. An uneasy feeling closed in on her and she knew in an instant that Jace had been born as the result of that attack.

Fingers trembling in horror, the wallet fell from her hands. The sound of Jace running water in the bathroom pulled her back to the present.

Taking deep breaths, she remained still as she relived and rationalized the shocking vision. The reality of the situation seeped into her brain. Jace's father was a werewolf, which meant Jace was a werewolf too!

Her skin broke out in a cold sweat as her stomach clenched. Panic shot through her. Oh God! She glanced at the closed bathroom door.

She pressed her forehead into her hands and fought to clear her head. She had to fight to think, to breathe. Her chest throbbed as her stomach dropped. Shocked and numb, she forced herself to stand.

How could this be? How could she not have sensed it? Read it? She already knew the answers to her questions. Jace was a half-breed and had learned how to hide that part of himself. That small area inside him that she couldn't penetrate was the animal in him.

Gut instinct and self-preservation urged her to run. She stumbled to the door and inched it open as her mind assessed the information.

God, why hadn't he told her? She loved him and felt his love for her, too. So why hadn't he told her *what* he really was? She pinched the bridge of her nose as understanding dawned on her. After she told him about her murdered family and the attack on her, Jace knew how much she hated werewolves.

Skylar glanced out the window. The thick clouds were parted, exposing the full, pale moon. Her gaze darted back to the bathroom door. She understood why he'd been so restless, so aggravated tonight. He was fighting the inevitable.

What would happen to him during the change? Weren't all werewolves killers when they turned into their primitive form? Would he become violent and unaware, or could he control his actions? Surely the task force wouldn't have him on the team if he became a murderous beast once a month. But what if they didn't even know?

A sick, apprehensive knot tightened in her stomach. Skylar tamped down the overwhelming feeling of anxiety and worked hard at figuring out what to do next. She loved this man, had faith in him. She had to trust that he loved her in return and wouldn't harm her. He was warm, tender, caring and touched her with such gentleness. *Surely* a part of that remained with him when he turned. The pair of handcuffs sitting on the nightstand caught her eyes. Perhaps he used those when he changed. She drew a deep breath and knew what she had to do. She couldn't flee and leave the man she loved with all her heart when he might need her the most.

She let the door slip shut. To gain additional security she reached for the dead bolt.

Just as her fingers closed over the brass lock, she heard a keycard slip into the electronic lock. The door pushed in before she had a chance to react. Skylar blinked and watched Tamara stalk toward her with the ferocity of a wild animal. Skylar opened her mouth to scream but no sound came as she inched backwards. Before she had a chance to get away, she felt the cold chill of darkness take over as Tamara's hands closed over her throat.

* * * * *

Jace stepped out of the bathroom and quickly perused the room. The suite door was wide open. A cool breeze swept through the room as an uneasy feeling began zinging through his veins. He pinched his lids shut then quickly opened them again.

Skylar was gone!

He swallowed the panic that rose in him and stole a quick look at the monitor. He felt his blood run cold. Lucas and Tamara were gone too. Grinding his back teeth together, his nostrils flared as he fisted his fingers.

He knew it in an instant—they had Skylar.

Jace also knew the situation was escalating beyond his control. He pulled his gun from his holster as he ran to the phone. He had to call for backup.

He didn't care if the task force came and found him in his primitive form. None of that mattered now that Skylar was in danger. The only thing he was concerned about was her safety.

After quickly making the call, he ran from the suite and bolted down the stairs two at a time. He could feel his skin crawl as the beast within him itched to get out. It was hard to think straight while trying to fight off the changes occurring deep inside him.

His muscles and joints ached as the full moon grew higher in the sky. He concentrated hard to keep the wolf at bay. He had to find Skylar before he turned or all would be lost.

Dread filled him. The thought of Lucas hurting her, or worse, killing her, was so chilling it turned his blood to ice.

He pushed the stairwell door open and bolted through the main lobby. He didn't slow down until he reached the outdoors. The cool night air washed over his face and helped clear his thoughts. He glanced around looking for anything unusual.

Where in the hell were they? How was he going to find her? He knew if he changed into his wolf form he could easily track her by her scent, but once he found her what would he do? Kill her? If he didn't find her, she was as good as dead anyway.

He drew in air to help clear his mind. Where would Lucas take her? It had to be someplace nearby. Someplace where no one would hear her screams. Jace ran flat out into the forest that surrounded the resort. The full moon, high overhead, broke through the canopy of leaves and lit his path.

He desperately searched for signs of Lucas' lair. Branches sliced his face and arms. He ignored the sting as blood dripped down his cheek, and pushed forward. Near the far end of the forest he spotted a large mound of earth. Was it possible that Lucas' lair was buried beneath? There was only one way to find out.

As he sprinted through the trees he heard a cry in the distance. Skylar. Bile pushed into his throat. Her cries of fear reached his ears and filled him with panic. He gripped his gun harder as he darted toward the sound of her voice.

The seductive pull of the moon was powerful. It beckoned him, enticing him to change into his wolf form. He ran harder and harder until he could barely breathe. His heart pounded like thunder as his lungs gasped for more oxygen.

When he glanced up at the moon, heated blood pulsed through his veins. He could feel his muscles twitch, his bones crackle and pop. Suddenly, the two legs he'd been running on turned into four.

Chapter Ten

ꙮ

The pungent smell of musty earth and rotting leaves pulled Skylar from her slumber. Lying flat on her back, she moaned and tossed her head to the side. Her jaw connected with something sharp. The stabbing pain shot through her body, forcing her to open her eyes. It was dark and dank, with the scent of death lingering in the air. Skylar pinched her eyes shut, letting them adjust to the dim light.

Where the hell was she?

Suddenly the memory of Tamara's hands closing over her throat raced through her mind. She tore her eyes open and frantically looked around. She seemed to be in some kind of cave.

She screamed and struggled to stand. A heavy chain binding her ankles pulled her back onto the damp, cold ground. She fell with a thud. The same rock she'd banged her jaw on only moments ago now jabbed her in the ribs. She cried out in pain and pressed her palm against her aching side.

"Shhh," a female voice whispered.

Skylar turned in the direction of the sound. She peered into the darkness and listened to the soft footsteps coming closer. She didn't recognize the feminine voice, but knew it was Tamara. She reached down and pulled on the chains, testing their durability.

"Lucas doesn't like loud noises," Tamara warned.

Skylar heard a deep, primal growl and a shifting movement in the dark corners of the cave. She cringed and turned her head. Her heart pounded in her chest.

"What…what is he doing?" There was a desperate edge to her voice.

Tamara chuckled softly, her voice growing closer. "He's waiting."

"What's he waiting for?" she whispered into the dark.

"For his brother to join him in the kill," she murmured seductively.

"His brother?"

Tamara gave her a sly grin. "Yes, his long-lost brother. He's been searching for him for years."

A strangled cry caught in her throat. Her eyes widened as the truth dawned on her. Jace was Lucas' brother. The beast who had sexually assaulted Jace's mother was also Lucas' father. She drew a quick sharp breath, as her pulse leapt. Now she understood why their eyes were strikingly similar. She swallowed hard as her mouth went dry.

A low chuckle rumbled in Tamara's throat. "Come now, Skylar. You're the *psychic*. I'm sure you've figured it all out already."

"How do you know who I am?"

"While you've been watching Lucas, I've been watching you and Jace." Her voice was low, harsh and growing increasingly closer. "You underestimated our predatory senses."

"Why haven't you changed yet?" An uncontrollable shiver racked her body.

"Because, like Jace, I'm not a purebred and can control it longer."

Panic rose in her throat. "Why are you doing this? Why are you helping him?"

"Because he lets me have a little fun with his women before he kills them." Tamara stepped out of the shadows and came closer. "Do you want to have a little fun with me, Skylar, before you die?" Tamara knelt down beside her and ran her icy fingertip over Skylar's cheek. Her hand trailed lower and lower until she dipped into her cleavage.

Skylar screamed, flinched, and tried to pull away.

Tamara narrowed her eyes to mere slits. "I told you to be quiet." Her voice grew angry, darker. "No one can hear your screams." Using her long fingernail, she ripped the buttons from Skylar's blouse. Her shirt fell open. "Your fate has been decided, Skylar. Stop struggling and enjoy the pleasant things I am about to do to you."

Just then a noise at the opening to the cave drew her attention.

She turned in the direction of the sound.

When she looked into the eyes of the wolf approaching, she knew it was Jace.

Their eyes connected as he stalked closer. His thick, meaty paws left heavy prints in the muddy floor. The look in his eyes was frightening. From the dark corner she heard Lucas growl. Tamara stepped back into the shadows.

Skylar sucked in a tight breath and prayed he could understand her plea in his wolf form. "Jace, please, help me." Her voice was a low, strained whisper. She squirmed beneath his hungry gaze. Her whole body trembled when it became apparent that his inner beast ruled his actions. Fear closed in on her, as he continued to come closer. His dark eyes locked with hers. They burned with intense rage. He bared his long sharp fangs. His low growl seeped into her skin and filled her with panic.

He was so close to her now, she could feel his hot breath on her neck. Her stomach curdled as bile pushed into her throat. She cringed and twisted when she felt his hot wet tongue trail a path over her neck. She clutched her stomach as fear and nausea overcame her.

Her hands turned into fists, but she knew she was no match for him. Tears pooled on her lashes and she feared she was fighting a losing battle.

Fueled by desperation, she made another attempt to reach the tender, gentle man locked inside the wolf's body.

"Please, Jace. Don't," she whispered and looked deep into his dark eyes. He flinched and pulled back. Somewhere in the depths of his angry eyes she caught a glimpse of the Jace that she'd grown to love. He was still in there. Her heart leapt with hope. She had to find a way to bring him out.

With her heart slamming in her chest, she summoned her courage and reached out to touch him. When her hand made contact, he reacted as though he'd been struck. He snarled as a low growl rumbled deep in his throat.

She tried to remain calm as she smoothed her hand over his rough, textured fur and whispered their special words of love. "Only you, Jace, *only you.*"

He stared at her for a long moment. Seconds crawled into minutes as she continued to stroke him. Suddenly he shook his head as if to clear his thoughts. It was as though something clicked inside him, as though her words had triggered a memory.

"Only you," she whispered into the still night.

At the sound of her soft, reassuring voice she felt him back away. Skylar turned to see Lucas creeping up behind Jace.

Lucas growled, circled Jace, and threw himself at her. Horrified, she cried out. In a motion so fast it took her by surprise, Jace leapt in between them and deflected Lucas' powerful body.

Lucas instinctively struck back, knocking Jace to the ground, pinning him with his deadly claws. When Lucas turned back to her, he seemed to be smiling. He stalked closer. A shiver of fear rushed down her spine.

Jace quickly recovered from the initial attack and retaliated. His growl pierced her ears. Positioning himself between Lucas and Skylar, he drove his sharp canines toward

Lucas' throat. Skylar gasped when Lucas let out a growl of fury and launched into Jace.

Skylar watched in horror as wolf battled wolf. Brother against brother. Their cries of pain and agony as they bit into each other's throats reached her ears. Shimmying backwards as far as she could go, she pressed her back against the dirt wall and covered her ears, trying to block out the excruciating sounds.

Jace moved like a bolt of lightning and threw Lucas across the room. He hurtled through the air and landed with a thud. He staggered to his feet and then slowly collapsed. Skylar's senses told her that the throw had killed him. She peered into the dark corner in search of Tamara. She was no longer there.

When Jace turned back to face her, her heart stilled. He crept closer and closer until she felt his hot breath on her face.

"Jace," she whispered.

He'd saved her. He'd been able to control the beast inside him and save her.

She felt her heart go out to him.

Jace curled up beside her and rested his head on her lap. The heat from his fur warmed her chilled body. They remained that way long into the night, waiting for him to change back to his human form.

* * * * *

At the first sign of dawn the wolf retreated back inside the man. Off in the distance Skylar could hear the faint shouts of approaching agents.

When Jace opened his eyes and looked at her, her heart caught in her throat. His eyes were filled with turbulent emotions.

"Are you okay?" he asked, his voice a soft, intimate whisper.

She struggled to find her own voice. "Yes," she admitted honestly. She'd spent the whole night coming to terms with what happened.

Jace stretched the kinks from his limbs and climbed to his feet. "Let's get you out of here."

"I can't." She nodded toward her feet. "I'm chained."

Jace glanced around the cave. Lucas' dead body was sprawled across the floor. A heap of clothes lay beside him. Jace padded across the dirt room and pulled on Lucas' clothes. He rifled through the pockets until he found the key. After he released Skylar's ankles, he carried her outside, into the fresh morning air.

He set her down on a soft bed of grass, took a seat beside her and bellowed to the approaching agents.

Skylar listened as Jace explained the situation to Agent Blair McCade, giving a description of Tamara. Agent McCade grabbed his comm unit, reported that Jace and Skylar were both safe, Lucas had been taken out and that he'd found footprints and was hot on Tamara's trail.

Jace turned his attention back to Skylar. "Blair is one of the best. He'll find Tamara and make her pay for what she did to you." When he noticed the apprehensive look on her face, he frowned and said, "I'm so sorry." He threaded his fingers through her hair and looked deep into her eyes.

She saw pain and regret lingering in his gaze. "What are you sorry for?" she asked.

"For everything." His voice was rough with emotion. "For not telling you what I was. For bringing you here and putting you in danger. For almost killing you."

She looked deep into his eyes. The love she saw there filled her with warm longing.

"I wouldn't have come here with you if I didn't want to. And you saved me, Jace." She reached out and caressed his face. He leaned into her touch and let out a low growl of longing. "I always had faith in you."

"Always?"

She grinned. "Well…maybe there was one small second where I was worried."

"I'm so glad you're safe, Skylar. I don't know what I would have done if anything had happened to you." She watched his throat work as he swallowed. "What if I had hurt you?"

"But you didn't hurt me," she reassured him, stroking her hand over his face.

Suddenly, his eyes brightened. "That's right, I didn't hurt you. I protected you…because I love you."

"You…you love me?"

He put his arm around her and hugged her to him. "I have from the minute you set foot in the Captain's office. I couldn't tell you, or offer you more, because I thought I would hurt you when I changed into my wolf form. That's why I tried to keep my distance. Now I know, Skylar. When we're married and living together I *know* I'll never hurt you."

"Married?" she asked hesitantly.

His eyes were as bright as a child's on Christmas morning. "Yes. Will you marry me, Skylar?"

Was she hearing him right? Love! Marriage! She'd never expected anyone to feel that way about her. She felt as though her heart would explode with the love she felt for him.

She'd always longed for everything he was offering. No longer would she be looking in from outside, watching and wishing it were her walking hand in hand through the park with the man she loved.

Jace was offering her everything her heart had ever desired.

His hands moved to her face. He cradled her cheeks in his palms. His expression turned serious, his voice deep. "Only you, Skylar, only you." He drew her in closer until his lips were a breath away from hers. "Please say you'll marry me?" There was so much love in his expression. He gently stroked her hair, her face and her arms as he waited for her to sort through her feelings.

She couldn't find her voice, so instead of answering him, she kissed him. His mouth was so hot, so inviting. He sank his tongue into her mouth and she greedily drew it deeper. The air around them instantly charged with sexual energy as Jace deepened the kiss. Fire curled a lazy path to her loins as his hands began skimming her curves.

Skylar tilted her head back as Jace rained kisses over her chin, her jaw, her neck and lower. Her senses exploded as he dipped his head and buried his face between her breasts, lashes fluttering against her skin. Her nipples quivered in response to his seduction. He pushed gently on her shoulders in a silent message for her to lay back.

After she obliged, he leaned over her, being careful not to crush her with his body weight. Her heart reached out to him.

He finger-combed her hair as his eyes moved over her face. "God, you are so beautiful," he murmured. His cock pressed insistently against her legs and bombarded her body with love and desire.

Skylar reached out and closed her hand over his, guiding him to where she needed his touch most. "I ache for you, Jace. I ache to feel you inside me."

His smile couldn't have pleased her more.

He turned his attention to her pussy. Skylar widened her legs as he stroked her through her clothes. "And you should always have what you want, Skylar. I will always see to that."

His deep voice played down her spine like a powerful aphrodisiac. His mouth found hers once again. They traded kisses for so long it left them both shaking. By the time they came up for air they were both breathless.

She twined her arms around his neck and held him to her. She couldn't seem to get him close enough. "I love you, Jace," she whispered into his mouth.

"I love you too, Skylar." He buried his face in the crook of her neck.

She broke free from the circle of his arms and looked deep into his eyes. A smirk played on her lips. "I think you should take me inside, so I can show you how much," she murmured playfully.

He smiled. "Like I said before, we should leave all the thinking to you."

Also by Cathryn Fox

Liquid Dreams
Web of Desire

About the Author

If you're looking for Cathryn Fox you'd never find her living in Eastern Canada with a husband, two young children and a chocolate Labrador retriever. Nor would you ever find her in a small corner office, writing all day in her pajamas.

Oh no, if you're looking for Cathryn you might find her gracing the Hollywood elite with her presence, sunbathing naked on an exotic beach in Southern France, or mingling with the rich and famous as she sips champagne on a luxury yacht in the Caribbean. Perhaps you can catch her before she slips between the sheets with a man who is as handsome as he is wealthy, a man who promises her the world.

Cathryn Fox is no ordinary woman. Men love her. Women want to be her.

Cathryn is bold, sensuous and sophisticated. And she is my alter ego.

Cathryn welcomes comments from readers. You can find her website and email address on her author bio page at www.ellorascave.com.

LION IN THE SHADOWS

Delilah Devlin

Trademarks Acknowledgement

ஐ

The author acknowledges the trademarked status and trademark owners of the following wordmarks mentioned in this work of fiction:

Genuine Wrangler: Wrangler Apparel Corporation

Maglite: Mag Instrument, Inc.

Viagra: Pfizer Inc. Corporation Delaware

Chapter One

ꟸ

The earth shook and the air stirred.

Sounds other than the usual chirping of cave crickets and the incessant drip of water intruded on the sleeper's dreams, echoing down the cavern. Voices, laughter, feet scraping over stone.

The sleeper opened his eyes and found that, for once, the exercise wasn't futile. A sliver of grayish light penetrated the gloom.

He stretched, willing blood to quicken through his body, to heat and ease muscles that had remained dormant too long.

Then a new scent—musky, warm-blooded, human—entered his tomb. He rolled to his feet. Then gathering his strength he roared up the cave wall.

* * * * *

Lani Kimmel drove over the cattle guard onto the gravel road that marked the beginning of rancher McKelvey's property. She followed the ridgeline of the steep, oak and cedar-covered hill, bouncing in her seat despite her truck's heavy-duty shocks. The tires churned in caliche, the fine sandstone gravel pinging on the wheel wells.

She tried to keep her mind focused on the task of keeping her pickup on the rough road and away from the reason she climbed to the remote spot. But her stomach already burbled, her palms grew moist and that little voice in the back of her mind—the one that sounded like her father's—taunted her, "What do you think you're playin' at, little girl? You aren't strong enough."

As she rounded a curve, a long line of parked vehicles forced her to pull onto the shoulder to continue forward.

Further along, she passed an EMS unit, two county squad cars, and the trucks and SUVs belonging to other members of the volunteer fire department. Parking in a narrow space between two vehicles, she had her door open before the engine finished chugging to a halt. Heat blasted her, and she grabbed her volunteer's baseball cap to shield her eyes from the bright afternoon sun. Then she slid her duffel from behind her seat, kicked a booted heel against the door of her truck, and headed toward the mouth of the unnamed cave.

She nodded to the EMS team crouched beside two boys huddled beneath blankets, shivering despite the late afternoon heat. Compassion could have swamped her, but she quickly tamped down the emotion. If she thought too much about it, she wouldn't be able to get through the next few hours. Their buddy likely lay on the bottom of the cave floor, and it was her job to bring him up.

Lani approached the group standing in front of a narrow black hole. Stones and gravel were already piled to the side as the men worked at widening the opening. She took a deep breath to calm her nerves. "Anybody looked inside yet?"

Cale Witte, the captain of the volunteer fire department, turned and gave her a crooked smile that creased his suntanned face. "Glad you could make it, Lani. Did you bring your vertical pack?"

Lani lifted her duffel. "Got it here, boss. So, we have a drop-off? Anyone hear from the kid inside?"

He shook his head, his grave expression telling her he expected the worst. "Those skinny runts shimmied through that hole carrying ropes and Maglites," he said, sounding disgusted. "Said they didn't know there was another level until their friend dropped out of sight."

Lani swore under her breath.

Cale spat a stream of chewing tobacco. "A couple of us crawled in. The entrance is blocked with loose-packed gravel and stone. It's pretty unstable, but the cave opens wide once you're through the mouth. About twenty feet inside, it bottoms out. We shined our lights around, but it was too deep to see much. We need to climb down."

"Well, that's what I'm here for, huh?" Lani said, willing confidence into her voice.

He nodded. "No one knows caves like you do—that's a fact. You better have a look for yourself."

Randy Brandt, another member of the department, leaned on his shovel. "Think we've got this hole wide enough for your butt now?" His grin stretched across his handsome face.

Not for the first time, Lani thought Randy's lean, muscled frame and sun-tinted brown hair belonged in a firemen's calendar. "Better put your back into it." Lani gave him a teasing glance. "Gotta make room for that big head of yours, too."

The men chuckled.

Lani took no offense. She'd long ago figured out she was one of the team when the men included her in the insults they traded. Besides, the banter helped drown out the voice that ate at her composure. The sooner she was in the cave—her world—the sooner she'd be in control.

"How are you, Lani?"

Lani stiffened at the low-pitched voice, rough as sandpaper. She didn't turn. "Just fine, Sheriff," she said, her own voice gruff as she forced the words past her frozen vocal chords. She'd known sooner or later their paths would cross in the line of duty, but had hoped for more time to steel herself against the pain. "Give me a minute to get out my gear, and I'll see about bringing up that boy."

His hand fell on her shoulder, and she finally turned to meet his gaze. No one else was close enough to see the heat in his angry glare. If anyone did look their way, all they'd note was his usual hard-edged mask. Only she could see the turmoil roiling in his eyes. Why was he making this so damn hard?

"You're not thinking of going down alone, are you?"

"Probably." She lifted her chin. "I do my best work in the dark, don't I?" she said softly. No way could he miss the sarcasm in her voice.

His expression didn't change, but his hand tightened.

Lani shrugged him off and stepped away. She slung her duffel to the ground, ignoring him and the slight tremor in her hands as she unzipped the bag. From the corner of her eye, however, she was aware of every breath he drew, of the tension that stretched his tan and black uniform taut across his shoulders and of the strength of his tall, hard body.

A body she knew too damn well. One she'd clung to in the darkness.

Randy came up, squatted beside her, and reached inside the bag for webbing and a carabiner clip. "I'm gonna anchor the rope around that oak." He pointed toward the tree just to the right of the cave entrance.

Lani nodded and swallowed to ease the dryness in her mouth. "Be sure to make two loops around the base with the webbing."

"Think I don't know what I'm doing? Maybe I should make it three since it's your ass going down there."

She forced a grin and shoved at his shoulder. "Just make sure you don't tie it off with a slip knot, rookie."

As Randy walked away, the sheriff's long shadow fell across her gear. "The kid's name's Matt Costello. He's sixteen."

Lani's stomach tightened. "What the hell were those three doing out here on private property, anyway?" Determined not to let him rattle her further, she kept her gaze averted.

"Having fun. Danny McKelvey hired them to move his cattle to the last stock pond he has with any water in it. They were wrangling livestock on this hill yesterday. Someone nearby was dynamiting—it shook the ground and opened up that cave." His booted feet shifted in the sand. "Matt and his friends decided to make an adventure of exploring it today."

Lani drew out her vertical pack and stuffed a first aid kit inside. "Some adventure. Let's hope Matt isn't already dead." Then she pulled out a long length of new kernmantle rope and threaded one end through the metal slats of her brake bar rack, leaving a tail to tie off the rope.

"Lani..." His voice dropped—intimate, tight.

She didn't want to look up, didn't want to see the accusation in his dark eyes. "Can we leave this 'til later?" The pain of their last parting was still too raw.

"Dammit, when will 'later' be?" he said, his voice hard-edged and bitter. "You don't answer my calls."

"Later," she said, the word sounding like a curse. She needed time and distance to remind herself why it had to be this way. His husky voice and warm, spicy scent tended to steal her resolve. If she closed her eyes, she could still remember how it felt to lie inside the circle of his strong arms—cherished, safe.

"Fine, but I'm going inside the cave with you," he ground out.

She jerked up her head. "You hate caves. You won't go ten feet without breaking into a cold sweat."

A flush colored his sharply defined cheekbones. The man didn't like betraying his weaknesses any more than she did. "I won't get in the way."

His tacit admission to his failing found a chink in her armor, but she hastily reminded herself she needed to push him away for his own good. "Well, I don't need to worry I'll have to rescue your ass, too."

His jaw tightened. "You're a stubborn cuss, you know that?" He took a step toward her, forcing her to tilt her head to look up his long body. "I'll only go as far as the drop-off. This case is my jurisdiction."

"But it's not your rescue." Angry at the flare of panic his intimidating stance produced, she bent and shoved the rope, carabiner clips, rope climbing devices and a spare harness into her pack. It wasn't his fault—the man hadn't a clue how his large, rigid body affected her.

Pretending indifference, she stood, stuffed gloves into her pocket, then unbuttoned her overshirt and let it drop to the ground. Any object or clothing that might get bunched up or caught in her rigging had to go. Next, she removed the leather belt from the loops of her uniform pants.

The hiss of his indrawn breath brought an unwanted reminder of just how easily he could be aroused—by her.

Worse, she was reminded how close to the surface her own unwanted desire remained. Sweat dampened her shirt, and it stuck to her skin. Her nipples tightened, visibly pushing against her sports bra.

His gaze flickered over her chest, and his mouth thinned.

Wishing her long-sleeved T-shirt was thicker and appalled at her body's betrayal, Lani reached for her seat harness and stepped into it, jerking it up her hips. She adjusted the loops around the tops of her thighs and cinched it closed around her waist. Then she picked up the vertical pack and slid her arms through the straps.

When he reached for the strap at her waist, she forgot how to breathe. Pulling it tight, he buckled the ends together, and the backs of his knuckles grazed her belly.

So close now that his lips were level with her gaze, Lani swallowed.

"Later," he whispered.

After one step backward and a deep, ragged breath, she turned sharply on her heels and headed back to the cave.

"Lani!"

She wanted to resist his command, but she halted and looked over her shoulder. Her yellow helmet sailed toward her, and she grabbed it.

"I'll be right behind you," he said, his dark gaze steady and his square jaw clamped tight.

She turned away and tipped her baseball cap back, letting it fall to the ground, then slammed her helmet on her head and adjusted her chinstrap.

"Hey, was Sheriff Chavez hittin' on you?" Randy stood so close she jumped.

"Course not," she lied, flashing him an incredulous look. "He thinks he wants to go down there with us."

His blue eyes narrowed. "Let me know if you want him to make an air rappel."

Relieved Randy was there to buffer her anxiety, Lani dug her elbow into his ribs. "You can't push him over a ledge. He's too damn big to carry back up."

She made a quick inspection of the anchor wrapped around the tree, and then followed the line to the cave entrance, looking for abrasions and dirt—anything that might compromise the strength of the rope she'd dangle from.

Randy dogged her steps all the way to the mouth of the cave. "It's all good, right?"

"Perfect." Lani picked up the coiled end of the rope and flipped on the lamp on her helmet. "Get the Stokes litter and some blankets and follow me down." With one look at the sheriff who trailed behind, and a nod to the crew who'd keep watch from outside the cave, Lani knelt and crawled through the opening.

Inside, she stood and flung the coil in front of her. She tugged on her gloves, and then lifted the rope and let it feed through her hand at her side as she moved forward, the gravel and sand shifting beneath her feet.

Once she stepped beyond the meager light that spilled through the opening of the cave, she paused, listening to the silence, breathing in the cool, moist air that wrapped around her like a blanket. Already, she felt the tension in her shoulders release. She stood taller, stronger—comforted by the darkness beyond her lamp. And free.

Lani knew some cavers did it for the thrill, but to her the dark, confined spaces meant comfort, peace. She lived for the moments she clung to a rope, descending into a black pit or wriggling through a narrow opening on her belly, clawing at rock and dirt to inch her way to the next dark hole.

Humid, musty air, inky darkness, spaces so tight the sound of her breathing couldn't echo. Except for the chill, like a mother's womb.

With no time to savor her environment, Lani kept moving until she'd reached the end of the spill of rock and gravel. Some long ago cave-in had likely closed the entrance to the cave behind her. The solid rock beneath her feet and the surrounding formations that glistened like ghostly pillars where her light touched, were very different from the debris around the mouth of the cave.

The walls of the cavern to her left and right were curtained with calcified rock that rippled like drapery. Stalactites hung like icicles, and curved pedestals of rock on the cavern floor reached toward the ceiling.

She continued forward, filing her observations, already planning return trips to this underground wonderland. But for now, she had a boy to find.

The shuffle of rock behind her reminded her she wasn't alone. Another step and she stood poised on a ledge that overlooked a deep, black abyss. Needing a stronger light, she unclipped a flashlight from the side of her pack and shone it downward. The light barely penetrated the gloom, like it was sucked into a celestial black hole.

"Matt!" she shouted, but her voice didn't echo back. The sounds of her feet scraping rock, even of her breath, hung in the air next to her.

"Lani!" Randy called.

She turned, surprised again by how close he stood.

He dropped the Stokes on the ground. "I was shouting at you. Didn't you hear me?" The sound of his voice was muffled as if her ears were stuffed with cotton.

She shook her head. "Sound doesn't seem to carry in this place."

Randy's forehead scrunched. "Weird place. Have you heard of anything like this before?"

Lani shrugged, puzzled herself. "No. It's like the cave is…super-insulated."

He stepped to the edge of the drop-off. "Man, I can't see the bottom."

Lani's gaze slipped beyond Randy's shoulder to the sheriff. His swarthy skin was sickly pale. "You shouldn't have come."

"I'm fine." He nodded to the pit. "That's where you're going?"

"Looks like it."

His jaw tightened. "We need more men down here."

"Probably, but first I need to find the boy and assess what equipment we'll need."

Lani didn't like the look of the sweat beading on his forehead. He looked ready to puke or pass out. "You better sit."

"It's so damn…close in here," he said, tugging at his collar.

"Dammit, Rafe," she said. "Just sit down."

One corner of his mouth lifted in a crooked smile.

Did he think her saying his name was some kind of endearment? She stared, feeling as though her heart were lodged in her throat. Hell, she did care. But she couldn't love him. He deserved better than her.

Lani turned away and removed her pack. Time to get to work.

Randy, under her direction, formed a loop at the end of the rope and knotted it, and then clipped on a carabiner.

Lani pulled out the other rope with the brake bar rack, attached it to the carabiner clip, and tossed the end over the ledge. Then she removed extra rigging from her pack, attached it to her seat harness, and clipped it to the rope. She stuffed an ascender device into a side pocket of her pants. "Randy, drape a blanket over the edge beneath the rope."

"Sure you don't want me to belay you down?" Randy asked.

Lani didn't want to wait to attach the extra hitches and pulleys. Besides, she preferred to control her own descent. "You go ahead and prepare the hitches we'll need for the belay when I take the basket down. I'll be faster making this trip on my own."

Randy shrugged. "You're in charge. Got your whistle?"

Lani tugged the cord from beneath her shirt. "Yeah, I've got it." Backing up to the edge, she leaned against the rope to test for any give in her equipment. She took another step backward, gave the two men a nod, and leaned back into the air. Then she bent her knees and simultaneously pushed off the edge, releasing the lock on her descending device to glide slowly downward into the darkness.

Once over the lip of rock, the wall receded, and she lost the advantage of a solid surface against her feet to control the direction of her descent. She twisted in a slow circle, her helmet lamp touching pale, limestone wall, a series of slanting ledges, a cavern so deep radiance found no boundary, then back again to the wall.

Deeper she descended, directing her light downward. She wondered whether she had enough rope to reach the bottom and despaired for the fate of the boy. She doubted there was any way in hell he'd survived the long fall.

Around and around she slowly spun, when suddenly her lamp caught the glitter of something shining from a rock ledge. She braked on the rope and waited another turn, until the light glanced upon a figure perched at the edge. When she spun away, she blinked, sure she'd only imagined what she'd seen.

One more full turn, and her breath stopped. Hunkered on all fours stood a large golden mountain lion, dark eyes gleaming like mirrors reflecting the lamplight. Beside him lay the still body of the boy.

Chapter Two

ꟷ

Lani froze. Mountain lions were rare aboveground in the Texas hill country. She'd never heard of one living in an enclosed karst habitat. Eyeless spiders and beetles, cave crickets and bats, yes. But never a lion.

How the hell did he get down here?

Another twirl revealed the cat, shifting from side to side on his large paws, the thick muscles of his shoulders and hindquarters revealing rippling shadows as he peered at her from the ledge. He leaned out and lifted a large paw, appearing ready to bat at her as she dangled from the rope. A scream ripped from her throat.

Terror made her hand shake as she slowly slid it down her thigh. She unbuttoned the side pocket and drew out the ascender and inched it up her harness, clipping it to the rope.

She cursed the spinning that made her head reel and her stomach plummet each time she lost sight of the huge cat. *Think!*

Darkness was her friend. She flipped off her helmet lamp and plunged herself and the lion into deepest night. Then she held her breath and waited.

A scratchy howl of frustration echoed around her, surprisingly clear after the cotton-thick sounds she'd experienced before. But she didn't have time to ponder the mystery. She followed her line upwards until she felt the rounded grip of the ascender, fit her fingers inside the grip, and slid it up the rope. Then she adjusted her rigging to take up the slack.

Closing her mind to the creature hovering on the ledge, she worked her way upward as soundlessly as the rigging and her ragged breaths would allow. Slide, adjust, slide, adjust. Without light she couldn't gauge her progress, but soon the muscles in her shoulders and arms burned. She had to be close.

Finally, a halo of light appeared above, and she reached for her whistle and blew. The rope shuddered, and then she felt one long tug and another, as the men pulled her upward. Hands extended to help her over the lip of rock.

Before she could utter a feeble protest, she lay cradled against a broad, rock-hard chest, strong arms pulled her close. She knew immediately whose arms held her in a bruising grip. His musky scent surrounded her, and she pressed her nose into the corner of his shoulder.

She was in the dark, in the one place where she'd learned to fight and truly be free of her monsters. Relaxing, she aligned her body on top of his and waited for the quivering to stop—as she had done so many times before.

"Lani, what the hell happened down there?" Rafael Chavez lay on the cave floor with his arms around Lani. He'd dropped his flashlight the moment he'd reached to drag her over the edge.

Randy was still peering over the side, the light from his helmet a misty, distant smudge.

For the moment, Rafe was alone with his woman in the darkness, and he savored it.

Her body shook as she clung tightly, her hands clutching his arms. He pressed her face deeper into the corner of his shoulder and drew in a breath to calm his racing heart. The moment her light faded as she'd disappeared down the rope he'd forgotten how to breathe—when he'd heard the whistle's trill his heart had stopped altogether.

For the first time since he'd stepped into this hellhole, the world felt right. "Did you find the boy?"

She nodded, her nose rubbing up and down against his neck.

"He didn't make it?"

She nodded again.

He swore and blew out a deep breath. *Poor bastard.*

"It's the weirdest damn thing," she said, her voice hoarse and tight. "He's on a ledge directly below us. No way he fell *under* the lip. He either climbed, or he was carried."

Her breath gusted sweetly on his face, and he knew her mouth was only inches from his. Then he realized what she'd said. "Carried?"

"There's a mountain lion on the ledge with him."

He didn't ask her how that was possible. Or if she was sure of what she'd seen. The woman had been steady as a rock when she'd lowered herself into the cavern—something had certainly rattled her.

"We'd better get help in here," he said, not wanting to move just yet. Her body was relaxing, and his was warming up. "We'll have to send an officer down with a shotgun. Did the boy look badly mauled?"

"Not yet. The cat didn't look like it was starving, either."

"Mustn't have been trapped down there long. Can he get up here?"

"I don't know. There are angled ledges, all the way down—or at least as far as I could see." Her breath was closer, blowing over his lips. "He might."

"We better move," he said, but his hands smoothed down her back.

"Yeah," she whispered, closer still.

Before he thought better of it, he fisted his hand in her hair and pulled her down.

Her mouth was open and ready, and she sipped greedily at his lips, suctioning softly.

He tore his mouth away and whispered, "Damn you."

Her hands cupped his face, and she sealed her warm mouth over his again, sliding her lips back and forth.

Then her tongue stroked his, and he was lost. He cursed her for teasing him like this when he knew she'd push him away as soon as they exited the cave.

She'd come to him in darkness—never in the light. He knew it. Knew she didn't feel the same need that ate a hole in his gut when he wasn't with her, that made him crazed to be inside her when she was near.

He hadn't a clue how to push his way past the wall she'd erected around her heart. She cared for him—he could see it in her eyes, even when she'd told him her door would be locked at night. Against him.

She didn't love him. Didn't trust him enough to share whatever in her past held her back. He'd hoped over time she would let him in—let him help her chase away her demons.

Even knowing that might never happen, he couldn't let her go. So he kissed her—here in the dark where she accepted him. Her mouth on his, their bodies pressed so close their heartbeats aligned. He tightened his embrace and wished the rest of the world would fade away.

"I knew I should have tossed you over the damn edge."

Rafe squinted against the light that shone down from Randy Brandt's helmet. He'd forgotten the fireman was nearby.

Lani pushed at his shoulders until he let his arms drop. Her motions rough and jerking, she couldn't scramble away fast enough. She never spared him a glance as she stared warily at the younger man. "We—we better go brief the team."

Randy shoved her helmet into her stomach and shouldered past. "You might want to wait a minute. Your mouth's swollen." He walked away, and the dark swallowed them again.

The silence that followed Randy's departure was leaden. Rafe sat up, wincing at the tightness of his groin.

Light flickered from Lani's helmet, and she offered her hand.

Knowing this touch might be their last, he let her pull him to his feet. He held tight for a long moment before releasing it.

She cleared her throat. "Put your hand on my shoulder, and I'll lead you out."

"Lani—"

"Not now." Lani's mouth tightened. "I'll leave the back door unlocked."

* * * * *

Four hours later, Rafe didn't give Lani a chance to change her mind.

He was through giving her space. He'd left her alone for twenty-one days, just like she'd asked. He'd spent twenty-one sleepless nights—that was ending now.

He followed her to the front porch only a step behind, his body so taut he couldn't think beyond the need to bury himself deep inside her.

His need was fueled in part by his desire, which was never far from the surface. But mostly, he had to assure himself she was safe, untouched by the tragedy they'd witnessed and the danger she'd put herself in.

She'd scared the hell out of him today.

He waited, impatient while she fumbled with her keys. His body was already hard as a post, ripe for sex—had been since she'd kissed him in the cave.

Lani didn't look back, and he was glad, sure his expression was feral, ferocious. She jerkily stabbed the key into the lock to unlatch the door.

As soon as it swung open, he came up against her back, pushing her through the door and kicked it shut. He didn't bother turning on a light—he knew she'd object. Instead, he reached around her waist and unsnapped her uniform pants, forced down the zipper, and jerked her clothing past her hips.

Another step and his pants were open, his cock springing free. Without a word he pushed her down, draping her over the arm of the sofa a few feet inside the door. The fingers of one hand found her soft, wet cleft while the other guided his cock. Without preamble, he drove into her as deep as he could reach.

Lani moaned a protest and wriggled beneath him. "Let me open my legs."

"Can't wait. Give me this," he pleaded, nuzzling her ear, dragging in her scent, dust mixed with sweat—and her. He pulled out and pushed his cock back inside, dying in sensation as he tunneled past the slick folds of her sex, gliding deep into the rippling channel that gloved him in cream and heat. Damn, this was going to be over fast.

"Fuck me, Rafe," she said, her words ending on a whimper.

"Christ! Don't talk," he said, gritting his teeth. He pulled partway out hoping to regroup his rapidly dwindling control.

But Lani squeezed her inner muscles around him, clamping hard around his erection, adding friction to the heat burning away his restraint.

His balls clenched. He was lost. "Baby, I'll make it up to you." Reaching around her slender waist, he slid his hands beneath her shirt and pushed up her bra. Her beaded nipples scraped his palms and he squeezed, not bothering to hold back a groan. He pulled out a few inches and slammed back inside.

He hammered—clumsy, fevered glides. So overcome with need, he couldn't think farther than the next stroke.

Lani's head sank to the sofa and her hands clutched at the fabric. Sexy little moans and gasps tore from her throat.

When his orgasm slammed through him, he cursed, gripping her breasts, his face pressed against her shoulder, his body heaving with each spurt of his release.

After the last pulse slowed to a gentle throb, he eased away, unable to meet her shadowed gaze as she reared up and stared over her shoulder. He'd wanted this to be perfect—needed a chance to show her how much she meant to him.

Instead, he'd proved he was like any other man—just more desperate than most, because she was slipping away.

He helped her up, seating her on the sofa, and quickly removed his clothing. Without a word, he knelt at her feet and quickly shucked her shoes and socks, then slid her pants down her long legs.

When he glanced up, he spotted the moisture in her eyes, gleaming in the dim light filtering through the window. His heart squeezed. "I'm sorry, baby. I'll make this time right."

She didn't reply, just shook her head and bent down, her lips sliding over his. Her kiss was sweet, her hot mouth wicked as her tongue glided over his, sweeping deep into his mouth. Then she leaned away and stripped her shirt and bra over her head and reached for him.

He held her hands away. "No, baby, I'm feeling like a bastard right now," he said, turning one wrist to kiss the pulse thudding beneath her skin. "I'm sorry I left you behind. Let me show you how much."

His hands smoothed down her sleek calves, and then gripped her ankles to force them apart.

Lani gasped, struggling against his hold. "No, Rafe. I need a bath."

His hands slid back up, clamping on her knees and pushed them wider apart. "Let me, baby. I'm dying to taste you." He bent and kissed her left knee and circled his tongue on her soft inner thigh.

Her hands gripped his shoulders and shoved.

He nipped her thigh, telling her without words he wouldn't take "no" for an answer, then continued to lap, stroking upward. Did she really think a little sweat would put him off? Her reticence only made him more determined. He licked and circled, drawing nearer to her core.

Lani's whimpered protests became interspersed with moans, but still she resisted his carnal persuasion. Her bottom wriggled on the sofa as she tried to move away. Her fingers slid through his hair and tugged backward.

He ignored the sting and gripped her hips to hold her still. "You won't stop me."

His tongue reached the crease between her thigh and plump labia. He traced its length, fluttering his tongue into the seam. Her scent was strong and ripening. He breathed her in and continued licking her skin, wetting her springy curls.

Lani moaned and shifted again on the sofa, her fingers spearing through his hair, tugging him close now. "Rafe, stop," she said, but her voice was wispy, unconvincing.

Pulling one plump lip between his, he suckled, and then stroked inside to lap the cream coating her tender inner lips. His cock stirred again, lengthening. He didn't pause, wouldn't give in to the urge to take her again. This time was for her.

He squeezed her buttocks and pulled her closer to the edge of the cushion, never letting up his ravenous assault. His tongue speared inside, and he held her while she bucked, forcing him deeper.

Her hands cradled his head, and her thighs trembled around him. Still he licked and sucked, then lapped upward until his tongue touched the hardened kernel at the top of her sex.

Lani's breath gasped and held.

Rafe closed his mouth around her clit and drew on it, flickering the point of his tongue across the rounded bundle of nerves until Lani's body quivered and spasmed as she came apart. He held her, determined to wring out every last moment of rapture. Then he rocked with her, his cheek pressed against her soft belly, his arms wrapped around her holding her tight.

When she quieted, he lunged upward, his arms encircling her back as he lifted her from the sofa. With her legs locked around his waist and her head resting on his shoulder, he walked down the black hallway to her bedroom, never hesitating to find his way in the darkness.

* * * * *

Rafe lazily caressed Lani's back and shoulders, enjoying the sight of her, replete and dozing in his arms. In the gray light creeping beneath her curtains, her chin-length blonde hair was delightfully mussed; her lush mouth was swollen from his kisses.

Her cheek lay on his chest and her body was snuggled so close, he wondered if she held him in her dreams. He dreaded the morning. Would she turn from him again? Tell him they didn't have a future together—that she couldn't love him?

From the first moment his gaze had settled on her, Rafe had felt "connected"—like he'd found something he hadn't known was missing.

Lani could deny it all she wanted, but he knew he'd never have gotten her into bed so fast after finding her if she hadn't felt it too. Now, everything he wanted for the future was riding on his belief he could wait her out.

He'd tried giving her time apart to think about them, but she'd only gone back to work on rebuilding her walls, while he hadn't been able to last a day without hearing the sound of her voice—even if it was for her to tell him she didn't want to see him again.

Well, he was back in her bed now, and she'd have a helluva fight on her hands if she tried to deny him, again.

Pressing a kiss to her forehead, he pushed aside the thoughts that burned a hole in his stomach and let his mind wander back to the cave. Too many unanswered questions kept him awake.

Lani had supervised the retrieval of the boy's body, accompanied this time by an armed officer. Autopsy results wouldn't be available for days, but it appeared Matt Costello had died from the injuries he'd suffered from his fall.

There'd been no sign of Lani's cat. No paw prints, although the ledge had been drenched in the boy's blood. More telling, there'd been no sign a hungry predator had mauled his body. Except for odd pressure marks on his upper torso and one shoulder, no hint that anything other than a fatal fall had occurred.

However, the mystery only deepened when the rescue team swung inward to the ledge where he lay. No way in hell the boy had landed there. But a mountain lion was still an unlikely explanation. If it had been anyone other than Lani who'd reported seeing the cat, he'd have questioned whether the story were true.

He wanted to believe her. Something had definitely spooked her. The proud, contrary woman was tough as nails—a professional. He'd never seen her flinch from danger, yet she'd trembled in his arms inside the cave.

Lani stirred beside him and her leg slid over his until her knee nudged his sex. "Thought you needed your sleep," she said, her voice low and raspy.

"I lied," he said, hugging her closer, a smile curving his lips. "You were the one yawning in mid-stroke."

"Impossible," she said, sounding grumpy. "This thing kept prodding me awake."

Rafe drew a deep breath and hauled her over him, until she'd settled her legs between his, her chin propped on her folded hands. "What's next, baby?" Jesus, could he have been more blunt?

Lani's eyes clouded. "I don't know. You're a hard man to shake loose."

"Why try?" he asked, surprised by the scratchy quality of his voice.

"You don't really know me…"

"I know I love you," he said baldly, his heart thudding like a dull drum.

Tears pooled, and she turned her head to hide them.

Rafe was determined this time she wouldn't shut him out. His fingers cupped her chin and lifted her head. "Tell me why that upsets you. You have to know by now how I feel."

Lani took a deep breath, but shook her head. "I can't. I just wish you didn't…love me, that is." Her eyes held a world of hurt.

Sure she cared, but confused about why she was so set on denying him, Rafe sighed. Tackling problems head-on might be how he handled most situations, but Lani wasn't an easy puzzle to solve. "If you don't tell me, how will I understand? Or is it that you just don't love me back?"

Her breath caught, and her mouth opened.

He thought her first instinct would be to tell him just that. "Don't," he said, pressing his thumb against her lips. "Don't say it. I'm not gonna believe you."

"If you have this all figured out, why ask me?" she said, resentment making her lips thin.

Anger was a helluva lot easier to face than hurt. Feeling relieved, and a bit like a coward, Rafe decided to let it go. "All right. I'll back off for now. But don't you try shutting me out again. It won't work, you know. I'm not going away."

Lani stared for a long moment. Rafe wished he could hear her thoughts. But Lani gave him a tense little smile, and then laid her head on his chest.

His arms tightened around her body, and he heaved a sigh of relief. At least for now, she wasn't pushing him away.

Chapter Three

ഇ

When his horse grew lathered and winded from the wild ride, he hauled back on the reins and slid from the roan's back in one fluid movement. Without a thought beyond the need to survive the next few minutes, he jerked his rifle from its scabbard and ran toward the mouth of the cave.

The three white men were almost upon him and fired shots at his feet, their laughter high-pitched with excitement. His soft-soled moccasins gripped the sand and gravel as he hunched down to make himself a smaller target, but he never slowed his pace. When they tired of harassing him as he ran, they'd kill him.

The cave loomed large and black. He ignored the prickles of awareness lifting the hairs on the back of his neck that warned him of mischievous spirits and plunged into the darkness. Finding the long skirt of the Mother, he hid behind the wall of rock and lifted his rifle to his shoulder to await the men who'd dogged his trail so many miles.

Not for the first time, he regretted leaving the rest of his people as they'd traveled northward. He'd been rash and foolish, and two of his brothers, friends since childhood, lay dead for their folly. Their way of life as they had known it was gone and would never be returned to them. Too many of his people lay dead as testament to a powerful and treacherous enemy.

He would have served his family better had he traveled north to the reservation. He despaired for his mother's health, and worried that she and his sister had no man to protect them. He'd been foolish and prideful – and selfish. Now he would die alone without anyone to sing a song for his spirit.

He waited with his rifle raised until his arm burned with the effort. Still the white men didn't venture near the mouth of the cave.

Then he heard scuffled footsteps, and a shower of rock and gravel fell from above the opening.

Before he had time to figure out the puzzle, he heard laughter again and the footsteps running away. Then a flash of heat and light exploded in front of him, and he was flying through the air, twisting and turning, falling backward until finally he landed, his body thudding dully on a bed of rock and sand.

He was dying, his spirit rising from his body, when he heard a snarl nearby.

Feet padded nearer and a low, raspy growl reverberated around the darkened tomb. The creature's breath washed over his face, then teeth bit deep into his throat. With a last silent prayer, he sank into the darkness…

Rafe awoke, sweat cooling on his hot skin. A suffocating feeling, like the one he'd felt inside the cave, closed around him. As the dream faded to shadowy remnants, he gently withdrew from Lani's warmth and crept from the bed.

He jerked open the door that led to her wraparound porch and pulled it closed behind him. Then he gripped the railing, dragging deep, cleansing breaths into his starved lungs. The dream, what he could remember of it now, had felt so real, down to the long hair that brushed the tops of his shoulders, the smell of his lathered horse, and the pain the man inside the dream suffered when the cat ripped out his throat.

Damn Lani and her talk of mountain lions! Rafe rubbed a hand over his face and wondered what the hell he was doing out here, shaking off nightmares, when Lani was still lying naked in her bed.

The early morning light filtered through the leaves of the oak trees, and Rafe closed his eyes and let the warmth sink into his skin. Then he heard a scrape and the pad of paws on the porch. Whatever animal was just around the corner of the house was sizeable.

Naked and feeling at a distinct disadvantage, Rafe reentered the bedroom and peered out the window.

"What's the matter?" Lani asked, her voice scratchy. "Bad dream?"

"I think there's an animal on your porch."

"Mmm. I live in the country, city boy—there are always animals on my porch. It'll go away. Come back to bed."

Rafe glanced over his shoulder. Lani had flipped back the covers, exposing her nude body and the mussed sheets. An invitation he couldn't refuse.

He gave the porch a final look, but all seemed quiet outside now. Leaving the curtain open, he hoped Lani wouldn't object to the light streaming through. She'd never allowed him to make love to her without shadows hiding her sweet form.

He walked to the bed aware her gaze swept over him. She wet her lips, and her breaths grew shallow. Nice to know some things were mutual. Her rosy-brown nipples beaded as quickly as his cock grew hard. By the time he climbed onto the mattress, he was ready to drive a nail through the wall.

But he held back, wanting to drink in the sight of her—her body, long-limbed and sturdy, the pale triangle of curls between her legs, breasts set high on her chest. When his gaze reached her face, he let out a breath.

Her eyes were moist, her expression a little shy. Not for the first time, she confused him. As strong and competent as she seemed on the job and outside the bedroom, she held a core of vulnerability that made his heart ache.

Cupping her chin, he swept his thumb over her soft lips. "You're beautiful, Lani Kimmel."

"I was thinking about what you said before. I don't want secrets between us, Rafe. Not anymore. I'd like to give this thing between us a chance." Her glance swept down again, and a little smile curved her lips. "Besides, you stuck closer to me than a tick on a hound dog."

"'Bout time you realized you can't shake me loose. I'm in for the long haul, baby."

Lani shook her head. "I can't make any promises about where this might lead."

"This is enough for now." He leaned over her and kissed her, glorying in her first tentative touches gliding over his shoulders.

Her fingers raked through his hair, tugging gently. "Love me, Rafe."

"I do, baby. You know, I do." He kissed her again and came down on top of her, resting the weight of his torso on his elbows. "We're gonna talk after we're done this time. I have to know what dragons we have to slay."

"All right," she whispered, her gaze holding his.

Unable to resist the temptation of her creamy flesh a moment longer, he leaned to one side and caressed a firm, round breast. Her skin was so pale, a fine tracery of blue veins was visible just beneath the surface. He rubbed the pad of his thumb over her nipple, and Lani's breath caught. He loved how damn responsive her body was to his touch.

He gently squeezed the tip, rolling it between his thumb and forefinger.

Lani made a little noise in the back of her throat, and her eyes closed tight.

He bent and nuzzled the velvety areola, then tongued the tip, a butterfly-soft flutter that produced a moan. Plumping her breast with his palm, he sucked the entire nipple into his mouth and drew hard.

She writhed beneath him—long, sinuous undulations, her legs opening to cup his sex.

Much as he would have loved to follow her sensual suggestion, he had a war to win. This was only one battle.

He moved down her body until his face was level with her breasts. He teased one then the other, drawing the tips to rigid little points. When her fingers clutched his head tightly, he bit a reddened, dimpled areola, determined this time he'd draw out their lovemaking to the point of physical pain—then maybe, she'd experience just a fraction of the mind-stealing desire he felt.

While Rafe's lips strafed and suckled her tender nipples, Lani gloried in the light that glinted in his thick, dark hair and the burnished tone of his skin as he labored over her breasts. The differences between them—light to dark, hard muscle to soft curves, man to woman—no longer made her cringe inside.

Rafe had banished most of her fears, first by the example of his steady, relentless pursuit, and finally, through the tender passion of his lovemaking. He'd seen to her pleasure, driving her to the point of madness time and again, but not once did his strong hands harm her. Not once had the near-violent desperation of his lovemaking caused her to fear him.

Oh, he'd drawn out her desire until she'd begged for release, her stomach clenching, and her vagina clutching around his tongue, his fingers, his cock, her entire body writhing like a wild thing. But he'd never hurt her, never let his frustration take a darker turn.

Sometime during the long night, she'd given him her heart. She'd only meant to open the door a crack, to test her comfort for this sort of sharing—but he'd muscled his way through, laying waste to all her defenses, leaving her shattered with the beauty and intensity of his loving.

She wouldn't deny him any longer. He'd branded her body and her heart.

Lani raised her knees on either side of his hips, tilting her pelvis to steal a glide along his thigh.

His mouth continued to suction, strong and biting, until her pussy wept with anticipation. Still, he didn't let up.

Scooting down her body, his lips and tongue left a wet trail of kisses, pausing to dip inside her navel, then moving lower to nip and torture her quivering belly.

Lani surrendered, letting her arms fall to either side of her head, her moans growing louder the lower he traveled, until his mouth was poised once more above her sex. She let her legs drop open, her breath catching, waiting for the first intimate touch of his tongue on her heated core.

Instead, he blew a stream of cooling air over her flesh, and gently parted her with his fingers. "You belong to me."

"Yes," she groaned. "Please, Rafe." Her eyes squeezed shut. His carnal kisses left no room for embarrassment, inciting her to an abandon she'd never thought herself capable of experiencing.

"Look at me," he said, his words gusting over her.

Her pussy pulsed, making a wet, sucking sound, and she opened her eyes, unable to deny the submission her body craved. She brought her hands to her breasts, cupping them, her fingers squeezing to raise her engorged nipples for his inspection.

His dark gaze, liquid chocolate framed by a face sharp-edged with need, held hers for a long moment. "Tell me you belong to me."

She drew in a ragged breath, and the sight of him blurred beneath pooling tears. "I'm yours."

He turned his head and kissed her inner thigh. "Baby, I won't ever let you down. Won't ever hurt you." Then he licked her, his tongue gliding in long strokes over her open pussy, flickering the edges of her thin inner lips, delving deep to drink her excitement.

Lani couldn't take her gaze from him. His forearms curved around her thighs, holding her hips still as she fought to squirm and pulse. His eyes were closed, his expression enraptured, and she *believed*. He loved her—craved the essence of her body and soul.

A fresh gush of pleasure pumped from inside her, and he burrowed his face between her legs, his nose and chin rubbing on her open sex. His coarse morning shadow added a delicious scrape to her sensitized flesh. "Rafe!" she gasped, as the first convulsions rippled along her vagina. "Please, come inside me."

The point of his tongue tunneled upward, delving beneath the hood protecting her clitoris to stroke the engorged nubbin. Each lap produced a tightening deep inside her belly, and her thighs closed around his head to hold him there. Her hips resisted his firm hold, and she bucked beneath him.

One hand moved between her legs, and he pressed a finger into her pussy, twisting as he pressed it inside.

Lani tightened her inner muscles around it, needing a deeper, thicker penetration.

While continuing to tease her clit with his tongue, a second finger joined the first, and he slid them in and out, delving deeper, pumping faster.

Her hips matched his rhythm, jerking up and down. Her cries grew louder.

Just when she felt her orgasm begin its tight spiral, he withdrew his mouth and fingers, and rose to sit on his haunches between her legs. He hooked his elbows beneath her knees, lifted her buttocks off the bed, and nudged her sex with his until the crown of his cock found her moist entrance.

His expression fierce, almost frightening, he plunged into her, deep and straight—all the way inside until his cock touched her womb.

Lani couldn't tear her gaze from the sight of him, his chest heaving, his eyes clenched shut. The powerful muscles of his chest and arms tensed as he held himself still inside her.

Then he drew a deep breath and pulled out, until the crown once more poised at her entrance.

Lani's fingers gripped the bedding as her body spasmed. Her cunt opened and closed noisily, wetly, trying to draw him deep.

"Jesus!" He groaned, and then let loose a short bark of laughter. "I wanted this time to last."

"I can't bear it," Lani whimpered. "I need you inside me. Please, give it to me."

"Everything I have is yours," he gritted out, driving deep. His hips flexed forward and back, his cock gliding in and out in powerful thrusts that raised her bottom higher.

Relieved the dance had finally begun, Lani let him take the lead and watched fascinated as his muscles flexed, while he drove into her again and again. The sight of his thick sex, glistening with her juices, disappearing into her body, seemed to add heat to the friction building inside her channel. Ruddy and veined, the longer she watched his cock play inside her cunt, the harder and thicker he felt.

The spiral tightened and suddenly snapped deep inside her belly. Her back arched off the bed, and she screamed—maybe his name, she didn't really know, couldn't think beyond the feeling she was shattering into a million pieces of sensation.

Her hands squeezed the bedsheets and her hips slowed, and eventually she remembered how to breathe. Her eyes fluttered open, and she found Rafe hovering above her, only a breath between their mouths.

His face was fierce and tender, and his cock was still hard and buried deep inside her.

Lani lifted a limp hand and fitted her palm to his cheek. "You love me," she said, cringing a little, knowing it sounded inane and wasn't really what she'd meant to say at all.

His expression reflected grim satisfaction. "You'll love me, too," he promised. "You'll also answer my calls, and I get my own damn key." The hard set of his jaw told her he wasn't backing away, no matter how many obstacles she might try to place in his path.

Still glowing from her orgasm, all she could manage was a nod.

He rested his forehead on her shoulder and groaned. "Now put your arms around me, baby. I'm ready to explode."

Lani slid her arms around his back and held tight.

With his hands planted on either side of her shoulders, Rafe flexed his hips, tunneling deep. Then he circled, grinding the base of his cock against Lani's swollen clitoris. He repeated the action, until Lani's fingers dug deep into his skin, urging him faster.

Sweat gathered between his shoulder blades; his breath grew labored. He pistoned his hips faster and faster, reigniting a passion that had Lani slamming her hips upward to catch the flame.

Soon the room was filled with the sounds of their moans and the sharp staccato of flesh slapping as their bodies met.

At the end, Lani dug her heels into the mattress and screamed as Rafe uttered a shout of triumph. While their heartbeats slowed, she pressed her face against his moist shoulder and thanked God for giving her the gift of Rafe's love.

* * * * *

A noise from beside the bed woke Lani from a deep, dreamless sleep. It came from the end of her bed—a scratching sound on the hardwood floor, like the scrape of claws accompanied by muffled footfalls. She reached for Rafe lying beside her to warn him, but he wasn't there. The bedding was cool to her touch—he'd left her some time ago.

She was alone with sunlight streaming through her curtains, and a wild creature paced at the foot of her bed. Then a purring, deep and resonant with each exhalation, rose from the floor, and before she could let out a startled cry, the creature leapt onto the bed, the mattress dipping beneath its weight.

The lion! The same one she'd faced on the ledge inside the cave—she was sure of it. It didn't make sense. Suddenly, she understood.

This is a dream—this isn't really happening!

She relaxed fractionally. The cat leaned down to sniff the bedding wound around her legs. This close, she noted the coarseness of its golden-beige fur, the black smudges that topped each of the hooded claws, the dark markings that transformed its face into a sinister mask.

Even knowing it was just a dream, terror clamored for her to move, to flee, but her body was paralyzed for the moment. She whimpered deep inside her throat, and the cat's head jerked up.

For a moment, its face shimmered and reshaped into that of a man—his expression no less feral. His long black-brown hair framed a well-tanned face. His features declared him an Indian—high, sharp cheekbones, a broad nose with a slight hook, a straight slash of copper lips, eyes so dark the pupils were indistinguishable from the irises.

Then as quickly as the vision had formed, the face was once again the lion's, the white tips of its fangs visible below the line of its upper lip.

The purring grew louder, echoing around the walls and the ceiling of her bedroom, until the vibration made her body tremble.

Perhaps, if she held very still, it would lose interest and leave—or better, she could wake from this nightmare. But neither happened. The cat sniffed at her, following the line of her legs beneath the sheet until it reached the edge tucked around her hips.

His hot breath fanned over her skin, and Lani gasped at the sensual quickening that gripped her body. His tongue flickered out, raspy and wide, to lap the top of her hip.

Her breath caught on a ragged hitch. She closed her eyes and fought her body's instant reaction. But heat curled in her belly, releasing a wash of desire that flooded her pussy. Her nipples beaded, tight and aching.

This is a dream. Just a dream! That was all she could think to explain her physical reactions.

Her legs moved restlessly, opening against her will, and the cat shifted, stepping in between.

Then fingers dragged down the sheet, grazing her skin, to expose her glazed and pulsing sex.

Lani's eyes shot open. The Indian knelt between her legs now, both hands coming up the inside of her thighs. His fingers spread open the folds of her pussy, and he stared at her glistening flesh.

She moaned a protest, but only the softest whimper escaped her mouth.

He bent over her and lapped at her exposed cunt, his tongue as raspy and hot as the cat's. The purring started again from deep inside the man and vibrated on her flesh. His tongue tunneled into her, drinking her desire.

No! she screamed inside her mind, but her body was already undulating, her knees coming up and splaying wide, encouraging him to delve deeper into her body. Rafe! she cried inside, but she couldn't resist the heat at her core that made her body tremble and writhe uncontrollably.

While his cat's tongue lapped and scraped, the Indian moved his hands beneath her to cup her bottom. They were rough with calluses, and his grip was strong. Another gush of desire seeped from her to meet his tongue and trickle lower.

Lani lifted her legs high, and her feet came off the bed. Her hips tilted to capture the fullness of his caresses.

With a final lap deep into her cunt, he withdrew and licked and nibbled at her pussy, sucking her lips into his mouth, chewing gently, until she jerked on the bed, so close to exploding she was mindless with desire. Then his tongue swept lower, and Lani mewled, her whole body shaking.

He circled her asshole, the odd sandpaper texture only heightening the excitement that threatened to devour her. When his fingers pressed on either side of her anus to open her ever so slightly, she sobbed. His raspy tongue dipped into her again and again, and her head thrashed on the pillows.

Her hands crept between her legs, and her fingers threaded through his long hair, clutching him closer.

A snarl startled her, and she found herself flipped onto her belly. His calloused hands encircled her to pull up her hips, and suddenly his thick cock drove deep into her pussy.

Frightened yet exhilarated, Lani felt the stirring of an orgasm burst over her, unwinding at her core as he pounded, fast and hard behind her, thrusting deep into her body. She rose on her hands, her back arching, and she pumped backward to meet his strokes.

This is a dream – only a dream, she said to herself. But God, please don't let it stop! He rocked against her bottom, hammering furiously, scooting her up the bed with the force of his strokes. His hands settled on her hips and squeezed hard.

Moans tore from her throat, deep and guttural, punctuated by gusts each time he thrust deep. Sweat beaded on her skin and eased the gliding motion of their bodies as they moved together.

As the tension in her belly wound tight once more, he came over her, his body blanketing her back, his hands sliding around her belly and down to the juncture of her thighs to tug and massage her pussy.

He nuzzled her neck, and she arched, rubbing her head and the side of her face against him. His body was hard, his skin hot as a furnace. He was burning her alive.

Then she felt the scrape of teeth at the back of her neck – long, sharp teeth that widened and clamped down. And his body was changing again, his slick flesh sprouting fur that chaffed erotically against her bottom and back.

He was becoming the cat! But Lani was past the point of caring. Her vagina convulsed around his cock, rippling, milking his sex – her channel so engorged and drenched, it suctioned on him, pulling him deeper.

The snarling grew louder as their bodies writhed together. With the first hot spurt of his cum, Lani shattered, gasping for breath, trembling with each roiling convulsion of her cunt. When the throbbing dulled, she collapsed onto the bed, shuddering.

Drugged with passion, her eyes closed.

"Sweetheart," Rafe's voice murmured against her hair. His arms wrapped around her tightly, pulling her close to cradle her hips, his cock still snuggled deep inside her body.

Lani had a last confused thought before she slept. Just when had her dream become reality?

Chapter Four

ꕥ

Showered and dressed, Rafe sat on the edge of the bed to tell Lani goodbye. He'd called the dispatcher earlier and wasn't expected at the station. But he felt restless and decided to head to his office to read through the day's reports, anyway.

As he ruffled her hair, he smiled. She didn't stir. Her head was buried between the pillows, and the sheets were tangled around her legs. He'd exhausted her—worn down her resistance, too.

Feeling hopeful for the first time in weeks, he let himself think about their future. Babies, white picket fences, a lifetime of waking with her head on the pillow next to his.

They still hadn't had their conversation—the one where he'd learn the secrets that had kept them apart for so long, but he didn't doubt it would happen soon. Lani loved him. He'd seen the truth shining in her eyes.

He bent and pressed a kiss to her shoulder, then grabbed his holster and strapped it to his waist. He'd call her later. Maybe he'd surprise her with dinner.

Setting the latch to lock behind him, Rafe quietly closed the front door and headed to his cruiser. Gravel crunched beneath his boots, and he reached into his pocket to hit the remote to unlock the doors.

The familiar soft snick of the lock was followed by an eerie growl.

Rafe stopped dead in his tracks and slowly reached for the gun strapped to his side. The creature that had been on Lani's porch that morning hadn't moved very far, and if his guess was right, it was a puma—a second in as many days?

With his weapon in front of him, Rafe carefully skirted the front of his sedan. The large cat sat on its haunches next to the driver's door.

In addition to the low growl coming from its throat, the mountain lion's tail twitched, a certain sign of its agitation. Rafe swore under his breath. He ought to shoot it. An animal unafraid of human contact was more than a nuisance, but he'd never seen a mountain lion outside a zoo cage. Perhaps, he could warn it away, and then he'd notify the fish and wildlife boys so they could set traps to relocate it.

He raised his weapon and fired off a shot into the air.

The cat didn't so much as flinch at the loud explosion. With an arrogant twitch of its long tufted tail, it turned and ran, seeming to melt into the bushes and tall grass just beyond the border of Lani's yard.

Rafe let out a sigh.

"What the hell was that all about?"

He glanced over his shoulder. Lani stood on the porch, dressed in a silky robe, the edges held together in one fist with the ties dangling. Her pale hair was tangled, her lips still blurred and red from his kisses. Her long legs tempted his gaze to roam lower. Damn, if his body wasn't responding already.

"Sorry about that," he said, giving her a lopsided smile. "Did you see him?"

"See what?"

"The mountain lion."

Her face blanched white. "There was a lion here?"

"Right next to the cruiser. And I think he was on your porch earlier this morning." He slid his gun back into his holster and walked over to her. He climbed the first step, and then slid his arms around her waist. "Don't worry. I chased him off."

Lani stood stiffly inside his arms. "It's too damn weird. First, the one inside the cave, then this…and I had a dream."

He pulled away and looked down into her face. Her eyes were wide, her mouth pinched. "Look, I know we're both rattled by what happened yesterday. Hell, I dreamt about a mountain lion, too. "

"I bet your dream wasn't anything like mine," she murmured, her gaze sliding from his. Color flooded her cheeks.

The rosy glow intrigued him. "Oh? My cat ripped the throat out of a man hiding in the cave. What did yours do?"

Her face twisted in disgust. "Nothing so gory." The color deepened.

"Hmm." Amused by her embarrassment, his hands slid down her back to cup her buttocks. "Maybe you should stay indoors today—or I might get jealous of that ole tomcat."

She shoved half-heartedly at his chest. "You're impossible. Is everything about sex?"

"I'm a guy. But judging from your blushes, I'd guess I scored a hit."

Her eyebrows shot up. "I'm not telling."

"You don't have to. Your body's melting all over me."

"You're…" she sputtered, "…impossible. And I'm still not telling." Her lips curved into a sly grin. "Besides, the Indian in my dream was pretty damn sexy, too."

Rafe held himself perfectly still. She'd dreamt of an Indian? "Baby, it's been a strange couple of days. Do me a favor, will you?"

Her arms came around him. "What?" She nudged the open collar of his shirt with her nose and pressed a soft kiss against his neck.

Spontaneous affection from Lani was a rare treat. He tightened his hold. An uneasy premonition crackled in the air around him. "Stay inside today and lock your doors."

Lani leaned back to stare into his face. "Lock my doors? That's not what you wanted yesterday. Besides, I'm in the boonies here. I'm safe."

"From the two-legged critters, maybe. Just humor me."

"And if I need to go to the fire station?"

"Then don't linger getting to your truck. It wouldn't hurt to put some bullets in that shotgun gathering dust in your broom closet either."

Her expression grew wary. "You're scaring me."

He sighed and pressed his forehead against hers. "Just humor me, huh?"

"All right. I'll keep an eye out." Her hands traveled up his back, drawing her chest flush with his. "And I'll clean the shotgun. I'll also find the bullets—but I'd really rather not load it unless I have to."

"Fair enough." His own hands stroked and kneaded the muscles of her lower back. "I'll see you at dinner?"

Her eyelids swept down before rising to give him a coy look. "You think you can go another round?"

He squeezed her lush bottom. "Baby, with you I think I'm Superman."

"You are." She groaned and her expression tightened. "Last night…"

"Yeah, it was like that for me, too." He kissed her hard. "Don't look at me like that, or I'll remember you aren't wearing a thing under that scrap of silk."

"You mean, you could be tempted?" Her voice dropped to a sexy drawl that curled his toes inside his boots.

"You know damn well all you have to do is crook your little finger—"

"Like this?" she said, scraping her finger in the underside of his chin. She gave him another sexy look from under her lashes. "Wanna frisk me, Sheriff?"

His cock filled instantly, pressing hard against the placket of his uniform pants. No way he could sit in a cruiser now. "Ever done it on your porch?"

Her mouth opened, but her eyes widened—the little vixen was intrigued.

He narrowed his eyes in challenge and unbuckled his gun belt. "Take off the robe."

Lani stared at Rafe. With his dark, leanly muscled good looks, standing there in his sheriff's uniform—crisp tan and black, knife-edged creases, shiny badge and buckles—he was any woman's wet dream. And all hers to play with.

Wondering at her temerity, she took a step backward and shrugged out of her robe, letting it pool on the porch, then waited for him to make the next move.

His hands were already opening his pants, sliding down his zipper. "Turn around and hold onto the rail," he said, his voice a scratchy purr.

Moisture pooled between her legs. She turned and grabbed the wooden rail.

When his hands closed on the top of her hips, she jumped and let out a nervous laugh. He was going to do her right here in broad daylight. Never mind the graveled driveway was off the road with trees and bushes to hide the view of the porch.

Anyone could come across them. The mailman could deliver a package to her door. One of the guys from the station house could drop by to say hello.

But here she was, naked as a newborn, the hot sun kissing her breasts—hell, all her parts.

His hands smoothed over her buttocks and squeezed, then a finger slid down the crease separating them.

She grew rigid with alarm and tried to pull away.

"Has anyone ever kissed you here?"

She almost said, "You did—last night." Had last night only been a dream? But if that dream was anything approaching reality she wanted more. "Nuh-uh," she denied, suddenly breathless.

He pressed his mouth to one cheek of her ass and gave her a wet, open-mouthed kiss. Then his tongue slid below and traced the line where her thigh and buttock met.

Lani couldn't help herself. She leaned forward, groaning.

Rafe gave a dry chuckle. "Like that, do you?" He caressed her bottom, providing her all the approval and encouragement she needed to raise her bottom higher to accept the next caress.

She wished she could tell him she wanted more than a kiss. But how could she tell him that the man in her dream did a helluva lot more, without sounding like a liar or an idiot?

Thankfully, Rafe was far from finished. He pushed at her shoulders until she leaned far over the railing, then he gently nudged apart her legs. "I'm gonna know every secret you've got, baby. There won't be a part of your body that doesn't know what it feels like to be claimed by me." Then his tongue swept between her legs, glancing over her juicy cunt to sweep higher over her asshole.

Lani rose on her tiptoes, bent as far as she could to give him free access to every aching part of her.

His wicked tongue lingered over her anus, fluttering at the opening, poking at it, teasing her until she squirmed. Smooth, not raspy like the Indian's, nonetheless his wet caress drove her crazy.

His hands closed around cheek each and held them apart. "I'm gonna fuck this, Lani."

"Please," she gasped, so hot for it, her pleasure ran down her thighs.

"No one's been inside your pretty little hole?"

"No one's fucked it," she said truthfully, liking the nasty words.

He rose behind her, and his cock slid between her legs. "You're so wet," he whispered in her ear. "Let's not waste this honey." Then he pushed inside her cunt, stroking side-to-side, gliding deep twice before pulling out.

Lani pushed back to take him inside again, but he bit her shoulder.

So like the cat—but not. She moaned.

Then his hands spread her buttocks again, and the thick round head of his cock poked at her asshole.

Lani whimpered. The crown was too thick—he'd never fit.

He continued to push, and the pressure grew unbearable.

"No! Stop!"

Her breath coming in shallow sobs, she felt moisture fall into the crease, and his fingers smoothed it around her entrance. Then something considerably smaller in circumference, pressed into her ass.

His finger glided inside without resistance, twisting in and out. There was discomfort, but no real pain. Still, her asshole burned.

"How's that? Not too much?"

"Better," she whispered, feeling like a coward she was so relieved he'd stopped trying to push his cock in that particular entrance.

"Don't get too comfortable there. We're not done." His cock came up between her legs again and slid between the folds of her pussy. At the same time, another finger pressed into her ass.

Lani lurched, her mouth opening around a loud moan.

"Is it too much?" he whispered.

She was so overcome, all she could do was shake her head.

"Good girl. Ride me, baby."

Lani began shallow backward thrusts. Her cunt squeezed around his cock, needing him deeper, but her ass burned so she limited the depth of her movements. Soon, she grew frustrated. "Rafe, take your fingers out. Fuck my pussy with your cock."

Instead of giving her what she craved, he pulled his cock all the way out.

"No, Rafe. I can't take any more. Fuck me, please."

To her relief, his fingers withdrew, only to be replaced by the familiar pressure of his much thicker cock.

Her sphincter tightened in resistance.

"Trust me," he said, his voice tight with strain. "And relax. Let me come inside."

More spit dropped between her cheeks. His finger smoothed it over her small opening, soothing her.

Then his cock pressed against her again. "Relax. Let it happen. I promise you'll like this."

Lani drew in a deep breath and tried to relax her muscles. His cock pressed and pressed until the pressure had her gasping, then suddenly, the head crowded past her opening. He paused, sliding no further.

Lani reached behind her to keep him from driving deeper. The sensation his thick cock produced lodged in her ass was pain mixed with the most intense pleasure she'd ever felt.

But she wasn't sure she could take anymore. Her asshole burned and squeezed around him. Her pussy oozed, making her inner thighs slick and sticky. He kissed her shoulder, and then licked a path up to her ear and nibbled at her lobe.

Her body quivered, tension building in her belly. She stopped pushing back on his hip and reached between her legs. She rubbed her clitoris, which was hard as a small, round pebble between her legs. Then her fingers dug into her cunt, trying to assuage the need that had her hips jerking now. "Now, Rafe. Give it to me, now!"

Rafe's hands held her buttocks in a bruising grip, and then he drove his cock deep inside her ass.

Lani screamed and writhed. Not quite seeking a deeper penetration, but unwilling to ask him to stop. Her asshole gloved his cock a little less tightly as her body clamored for release.

While her fingers fucked her sopping cunt, his cock glided in and out her ass. His belly slapped her bottom with the force of his thrusts. His groans were so loud, Lani had the whimsical thought that anyone driving by with their windows down would hear them—and it only made her hotter.

With one hand braced against the rail, the other inside her cunt—her ass filled with Rafe's hot cock—she let herself be swept along with the tide of an orgasm that threatened to make the top of her head explode.

Rafe hammered at her ass, his strokes shorter, harder, lifting her off her toes—then he shouted and a stream of liquid fire jetted into her.

That's all it took to push her over the edge, and she was falling, her body shattering like glass.

A long, keening sound ripped from her throat. The only reason she still stood was the railing biting into her belly and the strength of the cock still lodged deep inside her body.

"Are you okay?" he murmured against her shoulder.

She drew in a jagged breath. "Sure, but I think I have splinters."

"Sorry." He slowly withdrew and pulled her up against his chest, his hands closing around her breasts as he hugged her. "This is all your fault, you know. I really did intend to give you a bit of rest."

Lani rested her head against his chest, gratified his breaths were just as labored as hers. "I'm gonna be bowlegged for a week."

His mouth glided along the side of her neck. "You're a little sassy when you've had some."

"I'm just starting to realize the possibilities—I mean, there's the porch, the swing," she whispered. "There's this oak tree with a bent trunk that would be just about the right height..."

He pinched her nipple. "You're talking geography now—I'm thinking acts."

"Acts?"

"I've sucked you to orgasm—I'm dying to know what that nasty mouth of yours will do to my dick."

She grinned and lazily caressed the backs of his hands. "I didn't know you were such a sweet-talker. I like it when you get...specific."

"Baby, I can get downright explicit," he growled and bit her earlobe.

"I bet you can."

He nuzzled her neck while his voice rumbled in her ear. "Any bad moments there?"

Lani hoped he wasn't asking her what she thought he might be, and was very glad she wasn't facing him or her cheeks would be even hotter.

He plucked her nipple. "Did I hurt you?"

"At first," she said, in a tiny voice. "But I liked it." Then she had a thought about "acts". "Is that something you might like, too?"

"No."

Intrigued by his flat denial, she teased. "Hmmm. Doesn't seem fair."

"Nothing to do with fair."

"We'll see."

"No, we won't."

Lani turned in his arms and looked down his body. On any other man the sight of his pants shoved down to his knees might be comical, but on Rafe…

His muscled thighs and tight, washboard abdomen were sigh-worthy.

Rafe looked down too and grinned. "Guess I'd better go clean up again."

"Want some help?"

"No. I'll never get out of here if you do."

She wrinkled her nose. "Spoilsport."

He bent and drew his pants partway up and nodded toward the door. "After you."

Lani picked up her robe, and then his gun belt from where he'd tossed it on the railing. "All right. I think I like that you want to protect me. But don't get carried away."

"I know. You can take care of yourself."

She headed toward the bathroom.

Rafe cleared his throat.

"Just testing your resolve." She glanced over her shoulder. "Want breakfast before you go?"

"I'll grab *lunch* in town."

She raised one eyebrow. "Afraid of a little more geography?"

He blew out a breath. "I've created a monster. Where's the sweetly inhibited woman I thought I knew?"

Lani's smile stretched. "She left her last inhibitions on the front porch."

Still clutching his pants, Rafe strode toward the bathroom, muttering beneath his breath.

With a spring in her step, Lani headed to the guest bathroom.

Chapter Five

ꟾ

Rafe's first call was to the coroner. "So what do you know, Mitch?" He turned his chair away from his desk.

The sound of the other man's tired sigh had Rafe bracing for the news. "Well, the boy definitely died from multiple injuries suffered during his fall. He probably never recovered consciousness. He had massive head trauma."

"Okay." Rafe took a deep breath, and then asked the next question that had been burning a hole in his stomach. "Tell me there weren't any marks made by a large cat on that boy's body."

"I could…but it wouldn't be the truth."

"Damn."

The coroner took a deep breath. "It gets weirder, Sheriff."

Rafe's hand tightened on the telephone. "How so?"

"That cat carried the boy gentle as a baby. Its teeth never penetrated his skin. There were only pressure marks left in his flesh at the top of his shoulder. That mountain lion never took a bite."

After Rafe hung up, he stared out the window of his office for a long while. The boy hadn't fallen to the ledge, and he certainly hadn't crawled there.

The cat had dragged the boy to that ledge with his mouth clamped around his shoulder. Yet there had been no smears of blood leading to the ledge. It made no sense.

On one hand he was relieved the boy's death had been caused by the fall and not by being mauled by a cat while he lay helpless. On the other, he realized the chances of two different large cats appearing within miles of each other was rather remote, given the hunting range of mountain lions and their solitary habits.

The cat Lani had confronted on the ledge was likely the same one that showed up on her porch. For whatever reason, it had stalked her all the way to her home.

He should have shot the lion while he'd had it in his sights.

Rafe picked up the phone to call Lani, but there wasn't any answer. She'd mentioned she might pop in at the fire station, so he didn't worry too much. But tonight, he'd let her know she had a dangerous new pet.

Curious about the blast the boys reported hearing the day before the accident, Rafe paid a call to the McKelvey ranch. He found Danny McKelvey welding stock fence around a corral not far from his house.

As he approached, the rancher straightened and pushed his goggles up his forehead. "Sheriff, what can I do for you?"

Rafe took off his cowboy hat to wipe sweat from his face. "I don't know how you can work with that torch in this heat."

"Work has to be done." His broad, ruddy face formed a scowl. "I'm bringin' in my stud bulls until that mountain lion's killed."

Rafe glanced around the corral and barn. Both had seen better days—the roof of the barn sagged, older welds on the stock panels showed signs of rust. The barn and the fence needed more care than a slap of paint. "You have insurance on your cattle?"

"I do. But insurance won't pay for all my losses if that lion gits one." Danny's gaze narrowed. "But I'm sure that's not what you're here for."

Something about the rancher's wary stance raised Rafe's hackles. He was accustomed to being greeted with suspicion from the locals who'd lived here for generations. As the first elected sheriff who wasn't a hometown boy, he was considered a "blow-in", as were most of the people moving into the rapidly growing area. But Danny's demeanor was downright menacing. "You hear about Matt Costello?"

Danny nodded once. "I did. Damn shame."

Rafe didn't like the terseness of his reply. "Yeah, it is. The boys mentioned something that had me a little curious."

The big man's back stiffened. "What's that?"

"They said they heard someone using dynamite. It was close. The explosion's what opened that cave. I wondered if you had any idea who might be blasting?"

"No. Why you asking me?" he asked, his tone bordering on belligerent.

"Just curious." Rafe narrowed his gaze. "Wanted to make sure a permit was issued."

"Well, I'm not licensed to buy that stuff."

"Didn't think you were. Just wondered if you knew anyone else around here who might need it."

"You know there's a golf course goin' in on the other side of that big hill." Danny's scowl deepened. "Bought up several ranches to do it."

"I remember reading bout that when I was still in San Antonio. The company had you and some of the other ranchers pretty upset."

"Yeah, well, you would be, too, if some stranger dammed the only creek that feeds half a dozen ranches downriver and dumped a ton of chemicals all over your backyard."

"I understand they've only dammed for flood prevention—the creek's still flowing through."

"Well, that's water under the bridge." His smirk rankled. "They might be needin' dynamite for some of their construction, and I'm sure they'll have to use it to dig deep enough for a septic system."

"I appreciate the suggestion." Rafe put his hat back on his head. "One more question."

Danny's hand fisted around the torch he still held.

"What are you going to do about that cave?"

"Well, ain't that interestin'."

Rafe cocked his head.

"That pretty little fire-girl called me this morning to ask me that same question."

* * * * *

Lani forced herself to walk her natural gait, despite the swollen tissue between her thighs that seemed to grow puffier by the second. Why had she worn jeans? The material hugged her crotch, and the friction scalded despite the soft cotton panties beneath her jeans.

But she wouldn't complain about the cause. She still felt caressed all the way to her soul by Rafe's lovemaking.

The fire station was quiet today. Most of the men on shift were washing the trucks, polishing chrome, and repacking gear. She shied away from the group, giving them a friendly wave. She really didn't want to get into a conversation with those sharp-eyed guys. If they only knew…

Before last night, she sure hadn't had a clue. She'd never spent a night—or a morning—like the one she had with Rafe.

Oh, at first, everything had progressed just as she'd expected yesterday—the hot glances, the sly caresses. His pursuit had desire building into frenzied need before she'd made it through the front door. But throughout the long night, he'd shown her loving she'd never experienced before—sexy teasing and laughter—and conversation in a hushed, tender voice that wrapped warmth around her heart.

After she'd sated the hot passion, she'd sought his touch again and again—not because she craved the release he was so skilled and well equipped to deliver, but because she wanted *him*. And this wanting felt as natural and easy to her as breathing.

Of course, he could ratchet up that heat again in a heartbeat, she thought, remembering their little tryst on the porch.

"What's got you smiling like a Cheshire cat?" Cale said, devilment in his gruff voice.

Lani blushed and clamped her lips together before she turned to face the captain.

His eyes held a twinkle. "Wouldn't be that sheriff who followed you around like a birddog yesterday, would it?"

"What makes you think that?" *Certainly not the blush burning my cheeks hot as a wildfire!* She silently cursed her fair complexion, but figured she'd better get used to the teasing—she'd be blushing a lot from now on if Rafe kept introducing new "geography" lessons.

"Oh, I don't know," he said, not bothering to hide a smile. "I been married a lot of years. Seen that look a time or two on the wife."

"Well, you don't really expect me to comment, do you?"

"Hell no!" He waggled his bushy eyebrows. "Just gettin' you ready for when the guys come rollin' in. They're takin' a break."

Just as he predicted, laughter and the buzz of half a dozen male voices came from down the hallway as the men made their way to the kitchen.

Lani straightened her back, assuming her blandest poker face as the men shuffled past. She dipped her head in greeting.

"You come by to check on that Costello boy?" Cale asked.

Lani nodded.

"I called Rafe a little while ago." Cale's voice dropped. "Said the coroner determined the boy died from his fall."

The relief she felt confused her—dead was dead, whether he'd been mauled or not.

"Hi, Lani."

Lani glanced over her shoulder to find Randy standing behind her, a sheepish expression on his face.

"I didn't know you were working today," she said. "This isn't your shift."

"I'm not on shift. I just stopped in to help with cleanup. Didn't have anything better to do."

Lani smiled. Randy was young and eager—and he liked wearing his fireman's uniform. "Well, I wanted to talk to you anyway."

"Me, too." He rocked on his heels, and looked at the ground.

"I'll leave you two," Cale said. "Have to make sure the boys don't get too comfy in the kitchen."

"See you, Captain," Lani murmured, then turned back to Randy whose cheeks had flushed red. "What's up?"

"Look, I'm sorry about yesterday—about the way I talked to you…in the cave."

Lani shook her head, not understanding, then recalled Randy's odd behavior when he'd found her kissing Rafe. "Oh." Her own face heated. "Don't worry about it. You were right. It was definitely the wrong place…for that."

"No. I don't know why I got so mad."

Lani thought she might know. Randy followed her around like an eager puppy. She found his crush sweet. "Don't worry about it. We were all under a lot of stress."

He took a deep breath. "Well, I just wanted to say it."

"And I wanted to ask you if you'd like to make another trip back to the cave."

His eyes lit up. "Just us?"

"Yeah." She grinned at his eager expression. "I want to check out that second level."

"I'm in."

"All right. Tomorrow soon enough?"

* * * * *

"Sheriff, did I hear you talking earlier about that big cat Lani saw in the cave?" Deputy Johnny Ramos stood in Rafe's doorway.

"I was."

Johnny's expression turned dark. "A rancher east of McKelvey's property reported finding a dead calf. She said it was partially eaten. As far as she could tell, it was attacked by a mountain lion."

"Was the game warden notified?"

Johnny nodded. "I'm headed out there now. I'll let you know what I find."

"Call back the warden. Tell him I saw the mountain lion just west of town this morning."

"Will do. Although, he'll probably be a little late to capture it. The ranchers are planning a hunting party. Danny McKelvey's leading it."

Rafe knew that meant Danny's pit bulls would be along for the kill. Somehow, the idea of that proud cat being mauled or shot to death didn't sit right. "Well, let's hope the warden gets him first."

"I better get out on the road."

As much as Rafe would have liked to let the deputy take the call, it was still midafternoon—time enough to see to business before he headed back to Lani's place. "I'll head to the ranch and check out the damages."

"Thought you were taking the day off, boss."

"Yeah, I was. But I want to see for myself whether this is a mountain lion attack or whether folks are just getting nervous."

Johnny tipped the edge of his cowboy hat and left.

Rafe recognized the name on the report and made his way to the small ranch. Then he followed the trio of buzzards that circled overhead, silhouetted against the bright, Texas sky.

The calf, or what was left of its carcass, lay on its side, flies buzzing around gaping wounds.

Dressed in Wranglers and scuffed boots, her gray hair covered by a grimy straw hat, Kate Massey leaned against a fencepost. "This is just how I found it this mornin'. Least this one wasn't taken by drought. It was a faster death." Her lined face was drawn into a fierce frown.

"It looks like a lion did this, all right," Rafe said.

The ground around the carcass was free of tracks, which wasn't unexpected due to the hard, graveled surface. But the calf's throat had been laid open by a single, suffocating bite—the width consistent with the size of a mountain lion's jaws.

"My husband's bringin' the cattle in to the corral tonight. We'll keep watch in case he comes back."

"That's not a bad idea."

"Danny McKelvey said he'd come out later and let his dogs loose. He hopes to find scent they can track."

Uncomfortable with the methods, but understanding the rancher's concern, Rafe nodded. There wouldn't be any calls made to the game warden if the cat showed up here again.

"So what's your report gonna say?" she asked, blunt as a mallet, like always.

"Mountain lion attack. I'll have a copy ready for you tomorrow for your insurance claim."

"I'd be obliged." She straightened and tipped back her hat. "So, Sheriff, do you think this is the same lion what killed that boy in McKelvey's cave?"

Rafe's gaze narrowed. He wondered at the anger that sparked hot as a match to kindling. "The mountain lion didn't kill Matt Costello—a fall did."

Kate nodded, but the grim set of her lips told him she'd already made up her mind that particular version of the tale had been manufactured for public consumption.

Before he left the ranch, he called Lani's number on his cell phone.

"Hello?"

Rafe closed the door of his cruiser and stared out his window. "It's me."

"Rafe." Her voice changed, turning softer.

"Want some company?" He held his breath, hoping he hadn't dreamed the new intimacy he'd felt growing between them over the last day and night.

"Sure." She drew in a breath. "Have you eaten?"

"No."

"I'll make dinner."

The conversation felt awkward, and she sounded a little shy. His mouth curved—he knew how to bring her out of her shell. "How're you feeling today?"

"Fine," she said, a little too quickly. He knew her pale features would be glowing red right about now.

Unable to resist teasing her a bit further, he said softly, "Not sore?"

"Rafe!" She groaned. "You're a wicked man. What do you think?"

"I think we'll have to take it easy tonight. Maybe watch a movie. Keep it at kisses."

"Think you can?"

Her sexy drawl had his blood humming in a heartbeat. "I can be creative."

"Stop!" She laughed. "I'll need another cold shower."

"If you wait, I'll scrub your back."

"Kind of defeats the purpose, doesn't it?"

Her starchy tone had him chuckling. Then he cleared his throat. "Seriously, are you okay?"

After a moment's silence, she said, "Of course." She cleared her throat. "Sitting isn't very comfortable at the moment. I was afraid anyone who looked at me would know. I didn't stay long at the station."

"Why's that?"

"I think I'm wearing a permanent blush. And I've been thinking about...acts."

Recalling the sight of her lovely buttocks, quivering beneath his hands, Rafe leaned back in his seat to ease the ache centered in his groin. His hand tightened on the cell phone. "Any one in particular?"

"Maybe. I've been thinking about what you said."

"I said a lot of things."

"Yeah, and most of them X-rated," she muttered.

"Tell me you didn't like it," Rafe drawled, silently cursing the fact he was miles away.

She groaned and let out a gust of laughter. "You're impossible."

"So, what *acts* have you been thinking about?"

"You're going to make me say it?" Her voice rose at the end, a sure sign she was struggling with embarrassment and laughter.

"Yup," he said, a grin stretching his mouth.

"Well..." Her voice dropped to a sultry, smoky growl. "It's one that involves kisses...and tongue..."

"I'll be there in twenty minutes."

"Make it fifteen."

He heard a click and dead air.

Rafe jammed his hat on his head and cranked the engine into life. He churned gravel as he gunned his engine.

* * * * *

Lani met him at the door wearing only a smile. The embarrassment was worth it. His jaw dropped and the smoldering look that settled over his features told her she'd pleased him.

He reached for her, but she danced away. "I promised you dinner first."

"And if I'm on a liquid diet?"

Damn, if that growled double entendre didn't do the trick. Her body blossomed, her pussy creaming in response. She shook her head. He was not going to change the course she'd set. "Food first. Take off your hat and your gun belt…and whatever else makes you comfortable." She turned on her heels and headed to the kitchen, trying to ignore his low hiss and the snaps and slides that meant he was stripping at the door.

Once inside the kitchen, she leaned against the counter and waited for her heartbeat to slow. She'd greeted him stark naked! A giggle bubbled up, and she clamped her hand over her mouth. She only hoped she had the courage to follow through with the rest of her plan. Rafe had already pledged his love to her. Tonight, she'd show him what was in her heart.

She'd decided on simple, southwestern fare—Carne Asada, beef tips in spicy gravy, and tortillas. She poured a single glass of red wine and filled one bowl with the meat dish. Tonight, they'd share their meal, and she didn't want too many dishes getting in the way.

Pushing the door open with her hip, she carried the tray into the living room to find Rafe already seated on her sofa, unabashedly naked. Perfect.

She set the tray on the end table next to them and climbed onto his lap, facing him, trying not to note how the hairs on his upper thighs tickled the insides of hers.

Rafe's chest rose with the deep breath he dragged into his lungs. His face hardened, skin stretching across his sharp, high cheekbones. A muscle in his jaw flexed. "Something smells delicious," he said, his voice tight.

She knew he wasn't talking about the food, but ignored his suggestive comment and the hands that closed on her hips. She reached for the fork and speared a chunk of meat, twirling it in the gravy. Then she lifted it to Rafe's mouth.

His gaze held hers as he took her offering.

"What do you think?" she asked.

His gaze dipped, pausing on her breasts, then sweeping lower to her spread thighs. "Like I said, delicious."

She took a bite for herself while fighting the urge to grind her open sex on his cock. She could feel it hardening against her open slit. Her nipples tightened to exquisitely sensitive points—but she held herself away from the light furring on his chest.

While he remained watchful of her every move, Lani fed them both slowly, lingering over the meal.

"I'm thirsty," he said, nudging her open pussy with his sex in an unsubtle hint.

She took a sip from the wine and put her hands on his shoulders and bent to give him a drink, opening to let the liquid pass from her mouth to his. She chased the drink with a quick stroke of her tongue, and then pulled away.

Rafe followed her, leaning forward. "*Bruja!*" he whispered against her lips. "Are you going to let me have you?"

Her kiss was openmouthed, sliding over his mouth—but brief. "Baby, you're dessert."

Rafe cursed softly.

Lani laughed, setting the dishes aside, and rose from his lap. Her legs were unsteady, but she was determined.

Chapter Six

ꟹ

Rafe watched warily as Lani stood before him. It wasn't in his nature to submit, but he sensed tonight's "taking" was important to Lani, so he'd suffer through it. Besides, he was delighted with the evening's sensual turn. She had to trust him to believe he'd hand her the controls. He'd die before he disappointed her, however much his body screamed for release.

When Lani knelt between his open legs, Rafe knew she planned to take him, just as he'd hinted he wanted earlier in the day. Only at the time, he'd been well-sated—his body languorous after their sexual marathon. Unfortunately, he was primed for rougher sport.

Only now, he noted the early evening sun still gleaming through her open windows. Lani had set the stage well for her seduction, knowing the sight of her body limned in light would incite him. Her soft blonde hair was tucked behind her ears. Her body gleamed with a shimmering of gold flecks. The smell of a fresh-scented powder rose to tease his nose. Her lips still bore a faint trace of colored gloss, and looked ripe and innocent at the same time.

Christ, those lips! He tried not to think about what they'd do to him. He placed his arms along the top of the sofa and clutched the fabric, determined to withstand whatever sweet torture she meted out.

Her gaze sought his for a moment and color suffused her face.

"You can change your mind anytime you want," he said, praying she'd cry "uncle" now.

She tossed back her head. "And miss dessert? I like my sweet after dinner."

"Well, I don't know what you've been told," he said, gritting his teeth to keep his tone light, "but it's a little salty."

Her lips curved into a feline grin that set his heart pumping faster. "Trying to talk me out of it?"

He took a deep breath and lied, "Oh no."

"Nervous?" Her hands rested on his knees, her thumbs circling.

Rafe blew out the breath, unable to form a word. His cock was straining upward, a drop of pre-cum glistened on the tip.

Lani's gaze dropped from his face, and she licked her lips.

Rafe groaned, conceding the game. "Sweetheart, I can only take so much."

"Oh? Before doing what?"

"Before I fuck you all the way to oblivion."

She blinked, and then swallowed. Was her mouth as dry as his? "Maybe I have another idea."

His entire body was so hard with tension and desire, a throbbing pain had settled in his groin. All he could grind out was an honest, "Tell me quick, I'm dying here."

Lani licked her lips and held herself perfectly still. "Couldn't we both have our dessert?"

Rafe didn't give her a chance to change her mind. He pulled her up and kissed her hard. Then he lay lengthwise on the sofa. "Baby, give me your pussy."

Lani gave a strained laugh and climbed over him. He "helped" by guiding her hips backward, placing her knees on either side of his shoulders. "Come to me," he whispered, laying kisses on her open thighs as she scooted until her sex was just above his mouth. "There," he said, sighing as he pressed his lips to her cunt. She was drenched and fragrant, and for a moment he let the scent of her feed his appetite.

Lani was a fast learner and just as eager to explore. Her face and lips nuzzled his sex for long moments, and then her hands and mouth caressed his shaft.

Rafe pulsed upward to show his appreciation, then turned his attention to the sensual treat hovering above his waiting mouth. He licked and sucked her labia, lapping between to taste her honeyed pleasure. Soon her legs trembled and she sank lower, seeking his caresses in trembling pulses.

Rafe fought hard to pay attention to her need—his own rode him hard. Lani's clever mouth and hands glided over his sex, squeezing, sucking, stroking. When her lips surrounded his cock and her hot mouth sank to take him inside, his mind and body froze, every bit of his attention flying south to savor the sensations—moist heat, the soft scrape of teeth, strong hands stroking his shaft, delivering a wicked little twist that had his hips rising off the sofa.

Though it killed him, he kept his thrusts shallow. His reward was a strong suctioning that abated when Lani's mouth slid down his cock and drew hard again when she came up.

She moaned enthusiastically, the sound vibrating along his shaft. Her pussy pulsed on his mouth, and he remembered this was supposed to be a mutual giving. He renewed his assault on her moist, heated flesh, rimming her entrance with his tongue, bringing his hands into play to part her tender folds. Aware she suffered residual soreness from their long hours of lovemaking, he kept his touch gentle and well lubricated.

His efforts earned a quiver that began in her thighs and rippled through her sex. He carefully inserted two fingers into her vagina and kept on licking, while he pumped in and out.

Her hips pulsed in time to the rhythm of his stroking fingers. His free hand gripped a buttock to steady her. Lani's moans grew louder, and her head bobbed faster on his cock.

Together, they writhed against each other's mouths and the sounds of their coupling filled the room—groans, wet slides, and kisses.

Just when he thought he might last long enough to see to her pleasure first, one soft hand closed around his taut sac and gently kneaded his balls. Urgency tightened his thighs, and he bucked. His balls and cock clenched, and his release spurted into Lani's hot mouth.

As he shuddered in the throes of a powerful orgasm, Rafe kept only enough awareness about him to suction hard on Lani's rigid, little clitoris.

Fueled by her desire to please Rafe, as well as a niggling concern for her suede sofa, Lani drank his cum. She slid down his cock, opening her throat to receive the hot liquid gushing into her mouth. His powerful thrusts lifted her whole body, and she clung to his hips as he glided his cock in and out of her mouth. Taking great pride she'd driven him past arrogance and control, she reveled in his masculine vulnerability.

Then his wicked lips closed around her clit and sucked. All self-congratulatory thoughts of Rafe's orgasm flew as she jerked and spasmed against his mouth.

Her legs trembled while her body delivered fevered rolls of her hips beyond her control. Still he drew hard until her whole consciousness centered on the bud of bundled nerves sparking shocks that exploded through her core.

When she drifted back to awareness, Rafe lapped lazily at her cunt. He drew his fingers from her vagina and gave her ass a squeeze. "Come back around here. I want to kiss your mouth."

"I can't. I'm dead." She rested her head wearily on his hard thigh.

"Come here, and I'll revive you."

"A little mouth-to-mouth?"

"How about a lot of tender loving? I promise nothing's gonna poke around your pretty pussy."

Galvanized by the recollection her pussy was just what he was looking at, Lani scrambled to turn around. His arms opened, and she slumped against his chest.

"That's better," he said, hugging her close.

It *was* nice. His heart was just beneath her ear, pounding a comforting beat. The heat of his skin lulled her, nearly to sleep.

"Wake up, baby."

Lani opened her eyes and realized she really must have dozed off. "I thought you guys always slept afterwards," she said, feeling grumpy.

"We were going to talk," he said softly.

Lani froze. That had been part of her plan. But she'd chickened out just before he got to the door and decided to go for "dessert" first. She rose, her forearms supported on his broad chest, and met his gaze. "I'm only going to say this once."

"Does it hurt that much, baby?"

She nodded, and blinked at the tears that pooled with his tender expression. *God, where to start?* "I'm not from around here."

"I know." He arched one eyebrow. "I remember when you arrived."

Lani gave him a little, strained smile. "You didn't so much as give me a glance when I stopped at the sheriff's office for directions," she scoffed.

Rafe let her have her tangent, knowing she was still screwing up her courage to say what needed said. "I followed your sweet ass sashaying all the way back to your truck."

"I don't sashay."

"You did that day." Her blush delighted him.

"I knew you were watching me," she admitted. Her honesty pleased him more.

"Couldn't help myself," he said. "Knew I had to have you then and there."

"So you're into butts?" she quipped, then groaned and hid her face against his chest.

Rafe laughed softly, knowing he needed to keep a little lightness in their conversation to help her get through this. "You know I am," he growled. His heart ached for her. And if he could, he would take all her pain for his own.

Her cheeks pink, but expression solemn, she said, "You know I come from Uvalde."

"You mentioned it once."

"It's not very big. Everybody knows everybody else."

Rafe pushed back a lock of her hair from her cheek. "Sounds like here."

"Well, my daddy was the town drunk."

He held his questions, wanting her to offer her story.

She sighed and laid her head on his chest. "He was mean after he polished off a case, and the house always smelled of booze and his sweat."

He fought the flare of anger that had his arms tightening around her. He kissed the top of her head to reassure her. "Where was your mother?"

"At work. He couldn't hold a job—most days couldn't get out of bed before noon."

"What about you?"

"Mostly, I just stayed out of his way. If he fell asleep in the living room, I'd play in my bedroom or go play at the neighbors. I just tried to make sure I was…scarce."

Rafe glided a hand up and down her back, while imagining a blonde-haired little girl who had to keep beyond her father's reach. "You said he was a mean drunk. Did he hit you?"

"Not much, but I knew to stay out of his way. Mom never figured that trick out. She'd come home, see beer cans littering the living room and light into him. Then he'd be yelling back." She gave a cynical snort. "It was a very loud house."

"He hit your mom?"

Lani rubbed her cheek up and down on his chest. "Not often. But sometimes she just wouldn't shut up. She never learned to be quiet, like me. Never learned to hide."

Rafe took a deep breath, tamping down the sadness and anger that had him wishing her worthless father was in striking range.

"My favorite place was the coat closet," she said, her voice dropping to a whisper. "I'd crawl in between the coats where it was dark and the sounds of their fighting were muffled. I didn't care that the air was stale or that it got hot after a while. I liked disappearing inside there. I could stay a long, long time. Sometimes, I'd daydream and pretend I had a friend inside the closet with me. Someone I could really talk to."

"Didn't you have a real friend you could talk to about what frightened you?"

"Mom always said the neighbors didn't need to see our trash."

Rafe's anger washed over him all over again. Another person had a lot to answer for. "Sounds like your mom wasn't there for you, either."

"She had her own problems to sort through."

"Do you think that's an adequate excuse?"

"Not really. Looking back now, I can't figure out why the hell she didn't leave him." Her voice sounded raw. "She didn't need him. But at the time, I just thought that was the way it was supposed to be."

"What I want to know…" Rafe stopped to clear the lump in his throat. "…is how you turned out so strong."

"Strong?" Lani's brow furrowed. "I never thought of me like that. I was just surviving."

"Lani, you're the strongest woman I've ever known. Physically, mentally." He squeezed her again. "Hell, you withstood *me* for months."

Her laughter was husky. "Well, I guess I am. Look at me now." She stretched and slid her knee between his legs. "I have you just where I want you."

Rafe tightened as her thigh nudged his sex. "Witch! You trying to change the subject?"

"Spoilsport." She settled back on his chest. "When I was in high school it got better. I stayed away from home more. And I discovered caves. One of the guys' parents was into caving, so he asked if he could bring some friends along, sometime. His parents gave us classes, took us out to low bridges and had us learn to rappel and work with the ropes and rigging. Then one day, they took us to a cave they were very familiar with for us to practice what we'd learned.

"Most of the kids got a little freaked the deeper we went. They didn't like the darkness and the smells. They were afraid of the bats clinging to the ceiling. But I loved it. It was like crawling into my closet, but so much bigger. I felt free, and I was good at it. I couldn't wait to go back." Lani leaned away and looked into his eyes. "So now you know."

He nodded and threaded his fingers through the soft hair at her nape. "You came here. Why?"

"I couldn't change the way things were between my parents, so I decided to take charge of my own life. I liked rope work and I'm not afraid of heights. The thought of rescuing others appealed to me. I became a firefighter and took EMT training. When the chance came to be a full-timer training a crew of volunteers, I saw my opportunity to cut ties."

He kissed her shoulder. "Get your own life."

"Yeah. See whether I could do it any better." Lani's gaze was steady, but the raw vulnerability she rarely allowed to show was there in her face. Her eyes were moist, her mouth trembling. "I didn't want this, you know. Didn't plan to start any relationship with a man."

"I know. You don't need one."

She shook her head. "I didn't need any man—but I need you."

"Are you afraid?"

The corners of her mouth turned down and her lips trembled. "I hate it. I feel like a coward, but sometimes I think if I let my guard down and let myself love you, you'll change."

"Become a monster? Like your father?"

Her next indrawn breath sounded like a ragged sob. She nodded. "I know intellectually you aren't him—you're as far from him as any man can be. But it's still there." A tear welled in the corner of her eye and rolled down her cheek.

Rafe framed her face with his hands and held her gaze. "Lani, I won't change. I won't ever hurt you."

"I know." She sniffed. "I've tested your patience and acted like a flake. Please, have patience."

"Baby, I'm not going anywhere."

Her smile, tremulous though it was, lifted the shadows. He pulled her down for a kiss, telling her with his mouth and body he was in for the long run. No way, would he ever let Lani push him away again. She needed him. Needed to learn a man could keep his promises.

* * * * *

"Off belay!" Lani directed her shout upward, but the sound hung in the air next to her.

Lani opened her jaws wide, trying to pop her ears. Stepping into the limestone wonderland was enough to take her breath away, but while God had formed a visual marvel with a hundred thousand years of mineral-soaked water drops, the muzzy acoustics inside McKelvey's cave left a lot to be desired.

Yesterday, she'd been eager to return to the cave. But at the moment she couldn't remember why. She hadn't felt the sense of homecoming she normally did when she'd stepped into the darkness beyond a cave's entrance. Perhaps, she no longer needed her haven. Rafe's love and acceptance had given her that. After last night, she'd awoken feeling like she'd shed a lifetime of sadness and guilt.

Lani stepped away from the rope as Randy glided down the last few feet to the cave floor, then waited patiently while he unclipped the carabiner on his harness.

"So, what are we looking for?" he asked, his eagerness apparent in his expression. The younger man had definitely caught the caving bug.

"Let's try to find where Matt Costello fell," she said, not mentioning that she was also looking for signs the mountain lion had been this deep in the cave.

They trained their flashlights on the cave floor and worked their way in an ever-widening circle away from the rope.

"Found it," Randy shouted.

Lani hurried to his side. A large, dark stain and the dented, lens-less remains of small flashlight lay on the cave floor. She trained her light in the direction of the wall with the angled ledges. His body had been found on one about twenty feet above the floor.

"I don't get it," Randy said. "There's blood here and on that ledge where we found him, but not a drop in between. And how the hell did he make it up there?"

"I don't know. He was a hundred forty pounds. Can a mountain lion even carry that weight?"

Randy grimaced. "I'm glad I'm packin' a weapon today. That had to be one big, hairy moth—monster."

"Yeah, it was." Lani sighed. She'd hoped for answers. Now, she just had more questions.

"This is kind of a creepy place. Feels smaller down here. Kind of closed in."

She'd noted the anomalies before. The way sound didn't carry, how light seemed to be swallowed over a distance. Even she felt a little claustrophobic. "Want to take a look around before we head back up?"

Less enthusiastic this time, Randy merely nodded.

The lower level of the cave was as long as a banquet hall and bordered on one side by a rock formation that resembled a giant pipe organ and the other side by more of the calcified drapery. Further inside the chamber, the floor was littered with a dark layer of bat droppings and desiccated insect bodies contrasting with the pale walls.

In the distance, Lani heard a faint murmur. She cocked her head to the side. "Hear that?"

Randy's eyes widened. "Sounds like a creek."

"I think there's another level beneath us," she said, excitement stirring again. "I'll bet another room is being carved out of the rock right below our feet."

"Are we gonna try to find a way to get down there?" By his expression, he was game for the attempt.

"No." She lifted her eyebrows. "Maybe another time. We better head back, or Cale will send out a search party. He didn't like us coming down here by ourselves in the first place."

As they neared the rope, Lani's light glanced on something bright. "What's this?" She squatted beside a pile of white, fragmented objects.

"Shit!" Randy whispered from behind her, and she glanced back. His light illuminated a rounded shape. "It's a skull!"

She stood up and backed away. Splintered bones, some long—and human, by the shape of the few still intact—lay in a pile. And beside them, a complete skeleton. A mountain lion's if she had to hazard a guess.

"How long do you think this has been down here?" Randy asked, an edge of nervousness in his voice.

She lifted a flattened piece of fabric from among the fragments. "My guess would be quite a while. This is a moccasin."

Chapter Seven

ꟿ

Tired and disgusted, Rafe turned in his chair to stare out into the darkness. The sun had set an hour earlier, but he continued to run through the day's reports and taken calls from local ranchers who'd reported sightings of the cat.

The mountain lion was quickly becoming the Bogie Man. No single cat could be responsible for all the mischief that had been laid at its feet. Folks were convinced it had a part in Matt Costello's death and were ready to paint it a devil.

To top it off, the construction foreman at the golf course reported the theft of a case of dynamite from their warehouse—now ATF was getting interested in the blast that had set off the chain of events leading to Matt's death.

The one bright spot in the past couple of days was his blossoming relationship with Lani. Oh, they'd shared sex for months before the breakup—furtive, desperate liaisons. At first, he'd been content to keep things on the surface and scratch the purely sexual itch, but his feelings for Lani had grown, deepening without his notice. Not until she'd tried to end it, had he realized how deeply she'd burrowed into his heart.

Now, the future looked bright. Her smiles came more easily, the wariness he'd long thought of as part of her nature, was abating as he slowly peeled away her armor. The trust she'd shown during last night's revelations only increased his belief she was just about ready for the next step.

He'd made up his mind. He didn't know when he'd ask—but he was sure she'd balk. She might even try to close him out again, but he wasn't going to believe her when she said she didn't want it—didn't love him like that. He just had to get his skin hardened a bit for the battle to come.

One thing was certain—he was going to marry her.

His phone rang, and he turned back to his desk to answer one last call.

"Sheriff, you've got a call on line four," the dispatcher said. "It's Lani, and she sounds upset."

His heart thudded in his chest as he pressed the flashing button. "Lani? You okay?"

"Rafe, the mountain lion's on my porch."

"Stay inside. I'm on the way." He grabbed his hat and keys. As he left, he stopped at the dispatcher's booth. "Call the game warden. Tell him the lion's at Lani's place."

He drove with his blue lights strobing, his foot mashed on the accelerator. When he turned onto her driveway, he turned off his lights and crept the cruiser to about the midway point on her long drive, before cutting the engine.

Popping the trunk latch, he radioed back to the dispatcher to let her know he'd arrived, then opened the door quietly.

Except for the chirping of crickets, all was still, almost expectant. With only the bright lights of the porch lamps filtering through the bushes, he took out his shot gun and checked the barrel for cartridges, then headed to her house, keeping his ears open for any sound from the mountain lion.

As the porch came into view, he saw Lani in the window and waved. Then he heard a crunch in the underbrush and spun toward it, his shotgun raised.

The hairs on the back of his neck prickled and lifted, his heart slowed—all senses focused on what was hiding within the bushes. For a second, he debated whether he should go to the porch and wait for the warden or track the cat. If it escaped, Rafe worried it would return another day and catch Lani unaware. For whatever reason, the creature considered her property part of its territory.

He stepped off the driveway and into the trees, the stock of his weapon firmly braced on his shoulder. Ignoring the soft sounds his own feet made as he entered the thicket, he strained for a rustling or a telltale snarl. Rafe called himself every kind of a fool for tracking a lion alone in the dark. Still, he forged ahead.

The faint glow from Lani's porch lights faded, and soon he had only moonlight filtering through the leaves, painting everything around him in shades of gray shadows.

Beside him, a twig snapped, and he crouched, trying to discern an outline despite the dim light. He waited, slowing his breaths and his heartbeats, straining to hear. Then came a rumble, low and rhythmic.

In the distance, he heard the crunch of a vehicle turning onto Lani's gravel road. Thankful backup had arrived, he rose and retreated, choosing his steps carefully as he backed away.

"Rafe," Lani called, her voice surprisingly distant.

He hadn't thought he'd traveled that far from the road. Satisfied nothing stirred in the bushes before him, he lowered his weapon, still carrying it in front of him, and turned to head back.

That's when he spotted the mountain lion standing in his path. Its head was lowered to the ground, moonlight gleaming white on its bared fangs. A harsh growl, scratchy and resonant, rattled from its chest.

Knowing a sudden movement might startle it into attacking, Rafe backed away, hoping it would sense he wasn't a threat.

The cat matched his movement, coming forward a step.

"Rafe!" Lani called again.

But Rafe couldn't respond. The unblinking gaze of the animal in front of him told him he couldn't take his attention away from it for a second. But he couldn't remain frozen and have Lani walk up on them.

"We're at a stalemate, you and I," he whispered. He had to take the cat out now. He swung his rifle up to his shoulder, slid his finger into the trigger housing, and pulled back.

Just as the shot went off, the cat launched itself with a screaming howl. A hundred eighty pounds of mountain lion slammed into his body, carrying him to the dirt.

Then it seemed to fall right through him like water pouring through a sieve.

Rafe lay on the ground trying to catch his breath. What the hell had just happened? He rolled to the side and came up on his knees, glancing around him for a sign of the cat. But the clearing was empty. He picked up the gun, which had been knocked from his hands.

"Rafe! Are you all right?" Lani asked, from right behind him.

Without turning toward her, Rafe yelled, "Lani, get back to the house!"

As usual, she didn't heed his warning. She pushed past a cedar branch and rushed to his side. "Are you hurt? Why didn't you answer? You've been out here so long."

More footsteps crunched, "Sheriff, you okay?" The game warden had arrived.

Rafe dragged in deep breaths. He'd just been knocked stupid. And he'd missed the cat. "Damn!"

"What were you doing out here?" Lani asked, stepping close enough to put her arm around his shoulder. "You scared me half to death."

Rafe returned her hug and struggled to stand. "I saw the mountain lion."

She slipped her arm around his waist. "Well, I saw it too, but it was on my back porch just now."

"When the lion heard your gun go off," the warden said, "it lit out like lightning. Didn't have time to get a dart into the son of a bitch."

"What? But it was just here," Rafe said, shaking his muzzy head. "I fired my gun, and it knocked me to the ground."

"Are you hurt?" Lani skimmed her hands over his chest.

"I'm fine," he said, looking around him, "but it got away."

"Do we have two cats?" Lani asked, her eyes widening.

"Must be a breeding pair," the warden said, "They're solitary creatures except when they're ready to mate."

"So why'd they choose my place for their love fest?" Lani asked.

"Look, I don't like you standing around out here." Rafe grabbed her upper arms. "Let's get you inside."

Lani frowned. "Hey, I'm not the one who thought they could take a mountain lion on single-handed."

He let out a gust of air. "I deserve that. I feel like a goddamn fool."

"Well, you probably scared him to the next county," the warden said. "I'll head out now. I think it's gonna be a busy night."

Rafe let Lani lead him to her kitchen and press him into a chair.

"You're bleeding!" she said, staring above his eyes. "I'll take care of this." She turned to the cabinet above the sink and pulled down a blue first aid box.

Rafe touched his forehead and found a large lump. At least he understood now why he felt so dizzy. "Don't fuss. It's just a bump."

"It's a goose egg." She swabbed his forehead with peroxide, making him wince. "Don't be such a baby."

Rafe closed his hands around hers and pulled her between his legs. "I'm fine. I'm sorry I worried you."

"You were gone so long, I couldn't help worrying."

That was the second time she'd said that. Rafe shook his head. "I only stepped off the road. I was five minutes at most."

Lani leaned away and looked into his face, her eyes widening with concern. "Rafe, you were out there at least half an hour. I was so frantic I called the warden to make sure he was on the way. Then I heard growling on my porch and saw the cat outside my bedroom window. I couldn't come after you."

"That doesn't make any sense. I had only stepped off the road to follow the cat into the brush when I heard the warden arrive."

Her fingers brushed his forehead. "You must have really taken a whack to your head."

Rafe couldn't make any more sense of their conversation. His head throbbed. "Well, I am feeling a little fuzzy still."

"We should get you to a hospital. Have them check you out."

"I'm fine."

She pushed his face back and stared into his eyes. "Your pupils look okay. But I don't like that you seem to have lost time. Maybe, you should get straight into bed."

His hands settled on her hips. "Thought you'd never get down to business."

"Oh no." She pushed his hands away. "We've both had a couple of *strenuous* days—and I don't like the pastiness of your skin."

"I'm not going to the hospital," he said flatly.

Lani shook her head. "Anyone ever tell you, you're stubborn?"

"You." His hands slipped over her bottom. "My head is pounding. I'll just go lie down for a while."

"What if you're concussed?"

"I'm fine, but if it worries you, I won't sleep. I'd just like to get out of the light and let this headache dull a bit." He squeezed her bottom. "Join me?"

"And you think I'm stupid?" She leaned into him and hugged his shoulders. "Later, okay? I'll check on you. Right now, I want you to rest. I'm worried if you don't move soon, I'll be carrying you to bed."

"Think you can, little thing like you?"

Lani snorted. "You're the only man who'd say that. And yeah, I could even manage a rock like you."

"All right, I'll go to bed. For a while." The room was beginning to swim. "I hate to say this, but I think you're right. Give me a hand?"

Lani slipped her arm beneath his shoulder, and together they made it to her bedroom. Rafe let her strip him, chagrined that her handling never raised his ardor. He was definitely feeling out of it.

Lani pulled the cover over him. "I'll make something light. Soup, maybe. I'll let you know when it's ready."

Rafe nodded and closed his eyes—not to sleep—Lani'd have his hide.

He leapt to the floor, following the scent of the woman through the darkened tunnel to a bright space filled with scents that reminded him of his hunger. Peering from behind the door, he watched the woman, the woman from the cave, as she stood with her back to him. Her long limbs and sun-bright hair stirred a memory in him of richer, sharper scents—of sexual fervor and mating outside in the sunlight as he'd watched her with the man.

Her shoulders and arms moved accompanied by the sounds of sharp thuds. Light glinted from the thing held in her hands. Instinctually, he shied away from that shiny object and withdrew from the room. He padded away, seeking the source of a light breeze and pressed his nose against a scratchy surface that he could peer through.

Beyond the barrier, he could see the trees as they swayed in the wind, could smell the scent of deer as they moved, foraging within the thicket.

He pushed with his nose, but the barrier didn't shift. He reached up a paw and batted at it, but only managed to tear a hole in the surface. Feeling frustrated, he opened his mouth and emitted a growl – telling the barrier of his anger.

He heard a gasp and running feet coming from the bright space, so he turned and ran down the long tunnel to the place he had awakened.

The cat's growl echoed around the house, loud and angry. Lani dropped the knife she was using to chop vegetables for the soup and ran for the pantry where the shotgun stood now, propped against the shelves.

She shook bullets from a carton, letting them spill to the floor and quickly grabbed several, pushing them into a pocket in her jeans. Two, she jammed into the barrel.

The cat was inside the house! She had to get to Rafe.

Lani's hands trembled as she held the gun in front of her and crept from the kitchen into the living room, alert for sounds of the creature's footfalls. She toggled the switch to the light in the ceiling fan and quickly glanced around.

No sign of the cat, but the screen door was shredded. She cursed her own carelessness at leaving the oak door open when she'd led Rafe inside earlier.

A thump sounded from deeper inside the house. *Rafe!*

Lani sped down the darkened hallway, her heart thundering inside her chest. *Please let him be okay.*

The bedroom door was open wide and her heart stopped. She'd left it open only a crack. Her grip tightened around the weapon, and she lifted it to her shoulder. Never taking her gaze from the bed, she rubbed her back on the wall to flip the light switch, illuminating the room.

Everything looked exactly as she'd left it. Rafe lay on his side beneath the covers, turned away from her. His head was buried between her fat pillows, but his back and shoulders moved with his breaths. He shouldn't be sleeping—but right now she prayed he'd stay that way, so he wouldn't move and startle the cat.

Thinking the cat could be on the other side of the bed, her finger slid into the trigger housing as she slowly skirted the mattress.

She expected a noise, some sort of warning from the cat—but the only sound was her own blood pumping in her ears and the creak of the floorboards beneath her feet. When she reached the corner, she found the floor empty.

"Lani, what are you doing?" Rafe sat up, the cover slithering from his chest.

"The mountain lion." She barely spared him a glance, and looked inside the bathroom. Nothing. "I think it's in the house."

His expression went from sleepy confusion to fully alert in a second. "Give me that." He held out his hand.

"Dammit, are you up for this? Your head—"

"Just give me the damn gun."

He looked steady enough. Lani was only too happy to let him have it.

Rafe walked to the door and peered around the corner. "Close the door after me and stay put," he said over his shoulder, and then slipped out of the room.

Lani waited, listening for sounds of any trouble. Then she wondered what she'd do if she did hear anything, other than dial 911. Rafe had her only weapon. She glanced around the room. What else could she use?

Just when she'd decided to telephone for help, the door opened. Rafe strode inside. "It's all clear. No sign of it."

Lani launched herself at his chest.

Rafe's arms closed around her, hugging her tight. "You scared the hell out of me."

She breathed in his spicy man-scent and relaxed. "Did you think I was going to shoot you?" she asked, her voice muffled against his skin.

"No. I figured out real quick there must be trouble for you to be holding a gun." He kissed the top of her head. "But your hands were holding onto it so tight, I thought you might pull that trigger by accident."

She shuddered. "Guns scare me."

"They scare me, too—when you're holding 'em." He hugged her again, and let her go. "I looked all around. Your screen's a mess. I'm guessing that's where he came in."

She nodded and wrapped her arms around her middle, missing his warmth already.

"He must have high-tailed it back out the door." He broke open the barrel and removed the two cartridges, then propped the gun next to the door.

Lani glanced down his body, finally realizing he was naked. When she looked up again, his gaze was smoldering.

"Anyway, I closed the door," he said, amusement creeping into his voice. "He's not coming back inside."

Lani licked her lips. "How are you feeling?"

Rafe shook his head experimentally. "Better." He spread his hands and raised an eyebrow. "Shall I get dressed and help you in the kitchen with dinner?"

"I'm thinking...no." She stepped toward him. "You know, I never realized how phallic a gun looks on a man."

* * * * *

Rafe drew Lani back into the cradle of his thighs, fitting his hips snugly to her backside. Her head nestled on his shoulder, and her hair tickled his nose. He had the whimsical thought he was happiest when only a sheen of sweat separated their skins.

As his breaths grew less labored, his mind returned to the odd chain of events that had occurred over the course of the evening. The first being the cat leaping at him and suddenly disappearing. The second, the cat arriving on Lani's porch. Could it have been the same animal? Perhaps the blow to his head had skewed his memory of the order of events.

Then there was the mountain lion entering her house. That fact disturbed him enough. But even more unsettling was the dream he'd been having just before Lani woke him, creeping into the bedroom with the shotgun.

He'd dreamt he was the cat, and that he'd spied on her as she prepared dinner. His thoughts had been...primitive, possessive. Scents had seemed more acute—the odor of the deer foraging in the woods, the perfume and musk that was Lani's distinct fragrance. From the cat's perspective, Lani had been no less attractive as a mate. And the cat had definitely wanted her.

If he were a man given to superstition, he might think the dreams, the cave, the presence of the mountain lion, were all somehow related—and that tonight he'd somehow entered into the mix, as well.

"I can hear you thinking," Lani said, grumpily.

He smiled. "What do my thoughts sound like?"

"Well..." She turned around, sliding an arm over his side and a silky leg between his thighs. "Your heart beats fast, and your breathing gets quieter."

He pressed a brief kiss to the side of her neck. "I couldn't be on the verge of falling asleep?"

"No," she moaned and pressed her groin to his. "When you fall asleep, your breathing gets so loud, it rumbles in my ear."

He glided his hands down her back to her buttocks, and gave her a playful squeeze. "Are you saying I snore?"

"Course not. You just breathe loud…and sometimes you grind your teeth." She hid her face on his shoulder, but her voice held an edge of laughter.

"I wonder why you put up with me. If I were you, I'd make me sleep on the couch so I could get a good night's sleep."

"I like the noises." Her nose nudged his ear, and then her mouth pressed a kiss just below it. "They remind me you're here. Besides, you're a big guy. You should make noises proportionate to your…size." Her knee nudged his sex.

"I like being here." He brought one hand to her breast and cupped the fullness.

She surged into his hand, and her nipple pebbled.

"I'd like to be here all the time, Lani."

Her breath caught and held. "What are you saying?"

"You know I love you." He waited, hoping she'd give him a little encouragement to continue. But the longer the silence stretched between them, the more resigned he grew to the fact he still had an uphill battle to fight. He palmed the other breast.

"I love you, too."

The words were so soft he thought he'd only imagined them. He held himself perfectly still, but his heart galloped ahead. "Say it, again."

"I love you, Rafe."

He wrapped both arms around her and hugged her tight.

She kissed the side of his neck and whispered, "But…I'd like to take this a step at a time."

"Not a problem." The question would wait a while—but now he knew in his gut, she'd eventually say yes. "I don't want you to feel rushed off your feet."

She laughed. "Like you haven't already? You've been Viagra-man the past few days."

"I don't need a drug to keep it up for you, baby." As if on cue, his cock unfurled, filling rapidly.

"Same here. I want you so much I don't care if I can't walk straight for a week." Lani's fingers combed through the hair of his chest and tugged. Her hips undulated, her legs opening to let his cock slip in between. "Sure you're up for this? You got a nasty bump on your head earlier."

Rafe rolled over, until Lani's body was tucked beneath his. "Your pussy's the best medicine a man can buy. I feel invincible when I slide inside you, baby."

Lani's hands went straight for his ass. Her legs parted. "And I feel like the world's sexiest woman."

"You are." He flexed his hips and drove his cock upward, sliding easily between her slick folds.

"You have no idea how good that feels," Lani moaned.

He rested his head on her shoulder, forcing himself to remain still despite the heat caressing his cock. "You okay for this? Want me to take it easy?"

"No, I want it hard…fast." Her voice was thin and strained. Her hands squeezed his buttocks hard. "I want it now!"

Rafe groaned and pushed himself off her chest to give his hips better leverage. Then he stroked deep inside her.

Lani's breath left her body in a rush, and she widened her legs, planting her feet into the mattress to add resistance to his thrusts.

They slammed their hips together, countering each other's strokes. Soon, the sounds they made were wetter—the slaps as their flesh met, sharper.

For Rafe, this was a claiming. He slid into her tight channel, stroking upward to pound at the entrance of her womb.

He stamped his ownership with each fierce thrust. He branded her with his heat—and at the end, he left his mark, his seed, deep inside her body.

As the last tremors shook him, he rose on his arms to lift his body off hers.

"No, don't go," she moaned. "Let's sleep like this." Her legs tightened around his hips.

"I'll crush you."

"I'm a big girl." She kissed his mouth, framing his face between her palms. "I want to stay like this for a while."

Sated and pleased because he was reluctant to break the connection too, he slumped over her, resting his face on her shoulder. "Wake me, when you need to breathe."

Her arms slid around his back. She wasn't letting him go.

Chapter Eight

He stirred.

His bed was soft, yielding. His cock was surrounded by moist heat.

He breathed in deeply, dragging in the pungent scent of sex and…the woman. He didn't need light to know whose body cradled his manhood. Urgent, powerful desire flooded his body. His shaft filled instantly, stretching the walls of her tight sheath.

Her legs moved restlessly around his hips, pulling him deeper inside her. She moaned sleepily—her sweet breath gusted on his cheek.

His chest expanded, drawing richly scented arousal into his flaring nostrils. This was life! What he'd prayed for as he lay helpless in the jaws of his enemy.

The woman from the cave had given his spirit birth and drawn him from the darkness with her sensual scent and strength of will. Now, she caressed his cock into full arousal with the tremors that rippled along her channel.

He was powerful, immortal—in her arms, in her womb. He rose, hooked her legs roughly in the crook of his elbows and lifted her buttocks high to receive his life, his seed.

The power of his thrusts shook the soft bed beneath him, drove loud gasps from the woman's body. Her belly and thighs tightened, her sex squeezing to milk his cock.

In a powerful explosion of energy and heat, he surged into her, merging his body to hers, searing her soul with spurts of his immortality.

Light, shimmered around him, seeping from his skin, and he cried out as suddenly the woman shoved at his body, screams ripping from her throat.

The other raged within him, fighting to break through to the surface. He resisted, but withdrew from the woman, backing away on the mattress. Her horror wrenched at his heart, but he didn't reach out to her to comfort her as he wished.

He let her go, and she slithered backward off the bed.

Watching her recoil from him, he lifted a hand toward her, imploring her not to fear him. Then he let himself submerge beneath the other, to wait once more.

Lani scooted off the bed, falling to the floor, but she barely registered the pain. She kept moving away until her back came up against the wall. She stared in horror at the man whose skin shimmered like a golden sun—the Indian from her dream!

Only she wasn't sleeping now. And he wasn't a figment. His cum oozed from inside her body to slick her thighs.

She'd awoken in the dark, warmed by the body thrusting into hers. Her core had gushed its invitation, accepted his invasion. Her cunt had spasmed and clutched his cock trying to pull him deeper inside.

The orgasm he'd coaxed from her had shaken her entire body.

Now, she stared in horror at the Indian kneeling on her bed. His glowing body still shuddered. His cock glistened, coated with their release. His expression as he stared at her was primal, predatory—possessive.

Then the brightness dimmed, and she was once again in darkness, listening to the sounds of ragged gasps coming from the bed.

She sobbed, fear for her safety and worry over Rafe's disappearance holding her immobile.

"Sweet Jesus! Lani!" Rafe's voice, hoarse and strained, came from the bed.

It was a trick! She knew what she'd seen—the stranger on the bed—in her body. Lani put her hands over her ears and closed her eyes, wanting to disappear into the darkness. This wasn't happening. She wasn't really here. This was a nightmare, and she'd wake—she had to wake up!

"Lani, please." Hands—Rafe's hands gripped her shoulders. "Stop crying, baby. I'm here."

She shook her head and batted at his hands, trying to scoot away. Her sobs were broken, mewling. They sounded far away—she couldn't be making them. Someone else's heart was breaking.

Rafe's hands shook as he reached for her. He didn't understand what had just happened, but he needed to hold her. Christ! What had happened? What had he done? Weak and trembling though he was, he drew her into his arms and rocked with her, crooning into her hair.

Finally, her hands crept to his shoulders and she clutched him, falling against his chest. Her sobs lost the strained edge of hysteria, until finally, she quieted. "Turn on the light," she said, pushing against his chest. "Turn on the light!"

Rafe let her go and reached for the bedside lamp. The soft, yellow glow dispelled all shadows except those in her stark, pinched face.

He knelt in front of her again, flinching beneath her stricken gaze. Ignoring the knowledge that what had just occurred couldn't possibly be real, he reached to comfort her again. "Baby, are you okay? Did he…did I hurt you?"

Lani stared, then she hiccoughed and a fresh wash of tears glimmered in her eyes. "He was inside me, Rafe. He came inside me. I came. Then there was this light…"

A sharp bitter taste rose from his throat. "I know." Not wanting to alarm her, but needing to touch her, he lifted his hand to her face and gently wiped away her tears with his fingers. "Baby, I was there, too."

Her mouth twisted. "I don't understand."

"I don't either. I just know I was there."

She sniffed and shook her head. "I dreamt about him. He made love to me before..." She hiccoughed softly. "B-but I thought it was just...a dream."

"This is all crazy, but I think somehow he's inside me now," he said, lifting her hand to hold within his, "and so is the lion."

Her eyes widened. "I heard the lion run into this room last night, but I thought I'd been mistaken—"

"After I cracked my head, I dreamt I was the lion—"

"Then it disappeared." Her face crumpled. "Nothing makes sense."

"What's happening to me?" Rafe raked his hand through his hair. "I feel like I'm losing myself—losing my mind."

Lani leaned her head against the wall, looking weary. "Something happened in that cave."

"The cave..." Rafe grew still as memories swamped him. He remembered the dream—the men chasing the Indian inside, the explosion, falling. The lion. Only the images weren't fragmented dreams any longer—they were in his mind, his memories now. "He died in there. An explosion sealed the mouth of the cave, and he fell to the bottom of the second level. The cat killed him before his injuries did."

Lani straightened away from the wall. "I found him. His body. In the cave."

Rafe stiffened.

"I forgot to tell you. Randy and I went back in. We found the Indian's skeleton and the mountain lion's on the floor near where Matt Costello died." Lani wiped her face with the back of her hands, then crossed her arms over her belly, shivering. "So you think somehow, he and the lion merged? Are they spirits?" She laughed, but it was a harsh sound. "I don't believe in that shit."

"Baby, I don't know what I believe. Some Indians believed that if a man ate the flesh of his enemy, he took on his power."

"So, you think the Indian and the lion became a single spirit?" She closed her eyes and drew a deep breath. When she opened them again, her gaze was focused, even a little angry. "So, what the hell does it have to do with you? Why are they inside you now?"

Glad she seemed to be shaking off her shock, Rafe met her steady gaze. "I think it's because of you. You awakened something in them, down in that damn cave. They fixated on you. When I was the cat and seeing you through its eyes, I felt an overwhelming urgency to mate with you."

Her face blanched.

He didn't want to frighten her more, but he had to tell her the rest. "And when I was…there…with the Indian, I felt what he did—exultant, alive. He believes you're the key to his immortality."

"How the hell does he think I'll give him that?" she asked, her voice raw.

"By receiving his seed."

Lani's head jerked. Her eyes were wide with shock. "No!"

Rafe cupped her shoulders and smoothed his hands down her arms. "Lani, I don't understand this, but I think I *know* certain things. The dreams I've been having were this spirit's way of introducing itself to me. But I don't think it has the same ability to see through my eyes, to know what I know. Not like I could when they each…surfaced. And I also don't think they're evil."

Fresh tears welled in her eyes. "How do we get them to leave you? Or can they take you over? What will happen to you?"

Rafe shook his head. "I'm trying to think about this thing logically because it's scaring the shit out of me. But baby, I don't think that's their intention. And I'm not sure they're that strong."

Fear for him etched worry in the tightness of her lips and her pinched face. "But how can you know?"

"Think about the times I changed. I slept after I took a blow to the head—that was before the cat came out to play. Just now, I was asleep when the Indian surfaced."

"But I don't understand. They didn't need your body before. I saw the cat on the ledge—it had enough substance to move that kid up that wall."

"And it's been feeding on livestock." Rafe sighed. "I don't want to scare you more, but I think it wants my body because of my connection to you." He raked his hand through his hair. "Thank God, you're on birth control. He won't understand that."

Lani's eyes widened, and she shook her head. "But Rafe…I'm not."

Rafe felt his body still, but his heart thundered in his chest. In the back of his soul he felt a presence lingering, listening.

She drew in a jagged breath and tears filled her eyes. "I'm sorry. I'm so sorry."

"Lani, what did you do?" he asked softly.

Her face crumpled again and tears rolled down her cheeks. "I'm sorry. So sorry."

His hands closed on her shoulders, and he shook her. "Tell me," he rasped, anger blending with cold fear.

Her head fell back, and her expression pleading. "I stopped taking them a month ago." She closed her eyes, more tears leaking down her face. "I'm so s-stupid. I was afraid, but couldn't tell you."

He dragged her against his chest. "Tell me why, baby?"

Her back shuddered with each soft, shallow sob. "I wanted to be with you. B-but I was afraid. Christ! I'm such a coward."

"Lani, what were you thinking?"

"That if I got pregnant, I couldn't push you away anymore."

"Sweet Jesus!"

"I'm sorry…"

Rafe closed his eyes and hugged her. "Don't be. I'm not going anywhere. I love you."

"But what you said before…" she said, her voice muffled against his shoulder, "…about him wanting immortality… Can he make me pregnant?"

"I don't know," Rafe said, although he felt a glimmering certainty that was exactly what the spirit inside him believed he could do. Rafe had the sinking feeling his world was slipping from his arms. "If he surfaces again, hell, if the lion comes—you won't be safe."

"What do we do?"

"I have to keep away from you."

"No!" Lani shoved at his chest and leaned back. A fierce loving shone from her gaze.

"Baby, until I know how to fight this. You have to keep away from me."

"I brought them out of the cave—they tracked me down. I have to be part of this."

"And if I'm not in control—if he surfaces again? I won't take that chance. Don't you see? I'm becoming that monster you always knew I would be."

Lani shook her head, and her hands cupped his face. "Not you. Rafe, never you. And he won't hurt me. He let me go."

"He didn't want you frightened, but that doesn't mean he won't try to take you again."

"We're in this together. I won't let you do this alone." Her expression held all the love he'd waited so long to find.

Hell, she was going to make this hard.

"Please, don't shut me out."

Rafe kissed her forehead, and then pressed her face to his shoulder. He had to protect her from the monsters inside him. He just didn't know how. Not yet.

"I need to get a shower," she whispered.

His arms tightened. "None of this is your fault. You know that, don't you?"

"I do. I just…need a bath."

Rafe swallowed, feeling like his heart had lodged at the back of his throat. He'd seen enough in his line of work to understand some of what was going through her mind. He nudged up her chin with a finger. "Tell me what you're feeling."

"No way."

He stared into her moist eyes. "Just remember, I was there. I was inside you, too."

"Then why ask me?" He liked the edge of annoyance in her voice. She was fighting back. "You already know I came all over him."

"You thought I was the only one there."

"But it was different—the sex, I mean." Her fingers dug into his arms. "I should have known."

"How could you? I fell asleep inside you."

"He didn't speak—you're always saying sexy things. He smelled different. And he was a little rough."

Rafe wished he were better with words, better at understanding her woman's mind. A blunder now might shut her down. "You dreamt of him before—making love to you. And you liked it. That's why you're upset, isn't it?"

"That was just a dream. This time I thought it was you."

"Lani, don't beat yourself up. Do you think any less of yourself?" Lani was listening. He felt the tension stiffening her back and shoulders. "Do you think I think any less of you?"

"I don't know." Her words were so soft he barely heard them.

He threaded his fingers through her hair and gently tugged back her face so she could see his expression. "Well, I don't. What's happening here is beyond natural. We're both in this. What you said before—about me not shutting you out. Don't turn it around."

Her lips trembled, but she nodded. "Okay. But I still need to wash."

"Then let me come help you."

She nodded again, and her lips curved into a sad little smile. "We'll keep the light on. I want to know who's scrubbing my back."

Rafe bent to kiss her mouth. Lord, how he loved this woman.

Lani turned on the faucets and waited for the water to heat. She kept her back to Rafe, didn't want his keen eyes reading every emotion flitting across her face. Seemed like she couldn't hide a thought from the man anymore. When had he gotten to know her so well? When had he climbed inside her heart?

A few hours ago, she'd thought the worst was past—she'd shared her sordid history and her fears and come through unscathed, stronger even. Now this.

Rafe reached over her shoulder and pushed back the shower curtain. "I think the water's warm enough now."

Without looking back, Lani stepped into the tub, beneath the water, and let it sluice over her head, down her body. Rafe stepped in behind her, but she ignored him, needing silence, needing to be cleansed.

The shampoo dispenser slurped, and Rafe's large hands gently smoothed over her hair. His fingers kneaded her scalp.

Lani let her head fall back, closing her eyes against the spray washing over her face, and let Rafe soothe the ragged edges of her torn emotions.

His hands rubbed lower, soaping her back, rolling her shoulders gently, squeezing tension from the muscles flanking either side of her spine, and then lower.

Lani gasped, feeling the first sensual stirring and braced her hands against the tiles in front of her.

His palms massaged her hips, cupped her buttocks and kneaded, separating her cheeks, closing them, slipping for a moment between her legs, but never grazing the flesh that was quickly swelling with heat.

His fingers slid beneath her buttocks, tracing the creases, then smoothed lower over the backs of her thighs and calves.

When he reached to soap her toes, his hands entered her vision for the first time. Rafe's hands—square palms, long, thick fingers.

Tears intermingled with the spray to track down her cheeks.

Another slurp from the dispenser and his hands glided up the fronts of her calves. Now she felt his warmth lean into her thighs, the thick muscles of her chest and shoulders rippling as his hands worked the tension from her legs, moving ever higher.

When his fingers neared the juncture of her thighs, her heartbeat quickened and her breath caught, anticipating his intimate caress, but he glided past, his whole body caressing her back as he slowly stood.

When his hands reached her ribs, Lani captured them. Afraid he'd pass by the quickening tips of her nipples, she moved his hands over her breasts and held them there.

"Tell me what you want, Lani," he whispered in her ear. "Shall I dry you and hold you while you sleep?"

Lani couldn't calm the trembling that shuddered through her body. She shook her head and then slowly turned until she faced him.

Rafe's expression, so tight with need, made her want to cry. Her gaze swept lower to his cock. Reddened, engorged, he'd held that part of himself away from her while he'd washed her gently as he might a child.

Rising on tiptoe, Lani kissed his mouth, and then she slowly glided her palms up his chest and behind his neck to grip his hair. "I want you inside me Rafe—so deep you're part of me."

His mouth slammed over hers, and he stepped forward, carrying her back against the wall. He dragged his head away. "Tell me you need gentle, I'll go easy," he said, although the tightness in his voice told her it would kill him.

"I want you the way you are, Rafe. And you're not easy. Fuck me."

Grunting, he hefted her off her feet and slid his knee between her legs. Her fingers felt the play of muscle beneath his smooth skin, and she reveled in his strength as he drove her backward until his chest flattened against hers.

Lani raised her legs, sliding them around the tops of his hips. She read hesitation in his expression—wild eyes, flared nostrils—the man was barely holding onto his restraint. She inspired that kind of lust in him. She bit his chin. "Fuck me, Rafe."

His hands cupped her buttocks and pulled her up, his hips tunneled, his cock nudging along her slit until he found her entrance. "Don't let me hurt you."

"Baby, you're killing me. Fuck me!"

Rafe drove his cock straight up, his torso sliding up hers, his crisp chest hairs abrading her nipples. His thrusts were hard, sharp, and ended with a jerk—each accompanied by a guttural sound, dragged from deep inside him.

Lani writhed on his cock, relishing each long slide, clasping her inner muscles to increase the friction between his shaft and her channel. "Fuck me, Rafe. Fuck me," she chanted over and over.

His hands clamped hard on her ass, and he pushed her down to meet his upward thrusts. "Baby, I'm coming," he cried out, and his mouth closed over hers, his lips eating hers in drugging caresses.

Lani came apart, her hips jerking, a high-pitched whine escaping to mingle with his groans. Their movements slowed, all sense of passing time narrowing to the slides of their flesh, the beats of their hearts.

She held him, her arms and legs wrapped tightly around his body—their kiss ended in slackening glides of their lips. "Love you, love you," she moaned against his mouth.

Rafe's frame shuddered as his cum spurted inside her. "My seed. My child," he murmured.

Lani dragged her mouth away and stared at him.

Rafe's face was hard, but his eyes were moist. "Mine, Lani."

Chapter Nine

ॐ

Rafe awoke disoriented. Lani's room was dark, but his eyes saw into the darkness, discerning patterns as though objects were backlit by a glowing fluorescence, their outlines limned in green light. He tried to turn his head, but he quickly discovered he wasn't the one in control at the moment.

Lani sighed and stirred beside *them*, her bottom snuggling deeper into the cradle of *their* thighs.

Rafe watched helpless as a hand, *not his*, smoothed over her flank, and slipped beneath the bedding to follow the curve of her hips and buttocks. He felt the silkiness of her skin—and the arousal that coursed through the Indian's body.

Christ! He couldn't do this again. Couldn't watch Lani taken by another man. Couldn't witness her horror when she discovered her lover's identity one more time.

He railed inside his mind, trying to punch through, but could only watch and feel as the other man slid his fingers between her legs, combing through the curls at her mons, and dip into her moist sex.

Lani murmured sleepily and opened her legs a fraction, welcoming his touch.

His fingers twisted inside her, pushing deeper, generating more moisture that eased his penetration.

Lani moaned in her sleep, but her hips rolled, dragging on his fingers, riding them. His thumb flickered on her clitoris and Lani's pussy tightened, a ripple caressing the fingers sliding inside her.

The Indian's next action confounded Rafe. He pulled out of her body, despite her sleepy protest, and brought his fingers to his nose and inhaled.

No words, just an image of Lani's belly heavy with child told the story.

No! The Indian thought she was pregnant with his child. He leaned forward and kissed her shoulder, then withdrew from the bed.

Dazed, Rafe watched through the Indian's eyes as the other man crept through the house on silent feet to the front door. He opened it and stepped out onto the porch.

The night was quiet, the sky overcast with clouds. A billowing wind whipped his hair around his shoulders. The Indian looked over his shoulder through the screen door, and Rafe sensed his farewell.

He relaxed, knowing that, at least for now, Lani would be safe.

Lani heard the screen door thump and sat up. She reached for the bedside lamp and flicked it on. Rafe's clothing was still draped over the chair where she'd left them folded. Perhaps, he just couldn't sleep.

She rose and walked on bare feet into the living room. Through the open door she saw a silhouette of a man. Only it wasn't Rafe.

Her heart thudded dully in her chest. Broad-shouldered, stockier, shorter than Rafe, the Indian had surfaced again, and Rafe was trapped inside with him. As she watched, frozen by indecision, light burst through his naked skin, painting him in shimmering gold. He raised his arms to the sky and threw back his head, his long, straight hair falling between his shoulder blades. Then he bent forward, his legs and arms shortened, and fur sprouted from his skin.

If she'd blinked she would have missed the transformation it happened that quickly. Transfixed with terror, she watched the cat leap from the porch and pad to the edge of the forest where it blended into the trees and underbrush.

Lani stood for long moments, numb to pain. Then her mind kicked over and her heart lurched in her chest. Where was he going? If he crossed into any of the ranches in the area tonight, he'd be killed.

Where had he gone? To feed? To return to his lair?

Every fork in the road her mind took led back to one place. The place everything had started.

Something within her told her he was returning to the cave.

She rushed back to her room and threw on her clothes. Then she stuffed Rafe's clothing into a rucksack and headed to her truck. She prayed she was right, and she'd find him safe inside the cave. But to get there he'd have to cross onto Danny McKelvey's property.

As she pulled out of her driveway, Lani sent up a prayer that the rancher kept close to his homestead that night. The mountain lion might be a mystical creature, but he had substance, a form. He could be killed—and Rafe along with him.

The drive seemed endless. A storm was brewing and the wind picked up, battering her truck with gusts that jerked the steering wheel in her hands.

She almost missed the turn onto the gravel road that led up the winding track to the cave, but breathed a sigh of relief once she pulled up close to the entrance. The wind nearly tore the door out of her hands as she slid from the bench seat to the ground.

Cloud cover cloaked the moon and stars, and Lani had to prepare her ropes with a Maglite held between her teeth, while the relentless wind whipped her hair into her face.

All the while, she wondered if her instinct was correct. The cat could have wandered off in any direction, but her gut told her it would return here tonight. She hadn't a clue what she'd do if it did come, but she'd be there waiting. Somehow, she had to find a way to reach inside the creature for Rafe.

She wouldn't abandon him to the spirits inhabiting his skin. Rafe wasn't the monster—he wasn't responsible for what was happening to him. He wasn't like her father. She'd fight for him.

She anchored the rope to the same oak offset from the entrance of the cave and bent low to enter the cave. Once inside, she fed the line through her hand and walked to the end of the spill of gravel, her flashlight seeking the path that was familiar to her now. When she reached the precipice, she stared down into the darkness.

Now that she knew the mystical origins of the spirit inside Rafe, she accepted that a higher power had a hand in crafting this cave. The anomalies that had intrigued her, no longer required explanation. This place had never been meant to be explored or categorized. The acoustics and density of the darkness simply were.

Lani was breaking a cardinal rule—descending into the darkness without backup, without another living soul knowing where she was. This was a leap of faith—her faith in Rafe and the power that had crafted their destiny.

She stepped into her seat harness and adjusted the fit and slipped her arms through the straps of her vertical pack. Then she leaned back against the rope and stepped off the edge.

* * * * *

Dogs barked, the sound carried on the wind. Excitement made their voices whine. Winded from the chase, the cat paused at the edge of the long white road, careful to stay hidden in the foliage. He lifted his nose to scent the air. Had he outdistanced his hunters?

A familiar aroma wafted in the wind. The woman. His mate. And she was nearby. He followed her scent up the track—he knew where she waited. She'd followed him home.

The other yearned toward her as well, trying to push through. The cat ignored his pleas and raced alongside the trail.

* * * * *

Lani unclipped her harness from the rope and walked toward the pale pile of bones. The man she had seen on her porch with his broad shoulders and gleaming, night-colored hair lay here. He'd been devoured while he lay dying, and Lani could grieve for his pain, feel sorrow for his loss—but she wanted her man back.

She squatted beside the bones and sifted among them with her fingers. She found the stiffened, soiled remains of the moccasin and picked it up. The boot had been worked by loving hands. Bright turquoise and pale shell beads bordered the top and hung from tassels in the front. Someone who loved him had made the moccasin.

He'd known a woman's softness, a woman's love. She knew it because even through her own terror, she'd recognized the care with which he'd touched her. Guilt for the pleasure she'd taken from him warred with her anger over being tricked and used. She loved Rafe, but how could she reconcile her love with the heat the man-cat had raised in her? The depth of her pleasure would be a secret she'd have to keep from Rafe forever.

The crunch of footsteps alerted her she was no longer alone. Gravel skittered and fell around her, raising dust from the floor. As she slowly stood, her helmet lamp caught the golden reflection of cat's eyes on a ledge just above her.

Lani held her breath and returned *his* gaze. The cat was no longer a sexless creature to her—it had revealed its true nature, made love to her. When he leapt to the floor in front of her, she didn't flinch.

The purring started deep inside his chest, rumbling with each exhalation. He padded toward her, his head down, his fangs concealed.

She took that as a good sign, and wished she'd actually made a plan for what she'd do next, but all she could think to do was stand still as a pillar.

The lion greeted her—it was the only way she could describe his actions. He rubbed his muzzle against the fingers she clenched at her side, rubbed the back of his head on her calves as he slowly circled her. When he came in front of her again, he nuzzled the juncture of her thighs. The purring grew louder.

Lani trembled, not so much with fear, but an abundance of emotions that swirled inside her—regret, desire, sadness. When the cat's body shimmered with light, she waited, holding her breath, watching as he transformed into the Indian.

The light didn't dim, but glowed around his naked body, warming the color of his skin to a burnished gold. His face was an implacable mask, but his narrow eyes held longing. Her love for Rafe couldn't supplant her compassion for this man. Their essences had merged. When he opened his arms, she didn't resist his invitation and unclipped her helmet and pushed it off her head, then stepped toward him.

His strong arms encircled her, and the light leapt between their bodies to surround her as well. Heat and a quivering awakening broke like sunrise inside her.

She rubbed her cheek on his shoulder and felt the rise of his chest as he drew in breath. Her hand rested just over his heart, and she felt life thundering beneath her palm. His body ripened, his sex hardening against her belly, but she couldn't recoil. She was safe inside his arms.

His mouth brushed her forehead, and she turned her face upward to accept his kiss. When he drew away, his fingers touched her lips. She closed her eyes. His hand trailed lower, cupped her breast briefly, then his palm caressed her belly.

"You want my child," she whispered, and tears filled her eyes.

His hand cupped her head and pulled her back to his chest. Lani pressed her face into the crook of his neck. "I don't even know your name."

"You know my name, baby," Rafe whispered.

Lani jerked back her head and stared up into his face. The light was fading around them, but Rafe's face shimmered while it reformed. As darkness fell around them, his lips claimed hers. She clutched him, thankful for his return.

A rumble shook the cave, loosening rock and sand to rain down from the ceiling. Rafe pushed her back and swiped her helmet from the floor, shoving it on her head. Together, they slipped beneath the overhang of rock to wait for the last shudders from the explosion to die away.

"Who the hell is dynamiting in the middle of the night?" Rafe shouted.

Lani cocked her head to a sound that murmured and cracked in the distance, then grew louder. "There's an underground river beneath us. I think it's breaking through." She unbuckled her pack and dropped it to the ground. "Shine the helmet lamp inside my bag. We don't have much time." Lani drew out the spare harness she'd packed the day Matt Costello fell. "Put this on."

While Rafe slipped the harness up his naked thighs, Lani found her ascender clip. She took a moment to check his rigging, then hurried to the rope. "We have to go up together. You're stronger, you'll have to pull us both up."

As the sound of water washing through the back of the cave closed in, she clipped the ascender to the rope and his harness, then attached her harness to his. "Put your hand inside this," she said, holding the ascender, "slide it up the rope, then take up the slack in your rigging. Got it?"

He nodded, his face set in a determined mask.

"Hurry!"

Cool, rushing water swept them off their feet, and Lani fought the urge to grapple for the rope. She floundered, fighting the rushing water to hold her face above the surface and gave her trust to Rafe as he reached up the rope, sliding up the ascender, and then taking up the slack. What could only have been seconds felt longer as Lani bobbed on the surface, then she felt the drag on her harness as Rafe pulled them free of the roiling water.

Slowly, Rafe pulled them up the rope while the water rushed by beneath them, accompanied only by the rasp of the ascender and the clink of metal from their harnesses.

At last, Rafe reached behind him and grabbed her arm. He pulled her up his body.

Lani unhitched her carabiner from his rigging and climbed over him to the ledge. Then she turned to help him up.

Rafe collapsed on top her, his chest heaving, his head sagging against her shoulder. Lani clung to him, her hands running up and down his back. Once his breaths slowed, Rafe lifted his head. His gaze swept over her face, and he pushed her helmet off. The lamp blinked off.

With darkness wrapping around them, Lani gauged the direction of his lips by his breaths and sealed her mouth over his. Her hands gripped the back of his head as she glided against his lips. Her tongue lapped inside, skimming his teeth, stroking deeper.

It took a moment for her to recognize he accepted her kiss, but didn't participate.

She dragged her mouth away, but without light, she couldn't read what was in his heart, in his eyes.

Oh, God! Was he angry over the embrace she shared with the Indian? "Rafe?"

"This harness is pinching my cock," he voice rasped.

"Oh!" Lani's hands smoothed over his bare hips until she felt the straps. "You'll have to lift up."

He raised his body off hers, and Lani's hands slipped in front of the harness. She felt for the buckle, but encountered something much more enticing. His cock was hard, the satiny skin stretched taut over his rigid staff. Lani's heart raced, but she moved her hands up his shaft and reached beneath to unbuckle and remove the straps.

Rafe's hands shoved the harness down his hips. Then he felt along her chest until he found the top of her shirt. He made short work of unbuttoning the front, and jerked the cloth from inside her jeans to lay it open. All the while, he didn't utter a word.

Then his palms glided up her belly to her breasts. He cupped them, plumping her flesh. His thumbs scraped over her nipples, which were already beaded from the cool water. But the shiver that racked her body didn't have anything to do with a chill.

He shifted above her, and suddenly his lips closed around a nipple.

Lani arched her back, pushing her breast deeper into his mouth, but he resisted and pulled away.

"Take off your clothes." He said it without inflection—flat, hard.

Lani's hands shook, but she quickly complied, the task made awkward because he straddled her thighs and didn't budge. "You'll have to push my pants the rest of the way off," she said, anxiety making her breathless.

He did so, silent throughout. Then he lifted a knee and nudged it between her thighs.

Lani didn't consider this wasn't the time or place, or that his behavior scared her. She obeyed immediately, letting him slip first one, then the other knee between her legs, then widening her legs further when his hands pushed them apart.

His fingers found her opening, stroked inside once, and without any preparation or warning, he drove his cock up her channel.

Lani gasped, but didn't protest. She waited, her heart on the verge of breaking.

Rafe's breath gusted above her lips. "Do you even care whose hands are touching you? Who's fucking you?" he asked, his voice so harsh she flinched.

"Yes," she whispered, shock constricting her throat.

"Liar!"

Lani opened her mouth to deny it, but knew her words would sound hollow. He'd been there. He'd seen how she'd welcomed the Indian's kiss. She wrapped arms around his back, offering her apology the only way she could, and lifted her knees in acceptance of his storm.

Rafe's body tightened in resistance, but his hips pulled back. His breaths were loud, harsh, his body trembling as though he was fighting himself. She prayed he'd stop—or offer a gentler word, but he rammed forward, shoving the breath from her body.

He thrust deep again and again, his gasps ragged, his body poised above hers, meeting hers only where their flesh merged. At last, he shuddered, and his cum jetted inside her. He pulled out. "He's gone now. Do you wish he'd been the one to stay?"

Tears slipped down her cheeks, but Lani remained silent beneath him.

Hovering over her, his cock resting on her belly, he waited until the tremors of his release ended. Then he rose to his feet. "Get dressed," he said, his voice hard.

Lani fought the sobs that choked her. Her pride demanded she hide her agony. Too, she didn't want his pity—didn't want to add to his pain. After all, she'd betrayed him.

However confusing the past hours had been, she still believed deep inside that Rafe wouldn't abandon her. She'd give him however much time he needed to sort through his issues. Her own heart needed time to heal.

She'd grieve for the Indian later, when she was alone.

After Lani dressed, she led them out of the cave with the light of her helmet. The wind had died down, and the clouds had cleared. A full, yellow moon lit the night. She gave him the clothes she'd brought and waited beside the pickup truck while he dressed.

The passenger door jerked open, and Lani took that as her cue he was ready to leave. Together, they drove to her home in silence, the length of the bench seat might have been miles for the distance between them.

Before she cut the engine, he was out the door, heading for his squad car.

Lani wanted to call him back, but she remained frozen behind her steering wheel, watching through her windshield while he drove away.

Chapter Ten

ꟗ

Rafe stood on the banks of the creek overlooking the muddy remnants of the dam. Chunks of concrete and broken limbs from nearby trees clogged the creek bed now. Water burbled past, carving out new bends to skirt the debris.

But this tangled mess wasn't any worse than the mess he'd left in his wake last night. All morning his actions replayed in his mind. Guilt weighed heavy on his shoulders.

The construction foreman for the golf course carried his anger like an ugly red flag. His belly straining against his waistband, his ruddy face was animated as he voiced his litany of complaints. "Do you see this mess? These bastards set me behind a month!"

Rafe had listened to him rant for a good ten minutes. He was ready to put an end to it. "People around here are blaming you for the loss of their livestock when you dammed this creek," he said quietly.

The foreman's face grew redder. "I had the proper permits, and only excess water was diverted to the pond." Swearing under his breath, he kicked a block of broken concrete.

Rafe had written up the details of the damage and what little the crew could guess about what had happened. "Still some folks won't be unhappy you lost your dam."

"May I remind you a crime was committed here," the foreman said, shaking his finger angrily.

"Yes, sir. I'm well aware of that. And with your dynamite, no doubt. By the way, was it properly secured?"

Knowing full well the company had already been fined for that oversight, Rafe bit back a black grin at the scowl his jibe produced. "ATF'll be out here this afternoon. They'll have questions, too. Make sure your crew's available. No one goes home until they're through."

"Lot a damn good that'll do. I'll lose another day of work."

Rafe left the worksite in no hurry to get to his next destination. Besides, he was pretty sure he knew who was responsible. Kate Massey had already told her Danny McKelvey's alibi didn't hold water. The crusty old woman might agree the dam had to go, but she wouldn't conspire to save the other rancher's hide.

Danny had told Rafe earlier that he'd run his dogs all night after they'd caught the scent of the mountain lion on his property. It was strange to Rafe, hearing about the hunt when he'd been the quarry.

The dogs had been run all right, but Danny had made an error. The dogs had crossed onto the Massey ranch, and Kate's husband had joined the hunt led by Danny's brother. Danny hadn't led the hunt. He'd lied about where he was. And he had plenty of motives for wanting the dam removed and the construction halted. The man's hatred, no doubt based in his gut-deep knowledge his ranch was failing anyway, had spilled over on the golf course.

However much Rafe despised Danny McKelvey, he wasn't eager to be the arresting officer. He'd pass the information along and let another make the arrest. He had bigger problems on his hands to address.

Rafe drove west of town toward Lani's place, but he was relieved when he didn't see her truck parked out front. He wasn't really ready to face her. Didn't have a clue what he could say to make things right between them.

The sight of Lani's face lifting to accept the Indian's kiss burned in his brain. Perhaps, he wouldn't be so angry if he hadn't spent hours with frustration and fear building inside him as the cat had streaked across the countryside.

His joy when he'd finally seen Lani waiting in the bottom of the cave had turned to shock as she'd stared at *them*, tears welling in her eyes. Her look of wonder and acceptance had pierced his heart.

When the Indian had opened his arms, she'd flown to him. The joy the other man had felt, the sense of homecoming and love that had brushed his mind stunned Rafe.

Rafe had meant to wound Lani when he asked which man she would have preferred remain with her. He'd wanted to hurt her for her betrayal, but deep inside he'd wondered whether she really would have preferred the Indian.

Last night, his anger had come unbridled. He'd fucked Lani like a whore. Loosed a monster of jealousy on her he hadn't been able to rein in.

In the harsh light of morning, he regretted every word, every action. But how could he say he was sorry and have her know it was real and heartfelt? Was he really sorry? Or did he still harbor resentment inside him?

Rafe stared down at his hands and clenched his fists. He'd touched her with anger in his heart—for that he was deeply sorry. But did her transgression really warrant the punishment he'd meted out? When she'd lain beneath him, all he could think about was how sweetly she'd kissed the other man. Rafe had seen red and meant to brand her forever as his. Well, he had. He just hoped she'd forgive him.

He backed down her drive and headed to the fire station. He still had jealousy riding on his shoulders, but he couldn't wait another minute to tell Lani he loved her, even if she'd given part of her heart to a spirit.

* * * * *

Lani peeled potatoes at the sink in the fire station kitchen. She'd volunteered for kitchen duty. Anything to keep some distance from the boys today.

The men had groaned loudly because a few of her offerings had resembled the aftermath of a three-alarm fire. But she needed time alone. They must have seen something in her face, because they'd been quiet around her, careful even.

They'd had a busy morning—a kitchen fire and a brush fire beside the highway. But back at the station it was hard to wear a smile when her world was falling apart. She'd slept fitfully after Rafe left, hoping he'd show up at her door, ready to talk things out. But her alarm had woken her at six.

She'd even remembered to charge her cell phone and bring it with her, but it remained quiet all day. He wasn't going to call.

"Need any help?" Randy stood at the swinging door, his young face solemn.

She guessed her attempts at hiding her broken heart had failed miserably, since he'd guessed. She looked back at the potato in her hand. "No, I can handle it."

"Well, I'll just be out here…"

Feeling like the Grinch, she sighed. "I could use some help." She glanced back at him and smiled. "Know how to make meatloaf?"

"Sure." His devilish grin was quick. "Five minutes in the microwave?"

She lifted an eyebrow.

"Just kidding. Hamburger, bread crumbs, a little catsup." His smile turned sheepish. "My mom gave me a recipe book. Said I'd never survive the fire house if I poisoned the guys."

"Smart woman." Lani turned back to the potatoes.

The kitchen door shushed open again. Thinking Randy must have left to search for the cookbook, Lani nearly jumped out her skin when hands settled on her shoulders.

Hands she'd know anywhere from their weight and warmth. Lani didn't turn. She set her paring knife and the potato in the bottom of the sink.

"Hi, Lani," Rafe said, his voice rough as gravel.

She closed her eyes briefly, and tried to inject carelessness in her voice she didn't feel. "What are you doing here, Sheriff?"

"I need to talk to you."

Remembering Randy, she started to glance over her shoulder.

"He left when I came in."

"Well, I'm right here. Say what you have to say."

His fingers tightened. "I'm sorry, Lani."

Please, don't let this be goodbye. She shook her head. "You've nothing to be sorry about."

He leaned into her back, his mouth next to her ear.

It was all Lani could do to keep from turning and throwing her arms around him.

"Let me say this. I have a lot to be sorry about."

Lani's fingers curved around the edge of the sink.

"I hurt you. Used you rough." Rafe's voice grew harsher. "I took my anger out on your body."

Lani hung her head. "You had a right to your anger. I disappointed you."

"I was angry—but more because I couldn't reach you. Couldn't protect you." He turned her to her face him.

Sorrow was etched in his haggard face. "I think I understand. That kiss didn't have a thing to do with how much you love me, did it?"

Lani couldn't stop the tears welling in her eyes. She blinked and shook her head. "To me, he was part of you by that point, and so lonely. When I looked at him, knowing you were in there with him, I felt like your souls had somehow…blended. He's not coming back, is he?"

"I don't feel him inside me anymore."

Lani blinked again and a tear rolled down her cheek. She tried to smile, but her lips trembled. "I don't know what's wrong with me. I'm not usually such a crybaby."

"We've had a strange couple of days," he said softly and wiped away the tear with his thumb.

She gave a single laugh. "Unbelievable days."

"Forgive me?"

Unable to hold herself back a single second longer, Lani wrapped her arms around him and rested her cheek above his heart. "Rafe, I love you so much. Tell me, I didn't spoil things between us."

"Baby, I broke a promise to you. A couple actually."

She looked up, not understanding.

"I promised I'd never become a monster, and that I'd never hurt you. Can we get past that?"

All her fear drained from her. He wanted to move on—with her. "I'm not as fragile inside as you think. And I'm not naïve enough to think we'll never hurt each other again." She stared at him, hoping he'd see all the love in her heart. "Just love me."

Rafe drew in a deep breath and his arms hugged her tight. He pulled her up, so high her feet left the ground, until their gazes were level. "I love you, Lani. I want you for my wife."

Rafe didn't wait for her answer, he kissed her.

"I suppose this means I'm peeling the potatoes, too?" Randy's wry voice sounded from the kitchen door.

Lani grinned up at Rafe. "I'm afraid this shift doesn't end until the morning."

Rafe groaned and pressed the urgent part of him against her warmth. "I'll be waiting for you a minute after it ends."

"I'll hold you to that." Her happiness couldn't be dampened. "Staying for dinner?"

Rafe shot a glare at Randy who was leaning with his hip against the counter and a grin the size of Texas plastered on his face. "Not if he's cooking."

Lani picked up the paring knife and the potato and handed them to Rafe. "I hate peeling potatoes."

* * * * *

Rafe followed her home in his squad car.

Lani was glad he couldn't see the grin on her face as she kept the truck moving forward—under the speed limit. She wanted to build the urgency in him—wanted to see that taut, predatory look in his face as he stalked her through the house.

He didn't disappoint. He shadowed her steps up the porch and cursed while she deliberately fumbled with the keys. As soon as the door swung open, his hands reached around her and unbuckled her belt, forced her zipper down and shoved her pants down her thighs.

Once again, they made it no farther than the arm of the sofa.

Lani laughed, delighted as he drove his cock inside her. *Imagine! I inspire that kind of need!*

"Damn, I really did want this to last," he said, his voice hoarse and muffled against her shoulder.

"Rafe, I don't care if you're a one-minute man—the first time. You always make it up to me." She squirmed beneath him, encouraging him to move.

He bit her shoulder. "Don't move, baby. I'm barely holding on here."

She squeezed her inner muscles and felt him jerk.

"Dammit all to hell." Rafe pulled back and thrust hard inside again.

Lani groaned and clutched at the fabric, enjoying the heat he built inside her with each glide.

He leaned away and gripped her hips, improving the angle of his thrusts—as well as his leverage. His belly slapped her bottom—fast, sharp—warming her skin, raising her desire so that before long she pleaded for release.

Suddenly, he pulled out.

Lani glanced over her shoulder. His face was tight, hard. He'd managed to strip off his pants, and his legs were widespread behind her. His cock was red, engorged, and glistened with her juices.

"Strip!" he said, his chest rising and falling fast.

Her hands shook as she fought with her clothing, but moments later they were both naked. Rafe opened his arms, and Lani flew to him wrapping her arms and legs around his body.

He turned and pressed her back against the door. "You never answered my question," he said, as he nuzzled her neck.

It took a moment for her mind to grasp the change of topic. Like he didn't already have his answer two seconds inside the door! "It's yes, of course. Now, fuck me!"

His cock found her entrance, gliding easily past her slick cunt, and he rocked her on the door, sliding her up and down the smooth wood. "When?" His face was feral, a remnant characteristic he'd carry with him the rest of his life.

Not that she'd ever tell him.

Lani's eyes drifted closed, and she fought to catch her breath. "As soon as we get out of bed?"

"And how soon do you think I'll let that happen?"

A pleased smile curved her lips. "The justice might get a little embarrassed if we say our 'I do's' between strokes, lover."

"His problem." Rafe shifted her in his arms. "I need you under me."

"The floor," she gasped.

They slid down together, and finally with cool wood beneath her back, Rafe lifted her ass to give her the pounding she'd earned for all her teasing.

While her body shuddered and spasmed all around his hard cock, Lani counted her blessings. She'd have a lifetime of desperate, passionate loving.

"Aren't you supposed to be at work?"

Rafe smiled as Lani's fingers lazily traced the curve of his ear. "The dispatcher knows where I'm at. I told her I was having breakfast."

"Think she knows you aren't chowing down on doughnuts?"

Rafe smiled at her sassy words. "Probably. I don't think anyone hasn't figured out I'm crazy in love with you."

"I should rustle up something in the kitchen so you won't be a liar."

"Keeping up my strength?"

She grinned. "That too."

Reluctantly, Rafe rolled off Lani and she reached for the robe at the end of the mattress. He moved his foot onto it. "You need that?"

She lifted an eyebrow. "I guess not." She let it slip from her fingers. "I thought I'd be a little less distracting. Our meals together tend to get cold."

"I like watching you walk around naked."

"Better enjoy it now—before everything heads south."

"Think I won't still like what I see? I think it will be a new rule. This house is a no-clothes zone past the front door."

"What about the porch?"

Rafe gave her a wicked, teasing smile. "Want a little more porch, do you?"

Lani sighed and shook her head sadly. "I'm going to be wearing a permanent blush, aren't I?"

"It's part of the marriage vows—I promise to keep you bent over and bowlegged for the rest of our days."

She swatted him with the pillow and then strolled away—a definite sashay in her walk.

As her footsteps faded, so did his smile. He rose from the bed and opened the door onto the porch. The morning was bright, the heat not yet suffocating. A light breeze dried the last of the sweat from his skin. He gripped the railing and closed his eyes.

Rafe didn't consider himself a religious man—hadn't really given God much thought. But he recognized the hand of a higher power had been at work here. He'd thought he was chosen to receive the spirit of the Indian and the lion because of his connection to Lani, but that was only partially true.

He'd been chosen because he'd love her no matter whose baby she carried inside her body now. Lani didn't know she was pregnant yet, and he'd wait a little while to tell her.

She was going to cry.

He smiled at that thought. He'd found the gentle, soft core inside the strong woman. For him, she wore her emotions close to the surface, unafraid to let him see inside her heart.

He'd give it a few days, and then tell her. His child or the Indian's—she'd love either equally.

And he'd fulfill the ultimate role he'd been chosen for. He'd be a loving father to Red Wolf's son.

Also by Delilah Devlin

ஐ

Arctic Dragon

Desire 1: Prisoner of Desire

Desire 2: Slave of Desire

Desire 3: Garden Of Desire

Ellora's Cavemen: Legendary Tails III (*anthology*)

Ellora's Cavemen: Tales from the Temple III (*anthology*)

Fated Mates (*anthology*)

Jacq's Warlord (*anthology*)

My Immortal Knight 1: All Hallows Heartbreaker

My Immortal Knight 2: Love Bites

My Immortal Knight 3: All Knight Long

My Immortal Knight 4: Relentless

My Immortal Knight 5: Uncovering Navarro

My Immortal Knight 6: Silver Bullet

Nibbles 'n' Bits (*anthology*)

Ride a Cowboy

Silent Knight

The Pleasure Bot

Witch's Choice

About the Author

ꟾ

Delilah Devlin dated a Samoan, a Venezuelan, a Turk, a Cuban, and was engaged to a Greek before marrying her Irishman. She's lived in Saudi Arabia, Germany, and Ireland, but calls Texas home for now. Ever a risk taker, she lived in the Saudi Peninsula during the Gulf War, thwarted an attempted abduction by white slave traders, and survived her children's juvenile delinquency.

Creating alter egos for herself in the pages of her books enables her to live new adventures. Since discovering the sinful pleasure of erotica, she writes to satisfy her need for variety--it keeps her from running away with the Indian working in the cubicle beside her!

In addition to writing erotica, she enjoys creating romantic comedies and suspense novels.

Delilah welcomes comments from readers. You can find her website and email address on her author bio page at www.ellorascave.com.

Enjoy an excerpt from:

A CENTAUR FOR LIBBY

ꟷ

Up until now her dreams had been tame, even amusing. Like the one where she was screwing Randall Mason, the young district attorney, in front of an entire jury that had been charged with judging the quality of her moves. Or the one where she went down on Tony, the buff bailiff, unzipping his uniform trousers and pulling out his long snake of a cock, sucking it greedily into her mouth, hard and pulsing as Judge Cartwright banged her gavel screaming, "Out of order."

In comparison, her new dream was perverted. She probably should have asked for medication a while ago and maybe then she could have avoided the place she was at now, dreading sleep for fear of once again meeting and being seduced by the wondrous creature with deep as the sea eyes and long, dark hair that blew in the perpetual breeze.

It made her wet, just thinking about it.

"But I didn't get to tell you everything about work yet." She attempted a final, desperate diversion. "There's this new judge in Part B, right? Well, he's totally got it in for all us public defenders and last week he—"

Agatha cut her off, holding up a well-tanned, wrinkled hand. She did so with great dramatic flare, the warm glow of turquoise rings and mauve nail polish stopping Libby dead in her tracks. "Libra Daniels," said the sixty-three-year-old diva of psychoanalysis who could pass for forty-five on a good day. "Are we displaying avoidance behavior?"

Libby frowned. "You know you are harder on me than any district attorney, don't you?"

"That, my dear," she said, wrinkling her nose and pushing her herringbone glasses up, "is because I love you like a daughter. Also you happen to pay me a good deal of money."

"My insurance pays. I just sit here and suffer," Libby groused.

"And suffer you shall." Agatha waved an arm, bare feet tucked up underneath her Indian style as she held court on her pride-and-joy red leather couch, fifty-minute session clock beside her on a matching table, inoperable, no batteries in it for years.

A crocheted sign above it in a mahogany frame said "Waste not…and you're not really living". Everywhere on her walls were little pictures and signs. She had pillows, too—wild and loud—from her travels throughout the world.

Libby had always admired women like Aggy. So thoroughly professional and respected by males yet able to project as much femininity as they liked. For Libby it was a comical balancing act. One in which she was forever falling flat on her face. Her final answer had been repression, repression, repression. Severe hairstyle, pantsuits, minimal perfume, low heels and no dating. The price for all this according to Aggy—who insisted everyone call her by her first name—was the dreams.

Libby sighed. "I'll tell you my latest dream but only if you promise you won't freak."

"My dear girl," she chortled. "I've been in this business since you were in diapers. Do you really think there is anything I haven't heard by now?"

"You may have to eat your words, Aggy, this one is pretty kinky."

"Don't tell me, Brad Pitt and George Clooney fighting over you in the nude, Jell-O wrestling outside a café on the French Riviera while you sip champagne from a priceless flute?"

"No, though that would be normal in comparison to mine."

"Oh, thank the stars," she exuded. "Do give me all the gory details. I haven't heard anything juicy all day."

"It has a centaur in it," said Libby, giving her a last chance to beg off hearing it.

Her eyes lit. "Mythology, eh? Yummy. Herr Freud would have a field day. Does your centaur smoke a cigar by any chance?"

"No, he gallops up on me in the dark. I am standing on this beach and he rides up, the wind in his hair, beautiful dark hair." Libby could picture it so easily, she could slip away, she could touch herself, right here and now. "He has the most beautiful face, I can tell by the shadows, but I can't ever make out the details. Just the eyes, reflecting purple moonlight. The eyes are blue. His chest is bare, his skin is so healthy and rugged, he is very muscular and he wants me, Aggy, with a passion and desire I can't begin to absorb."

"I assume he makes it past the proverbial first base?" Aggy inquired. "Though I do have a question or two about logistics. Four-legged man, two-legged woman…"

"That's the amazing thing. I always ask him that right off and he answers, telling me not to worry. 'Let things be,' he says. 'Let it all fall into place.' Then he says more, speaking to me, with this magnificent deep voice, telling me I am the most beautiful creature he has ever seen and he will die if he does not make love to me.

"'Have you seen what your sex does to me?' he asks. And that's when he shows me his erection. He rears up on two legs on this amazing sand—clear and pure as diamonds—and reveals his cock and balls. The most wonderful shaft I have ever seen, long and tapered, completely human, reddish-purple from the veins crisscrossing the surface, surging with blood. His balls are so full and tight and high. He is uncircumcised, his cock points at me proudly, tapering like a carved Greek statue, cool and powerful. But I know there is so much heat in it. I want to touch it, I want to be touched. I'm still afraid. The centaur tells me not to fight it. We are going to make love and it would be wrong for me to resist. 'Where there is this much lust, nature will find a way,' he says."

"Some pretty impressive pickup lines," quipped Agatha, shaking her head, dangling turquoise earrings from the reservation she visited twice a year and where she was a certified shaman. "I half expected you to tell me the creature asks you your zodiac sign."

"Nothing nearly so corny. That's the strange part, Agatha. It doesn't feel like something I am making up. I mean I am not into astrology and I am not into bizarre sex."

"You're not into sex, period, dear. That's the problem with your whole generation—you totally overlook the value of a completely meaningless fuck."

Why an electronic book?

We live in the Information Age—an exciting time in the history of human civilization, in which technology rules supreme and continues to progress in leaps and bounds every minute of every day. For a multitude of reasons, more and more avid literary fans are opting to purchase e-books instead of paper books. The question from those not yet initiated into the world of electronic reading is simply: *Why?*

1. ***Price.*** An electronic title at Ellora's Cave Publishing and Cerridwen Press runs anywhere from 40% to 75% less than the cover price of the exact same title in paperback format. Why? Basic mathematics and cost. It is less expensive to publish an e-book (no paper and printing, no warehousing and shipping) than it is to publish a paperback, so the savings are passed along to the consumer.
2. ***Space.*** Running out of room in your house for your books? That is one worry you will never have with electronic books. For a low one-time cost, you can purchase a handheld device specifically designed for e-reading. Many e-readers have large, convenient screens for viewing. Better yet, hundreds of titles can be stored within your new library—on a single microchip. There are a variety of e-readers from different manufacturers. You can also read e-books on your PC or laptop computer. (Please note that Ellora's Cave does not endorse any specific brands. You can check our websites at www.ellorascave.com

or www.cerridwenpress.com for information we make available to new consumers.)

3. ***Mobility***. Because your new e-library consists of only a microchip within a small, easily transportable e-reader, your entire cache of books can be taken with you wherever you go.
4. ***Personal Viewing Preferences.*** Are the words you are currently reading too small? Too large? Too... ANNOYING? Paperback books cannot be modified according to personal preferences, but e-books can.
5. ***Instant Gratification.*** Is it the middle of the night and all the bookstores near you are closed? Are you tired of waiting days, sometimes weeks, for bookstores to ship the novels you bought? Ellora's Cave Publishing sells instantaneous downloads twenty-four hours a day, seven days a week, every day of the year. Our webstore is never closed. Our e-book delivery system is 100% automated, meaning your order is filled as soon as you pay for it.

Those are a few of the top reasons why electronic books are replacing paperbacks for many avid readers.

As always, Ellora's Cave and Cerridwen Press welcome your questions and comments. We invite you to email us at Comments@ellorascave.com or write to us directly at Ellora's Cave Publishing Inc., 1056 Home Avenue, Akron, OH 44310-3502.

THE ☥ ELLORA'S CAVE ☥ LIBRARY

Stay up to date with Ellora's Cave Titles in Print with our Quarterly Catalog.

TO RECIEVE A CATALOG,
SEND AN EMAIL WITH YOUR NAME
AND MAILING ADDRESS TO:

CATALOG@ELLORASCAVE.COM
OR SEND A LETTER OR POSTCARD
WITH YOUR MAILING ADDRESS TO:

CATALOG REQUEST
C/O ELLORA'S CAVE PUBLISHING, INC.
1056 HOME AVENUE
AKRON, OHIO 44310-3502

Cerridwen, the Celtic Goddess of wisdom, was the muse who brought inspiration to storytellers and those in the creative arts. Cerridwen Press encompasses the best and most innovative stories in all genres of today's fiction. Visit our site and discover the newest titles by talented authors who still get inspired - much like the ancient storytellers did, once upon a time.

ELLORA'S CAVE
ROMANTICA PUBLISHING